THE FINGER OF FATE

STORIES BY

SAPPER

HOUSE OF
STRATUS

This edition published in 2001 by House of Stratus, an imprint of Stratus Holdings plc, 24c Old Burlington Street, London, W1X 1RL, UK.

www.houseofstratus.com

Typeset, printed and bound by House of Stratus.

A catalogue record for this book is available from the British Library.

ISBN 1-84232-549-3

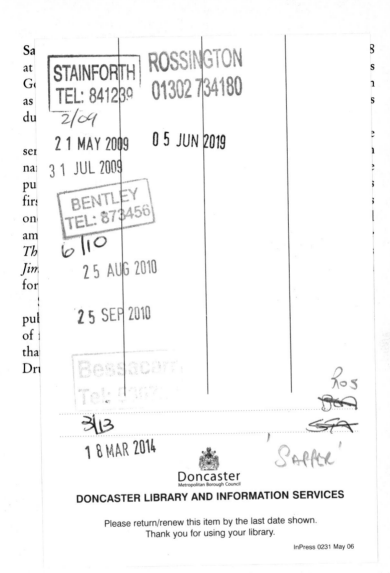

BY THE SAME AUTHOR
ALL PUBLISHED BY HOUSE OF STRATUS

CONTENTS

THE FINGER OF FATE

The funny thing about it was that I did not know George Barstow at all well. Had he been an intimate personal friend of mine, the affair might have seemed more natural. But he wasn't: he was just a club acquaintance with whom I was on ordinary club terms. We met sometimes in the bridge-room: occasionally we had an after-lunch brandy together. And that was all.

He had obviously a good deal of money. Something in the City, but a something that did not demand an extravagant amount of his time. His weekends were of the Friday to Tuesday variety, and I gathered that he was on the borderline of golfers who are eligible to compete in the Amateur Championship.

In appearance he was almost aggressively English. Clean-shaven, and ruddy of face, his natural position was with his legs apart on the hearthrug and his back to the fire. Probably a whisky-and-soda in his hand, or a tankard of beer. Essentially a man's man, and yet one who by no means disliked the pleasures of the occasional nightclub party. But one realised they must only be occasional.

He was, I suppose, about thirty-seven, though he was one of those men whose age is difficult to tell. He might quite easily have been in the early forties. His appearance was healthy rather than good looking: his physical strength was distinctly above the average. And to finish off this brief outline of the man, he had joined up in the earliest days of the war and finally risen to the command of a battalion.

I recognised him when he was a hundred yards away from the inn. He was coming towards me down the road, his hands in his pockets, his head sunk. But the walk was unmistakable.

"Great Scott! Barstow!" I said as he came abreast of me, "what brings you here at this time of year?"

"Here" was a little village not far from Innsbruck.

He glanced up with a start, and I was shocked to see the change in his face. He looked positively haggard.

"Hullo! Staunton," he said moodily. Then he gave a sheepish little laugh. "I suppose it is a bit out of my beaten track."

"Come and have a spot of this," I remarked. "I've tasted much worse."

He came across the road and sat down, whilst I studied him covertly. Quite obviously something was wrong – seriously wrong, but in view of the slightness of our acquaintanceship it was up to him to make the first move if he wanted to.

"August and Austria hardly seem a usual combination for you," I said lightly. "I thought Scotland was your habitual programme."

"Habitual programmes have a way of being upset," he answered shortly. "Here's how."

He put his glass down on the table, and pulled out his tobacco pouch.

"Personally, I think this is a damnable country," he exploded suddenly.

"Then," I said mildly, "is there any essential reason why you should remain?"

He didn't answer, and I noticed he was staring down the road through narrowed eyes.

"The essential reason," he said at length, "will shortly pass this inn. No, don't look round," he went on, as I turned in my chair. "You will see all there is to be seen in a moment."

From behind me I heard the jingling of bells, and the noise of some horse-drawn vehicle approaching at a rapid rate. And a few seconds after, an almost mediaevally magnificent equipage drew up at the door. I use the word "equipage" advisedly, because it was like no English carriage that I have ever seen, and I have no idea as to the correct local name for it.

The coachman was in scarlet: all the horses' trappings were scarlet also. But after a brief glance at the setting, my eyes fixed themselves on the man contained in it. Seldom, I think, have I seen a more arrogant and unpleasant-looking face. And yet it was the face of an aristocrat. Thin-lipped, nose slightly hooked, he was typical of the class of man who, in days gone by in France, would have ordered his servants to drive over a peasant in his way, rather than be delayed.

He waited without movement till a footman, also in scarlet, had dashed to the door and opened it. Then he stepped out, and held out his sleeve for an imaginary speck of dust to be removed. And for an instant the wild thought came to my mind that the man was acting for the films. The whole thing seemed unreal.

The next moment the landlord appeared bent nearly double. And my fascination increased. I'd forgotten Barstow's words about the essential reason in my intense interest. He advanced slowly towards a table, the landlord backing in front of him, and sat down. At the same time the footman, who had been delving under one of the seats of the carriage, came up to his table and put a leather case in front of him. He opened it, and I gave an involuntary start. Inside were two revolvers.

"Good God!" I muttered and glanced at George Barstow. There was nothing mediaeval about those guns.

But he seemed to be taking no interest in the performance whatever. With his legs stretched in front of him he was puffing calmly at his pipe, apparently utterly indifferent to the whole thing.

But now even stranger doings were to take place. With great solemnity the footman advanced to a tree, and proceeded to fix an ordinary playing card to the trunk with a drawing pin. It was the five of hearts. Then he withdrew.

The man at the table took one of the revolvers from the case, and balanced it for a moment in his hand. Then he raised it and fired four times.

By this time I was beyond surprise. The whole thing was so incredibly bizarre that I could only sit there gaping. If the man had now proceeded to stand on his head, and drink a glass of wine in that position, I should have regarded it as quite in keeping. But apparently the performance was not yet over. Once again did the footman solemnly advance to the tree. He removed the card, and pinned up another – the five of spades. And the man at the table picked up the other revolver. Once again did four shots ring out, and then the marksman, with great deliberation, leaned back in his chair after drawing a handkerchief delicately across his nostrils.

He accepted from the almost kneeling landlord a glass of wine: then he extended a languid hand for the two targets which the footman was holding out, and examined them with an air of bored indifference. Apparently the result of the inspection was favourable: he threw the two cards on the table and continued his wine.

Now I cannot say at what moment exactly a strong desire on my part to laugh was replaced by a curious pricking sensation at the back of my scalp. But it was the way George Barstow was behaving, more than the theatrical display of the other man, that caused the change. From first to last he had never moved, and it wasn't natural. No man can sit calmly in a chair while someone looses off eight shots behind his back. Unless, that is to say, it was an ordinary proceeding, which had lost its interest through constant repetition. Even then, surely, he would have made some remark about it: told me what to expect. But he hadn't: from the moment the man had stepped out of his carriage he had remained sunk in silence.

A movement from the other table made me look up. The stranger had finished his wine, and was standing up preparatory to going. He made a little gesture with his hand; the footman picked up the two cards. And then to my utter amazement he came over and threw them on the table between us, in a gratuitously offensive way.

"What the devil!" I began angrily, but I spoke to empty air. The man was already clambering up to his seat at the back of the carriage. And it wasn't until the jingle of the bells had died away in the distance that I turned to Barstow.

"What on earth is the meaning of that pantomime," I demanded. "Does he often do it?"

George Barstow removed his pipe, and knocked it out on his heel.

"Today is the sixth time," he said quietly.

"But what's the great idea?" I cried.

"Not very great," he answered. "In fact, perfectly simple. His wife and I are in love with one another and he has found out."

"Good God!" I said blankly.

And then for the first time I looked closely at the two cards. The four outside pips had been shot out of each: only the centre one remained.

And once again I muttered: "Good God!" Farce had departed: what looked very like grim tragedy had replaced it. With George Barstow of all people. If one had searched the length and breadth of Europe it would have been impossible to find a human being less likely to find himself in such a position. Mechanically I lit a cigarette: something would have to be done. The trouble was what? But one thing was perfectly clear. A state of affairs which caused a performance such as I had just witnessed could not continue. The next move in the game would probably be to substitute Barstow for the playing card. And no one could be under any delusion as to the gentleman's ability to shoot.

"Look here, Staunton," said Barstow suddenly. "I'd like your advice. Not that there's the slightest chance of my taking it," he added with a faint smile, "because I know perfectly well what it's going to be. It will be exactly the same advice as I should give myself to another man in my position. Still – if it won't bore you…"

"Fire right ahead," I answered. "And let's have another flagon of this stuff."

"It started in Paris three months ago," he began. "A luncheon party at Delmonico's. There were eight of us, and I found myself sitting next to the Baroness von Talrein. Our friend of this morning is the Baron. Well, you'll probably see the Baroness before you've done – so I won't waste time in trying to describe her. Anyway I couldn't. I can give a man a mental description of a golf hole, but not of a woman. I'll merely say that as far as I am concerned, she is the only woman in the world.

"She is half English, half French. Speaks both languages like a native. And to cut the cackle, I was a goner from the first moment I set eyes on her. I don't pretend to be a moralist: I'm not. I've been what I called in love with other men's wives before, but I'd always survived the experience without much difficulty. This was something totally and utterly different."

He paused for a moment and stared over the fields.

"Totally and utterly different," he repeated. "But, except for one thing, it would have ended as other affairs of that sort have ended in the past and will in the future."

He pulled thoughtfully at his pipe.

"One doesn't mention such things as a general rule," he went on, "but the circumstances in this case are a little unusual. You're a fellow countryman: we know one another and so on. And as I say, but for this other thing you would not have been treated to the performance this morning. I found out she was in love with me. Doesn't matter how: it was motoring back latish one night from Versailles. Well that fact put a totally different complexion on the matter."

"Interrupting you for one moment," I said, "had you met the Baron when you found this out?"

"No – not then. He arrived about three days later. She was stopping with friends in the Bois de Boulogne. And during those three days we were never out of one another's pockets. Foolish, I suppose – but there you are. We're dealing with what is, not what might have been.

"Then that specimen arrived, that you've seen today. And Eloise insisted that we must be terribly careful. She was frightened to death of the man – it had been one of those damnable arranged marriages. And I suppose I was in the condition where care was impossible. I mean affairs of that sort are given away by an intercepted glance, or something equally trivial. Or perhaps it was that the woman in whose flat Eloise was staying gave us away: I never trusted her an inch. Anyway the Baron had not been in Paris two days before he came round to see me at the Majestic.

"He was ushered into my sitting-room just before lunch, and I knew at once that he had found out. He stood by the door staring at me, and going through his usual elaborate ritual with his lace handkerchief. And at last he spoke.

" 'In my country, Mr Barstow,' he said, 'it is the custom for a husband to choose his wife's friends. From now on you are not included in that category.'

" 'And in my country, Baron,' I answered, 'we recognise no such archaic rules. When the Baroness confirms your statement I shall at once comply. In the meantime…'

" 'Yes,' he said softly, 'in the meantime.'

" 'Lunch is preferable to your company.'

"And so matters came to a head. I suppose I might have been a bit more tactful, but I didn't feel like being tactful. He got my goat from the very first, apart altogether from the question of his wife. And that afternoon I decided to stake everything. I asked her to come away with me.

"I suppose," he went on after a little pause, "that you think I'm a fool. If I were in your place I certainly should. But I want you to realise one thing, Staunton. I am not a callow boy, suffering from calf love; I'm an old and fairly hardened man of the world. And I did it with my eyes open weighing the consequences."

"What did the Baroness say?" I asked.

"She agreed," he answered simply. "After considerable hesitation. But the hesitation was on my account – not hers. She was afraid of what he would do – not to her, but to me. The man is a swine, you see, of the first order of merit. And he sort of obsesses her mental outlook. You've seen him: you can judge for yourself. Fancy being condemned to live with that for the rest of your life. However, I soothed her as best I could: pointed out to her that we lived in a civilised country in the twentieth century, and that there was nothing he could do. And finally we agreed to bolt next day. There was to be no hole-and-corner work about it: I was going to write him a letter as soon as we had gone.

"Well – she never turned up. A pitiful little scrawl came, written evidently in frantic haste. Whether he had found out, or merely suspected our intentions, I don't know. But he had left Paris early in the morning taking her with him. Back here."

Barstow waved a hand at a big château half hidden by trees that lay in front of us dominating the whole countryside.

"At first, I was furious. Why hadn't she refused to go? You can't compel a human being to do what they don't want to. But after a time the anger died. I met a friend of hers – a woman, and it was she who told me things I didn't know about this menage. Things about his treatment of her: things, Staunton, that made me see red. And then and there I made up my mind. I, too, would come here. That was a week ago."

George Barstow fell silent, and stared at his shoes.

"Have you seen her?" I said.

"No. The first day I arrived I went up to call. Rather putting one's head in the lion's mouth – but I'm beyond trifles of that sort. He must have known I was coming: as you saw by the landlord's behaviour he is God Almighty in these parts. Anyway, I was met at the door by the major-domo, with three damned great Alsatians on leads. The Baroness was not at home, and it would be well if I remembered that the next time I came the Alsatians would not be on leads. Then he slammed the door in my face.

"The next morning the performance you saw today took place. It has been repeated daily since. And that's the position. What do you think about it?"

"Well, old man," I remarked, "you started off by saying that you wouldn't take my advice. And so there's not much good my giving it to you. What I think about it is that you should pack, put your stuff in the back of my car – and hop it. My dear fellow," I went on a little irritably, "the position is impossible. Forgive my cold logic, and apparent lack of sympathy – but you must see that it is yourself. After all – she is his wife. And it seems to me that you have the alternative of a sticky five minutes with three savage Alsatians, or finding yourself in the position of acting as one of these cards. I quite agree with your estimate of the gentleman – but facts are facts. And it seems to me you haven't got a leg to stand on."

"I don't care a damn," he said obstinately. "I'm not going. Good God! man, don't you understand that I love her?"

I shrugged my shoulders.

"I don't see that sitting in that inn for the rest of your life is going to help much," I answered. "Look here, Barstow, this isn't England. They have codes of their own in this country. On your own showing that fellow is the great Pooh Bah here. What are you going to do if he challenges you to a duel? I don't know what you are like with a revolver."

"Hopeless. Perfectly hopeless."

"Well, I believe you'd have the choice of weapons. Are you any good at fencing?"

"Far, far worse than with a revolver. I've never had a foil in my hand in my life."

"Then," I cried, "you'd find yourself in the enviable position of either running away or being killed for a certainty. My dear old man, really – really, it isn't good enough. I'm extremely sorry for you and all that, but you must see that the situation is untenable. The man would kill you without the slightest compunction, and with the utmost ease. And here it would simply be put down as an affair of honour. All the sympathy would be with him."

He shook his head wearily.

"Everything that you say is right. Doubly distilled right. And yet, Staunton, I can't go. I feel that anyway here, I am near her. Sorry to have bored you with all my troubles, but I felt I had to."

"You haven't bored me in the slightest," I said. "Only frankly it makes me angry, Barstow, to see a fellow like you making such a fool of himself. You've got nothing to gain and everything to lose."

"If only I could get her out of this country," he said again and again. "He ill-treats her, Staunton. I've seen the marks of his hand on her arms."

I sighed and finished the wine. He was beyond aid. And then suddenly he sat up with a jerk: he was staring at a peasant girl who was making peculiar signs at us from behind a tree some fifty yards away. And suddenly he rose and walked swiftly towards her. I saw her hand him a note, and then dodge rapidly away. And as he came back towards me, I realised that I might as well have been talking to a brick wall. His whole face had changed: he had forgotten my existence.

"A letter from her," he said as he sat down.

"You surprise me," I murmured cynically. "From your demeanour I imagined it was the grocer's bill."

And then I stopped – a little ashamed of the cheap sarcasm. For George Barstow's hand – phlegmatic, undemonstrative Englishman that he was – was shaking like a leaf. I turned away as he opened the envelope, wondering what new complication was going to be introduced. And I wasn't left in ignorance for long. He positively jibbered at me, so great was his excitement. Unknown to her husband she had managed to get out of the house that morning, and she was hiding in the house of her maid's people in the next village.

I suppose it was foolish of me, but I think most men would have done the same. And to do him justice George Barstow didn't ask in so many words. He just looked, and his words came back to me – "If only I could get her out of the country" – I had a car: the Swiss frontier was sixty miles away.

"Get to it, Barstow," I said. "Pack your bag, and we'll hump it."

"Damn my bag!" he cried. "Staunton, you're a sportsman."

"On the contrary I'm a drivelling idiot," I answered. "And I wash my hands of you once we're in the Engadine."

"You can," he said happily. "Jove! But this is great."

"Is it," I remarked grimly, as I let her into gear. "It strikes me, my friend, that your lady fair's absence is no longer unknown to her husband."

Galloping down the side road that led from the château was the same barouche as we had seen that morning. You could spot the scarlet-coated coachman a mile off. But the main road was good, and a Bentley is a Bentley. We passed the turn when the Baron was still a quarter of a mile away. And then I trod on the gas and we moved.

"It's a race, my boy," I said. "He'll get a car as soon as he can. And if we get a puncture…"

"Don't croak," he answered. "We shan't."

We roared into the village, and there, standing in the middle of the road waiting for us was the most adorable creature I've ever seen. There was no time for rhapsodies: every second counted. But I did say to Barstow, "By Jove! old man – I don't blame you." Then we were off again. And as we left the village, Barstow, who was sitting in the back with his girl, shouted to me: "He's just come in sight."

Luckily I am one of those people who never forget a road. And in one hour and three-quarters the Austrian douane hove in sight. My triptyque was in order: the authorities were pleased to be genial. And a quarter of an hour later we were across the frontier.

"You might now introduce me," I murmured gently. "This is the first time in my life that I've assisted at an entertainment of this description, and I feel it ought to be celebrated."

And for a while we behaved like three foolish children. I know I was almost as excited as they were. The fact that half my kit and all George Barstow's was gone for good seemed too trifling to worry about. All that mattered was that the bus had gone like a scalded cat, and that somewhere on the road, miles back, a hook-nosed blighter was cursing like blazes in an elderly tin Lizzie.

It was the girl who pulled herself together first.

"We're not out of the wood yet, George," she said; "He'll follow us all over Europe. Let's get on."

And so we got on – a rather soberer party. George and his girl doubtless had compensations in the back seat, but now that the excitement of the dash was over I began to weigh up the situation calmly. And the more I weighed it up the less I liked it. It's all very well to do a mad thing on the spur of the moment, but the time of reckoning comes. And the cold hard fact remained, that but for me George Barstow would not have been able to kidnap another man's wife. For that's what it came to, when shorn of its romance.

It was as we drove into Samaden that George leaned over and spoke to me.

"Look here, old man," he said gravely. "Eloise and I want you to leave us in St Moritz and clear out. It isn't fair that you should be mixed up in this."

Exactly what I had been thinking myself, which was naturally sufficient to cause a complete revulsion.

"Go to blazes!" I cried. "Anyway we can't discuss anything till we've had lunch. It's all hopelessly foolish and reprehensible, but I've enjoyed myself thoroughly. So we'll crack a bottle, and I will drink your very good health."

It was stupid, of course, leaving the car outside the hotel. And yet, as things turned out it was for the best. The meeting had to take place some time: it was as well that I should be there when it did. It was also as well that we were late for luncheon: the room was empty.

We'd all forgotten the Baron for the moment – and then, suddenly, there he was standing in the doorway. George Barstow saw him first, and instinctively he took the girl's hand. Then I turned round, but the Baron had eyes for no one but Barstow. His face was like a frozen mask, but you could sense the seething hatred in his mind. Quite slowly he walked over to our table still staring at George Barstow, who rose as he approached. Then he picked up a glass of wine and flung the contents in George's face. The next moment George's fist caught him on the point of the jaw, and the Baron disappeared from view.

But he rose to his feet at once, still outwardly calm.

"I shall kill you for that," he remarked quietly.

"Possibly," said Barstow, equally quietly.

"I challenge you to a duel," said the Baron.

"And I accept your challenge," answered Barstow. I heard the girl give a gasp of terror, and I gazed at him in blank astonishment.

"Good God! man!" I cried, "what are you saying? Surely the matter is capable of settlement without that?"

But George was speaking again.

"I shall not return to your country, Monsieur le Baron," he said. "We will find some neutral *venue* for the affair."

"As you please," said the Baron icily, but I saw the triumph that gleamed in his eyes.

"And before," went on George, "leaving the details to be settled by our seconds, it would be well to have one or two matters made clear. I love your wife: she loves me. The only reason – I admit an important one – that brings you into the affair is that you happen to be her husband. Otherwise you are beneath contempt. Your treatment of her has been such as to place you outside the pale. Nevertheless you are her husband. I wish to be. There is not room for both of us. So one of us will die."

"Precisely," agreed the other with a slight laugh. "One of us will die. I presume this gentleman will act as your second."

Without waiting for my answer he stalked out of the room.

"Barstow," I almost shouted at him, "are you mad? You haven't a hope."

And the girl turned to him in an agony of fear.

"Darling," she cried, "you mustn't. You can't."

"Darling," he said gravely, "I must. And I can."

"It's murder," I said dully. "I absolutely refuse to have anything to do with it."

But on Barstow's face there flickered a faint smile.

"Or bluff," he remarked cryptically. "Though I admit it's a bluff to the limit of my hand."

And not a word more would he say.

"I'll tell you everything when the time comes, old man," was the utmost I could get out of him.

Now various rumours have, I know, got abroad concerning this affair. Whether my name has been connected with it or not I neither know nor care. But it is in the firm belief that nothing but good can come from a plain statement of the truth, that I am writing this.

I suppose, strictly speaking, Barstow could have refused to fight. Duelling is forbidden by the laws of England. But he was an obstinate fellow, and he certainly did not lack pluck. Moreover he felt, and it was a feeling one couldn't help admiring, that he owed it to the Baron to meet him.

The girl, poor child, was almost frantic with fear. And for some strange reason he wouldn't tell her what was in his mind. He adopted the line with her that he was no bad shot himself, and I followed his lead.

And it wasn't until he had said good-bye to her, and we were in the train, bound for Dalmatia, that he told me.

(A certain uninhabited island off the Dalmatian coast was to be the scene of the duel.)

He had, of course, the choice of weapons, and when he first told me the terms on which he intended to fight I felt a momentary feeling of relief. But that feeling evaporated quickly. For what he proposed was *certain* death for one of them.

They were to fight with revolvers at a range of three feet. *But only one revolver was to be loaded.*

"I see it this way," he said to me. "I can't say that I *want* to risk my life on the spin of a coin. I can't say I want to fight this duel at all. But I've got to. I'm damned if I, an Englishman, am going to be found wanting in courage by any foreigner. If he refuses to fight on such terms, my responsibility ends. It will be he who is the coward."

"And if he doesn't refuse," I remarked.

"Then, old man, I'm going through with it," he said calmly. "One does a lot of funny things without thinking, Staunton. And though I should do just the same again over bolting with Eloise, I've got to face the music now."

Involuntarily I smiled at this repetition of my own thoughts.

"He is her husband, and there's not room for the two of us. But if he refuses to fight, then in his own parlance, honour is satisfied as far as I am concerned. Only one proviso do I make under those circumstances: he must swear to divorce Eloise."

And so I will come to the morning of the duel. The Marquis del Vittore was the Baron's second – an Italian who spoke English perfectly. We rowed out from the mainland in separate boats. Barstow and I arrived first and climbed a steep path up the cliff to a small level space on top. Then the others arrived, and I remember noticing at the time, subconsciously, a strange blueness round the Baron's lips, and his laboured breathing. But I was too excited to pay much attention to it.

Barstow was seated on a rock staring out to sea and smoking a cigarette, when I approached del Vittore.

"My first condition," I said, "is that your principal should swear on his honour to divorce his wife in the event of his refusing to fight."

The Marquis stared at me in amazement.

"Refusing to fight!" he said. "But that is what we've come here for."

"Nevertheless I must insist," I remarked.

He shrugged his shoulders and went over to the Baron, who also stared in amazement. And then he began to laugh – a nasty laugh. Barstow gazed at him quite unmoved.

"If I refuse to fight," sneered the Baron, "I will certainly swear to divorce my wife."

"Good," said George laconically, and once more looked out to sea.

"Then shall we discuss conditions, Monsieur," said del Vittore.

"The conditions have been settled by my principal," I remarked, "as he is entitled to do, being the challenged party. The duel will be fought with revolvers, at a range of three feet and only one revolver will be loaded."

The Marquis stared at me in silence: the Baron, every vestige of colour leaving his face, rose to his feet.

"Impossible," he said harshly. "It would be murder."

"Murder with the dice loaded equally," I remarked quietly.

And for a space there was silence. George had swung round and was staring at the Baron. He was outwardly calm, but I could see a pulse throbbing in his throat.

"These are the most extraordinary conditions," said the Italian.

"Possibly," I answered. "But in England, as you may know, we do not fight duels. My principal has no proficiency at all with a revolver. He fails therefore to see why he should do a thing which must result in his certain death: though he is quite prepared to run an even chance. His proposal gives no advantage to either side."

"I utterly refuse," cried the Baron harshly.

"Splendid!" said George. "Then the matter is ended. You have refused to fight, and I shall be obliged if you will start divorce proceedings as soon as possible."

And then occurred one of those little things that are so little and do so much. He smiled at me, an "I told you so" smile. And the Baron saw it.

"I have changed my mind," he said. "I will fight on those conditions."

And once again there was silence. George Barstow stood very still; I could feel my own heart going in great sickening thumps. And looking back on it now, I sometimes try to get the psychology of the thing. Did the Baron think he was calling a bluff: or did he simply accept the conditions in a moment of uncontrollable rage induced by that smile? What did Barstow himself think? For though he had never said so to me in so many words, I know that he had never anticipated that the Baron would fight. Hence the importance he had attached to his first condition.

And then suddenly the whole thing was changed. Impossible now, for anyone or anything to intervene. Barstow's conditions had been accepted: no man calling himself a man could back out. The Marquis drew me on one side.

"Can nothing be done?" he said. "This is not duelling: it is murder."

"So would the other have been," I answered.

And yet it seemed too utterly preposterous – a ghastly nightmare. In a minute, one of those two men would be dead. George, a little pale, but perfectly calm, was finishing his cigarette: the Baron, his face white as chalk, was walking up and down with stiff little steps. And suddenly I realised that it could not be – must not be.

Del Vittore, his hands shaking, took out the two revolvers. He handed me a round of ammunition, and then looked away.

"I don't even wish to know which revolver it is," he said. "Hand them both to me when you've finished."

I handed them to him, and then turned round.

"I will spin a coin," I said. "The Baron will call."

"Heads," he muttered.

"It's tails," I remarked. "Barstow, will you have the revolver in the Marquis' right hand or in his left?"

He flung away his cigarette.

"Right," he said laconically.

I handed it to him, and del Vittore gave the other to the Baron. Then we placed the two men facing one another.

And suddenly del Vittore lost his nerve.

"Get it over!" he shouted. "For God's sake get it over!"

There came a click: the Baron had fired. His revolver was not the loaded one. For a moment he stood there, while the full realisation of what it meant came to him. Then he gave a strangled scream of fear, and his hand went to his heart. His knees sagged suddenly and he collapsed and lay still.

"What's the matter with him?" muttered Barstow. "I haven't fired."

"He's dead," said del Vittore stupidly. "His heart – Weak…"

George Barstow flung his revolver away.

"Thank God! I didn't fire," he said hoarsely.

And silence fell on us save for the discordant screaming of the gulls.

"The result of the exertion of climbing," said del Vittore after a while. "That's what we must say. And we must unload that revolver."

"There's no need," I said slowly. "It was never loaded. Neither of them were."

THE DIAMOND HAIR-SLIDE

"Pity one can't turn 'em on to fight it out like a couple of dogs." The doctor looked thoughtfully across the smoking-room.

"It won't be necessary to do much turning if this heat continues," I said. "As a matter of fact I thought they were going for one another last night."

As usual there was a woman at the bottom of it, and in this particular case it was aggravated by what appeared to be an instinctive dislike at first sight. Funnily enough I had happened to be a witness of their introduction to one another.

It was our first night out from England and I was having a gin and vermouth before dinner when one of them came in. A biggish red-faced man – the type who might have been in cattle in Australia. Mark Jefferson by name, and after he'd ordered a drink himself we started chatting. The usual desultory stuff: bad weather till we get to Gib – hot in the Red Sea, and so on.

Quite a decent fellow I thought – but the sort of man I'd sooner have as a friend than an enemy. Powerful great devil with a fist like a leg of mutton.

We'd just ordered the rest of the half section when the second of them appeared. Completely different stamp of man, but just as tough a nut. Tougher if anything. Hatchet-faced without much colour, but with an eye like a gimlet. His name was Stanton Blake, and at first sight you'd have thought him far the less powerful of the two. At second you'd have realised that there wasn't much in it. Different sort of strength, that's all. The sinewy power of the thin steel rope as against the massive strength of the big rope cable.

However – to get on with it. The ship gave a roll, and Blake lurched into Jefferson. And Jefferson spilt his drink on his trousers. A thing that might happen to anyone. But I've always believed myself that there is such a thing as instinctive antipathy between two people. I mean the sort of dislike that isn't dependent on any specification or spoken word. And it was present in this case. The spilling of the drink was merely the spark that brought it to life.

Blake said, "Sorry." That I swear.

Jefferson growled something about "Clumsy devil" and turned his back. Which he had no right to do.

My own belief, in view of what I've seen since of Jefferson's alcoholic consumption, is that those two cocktails were not exactly his first that day. Not that he was in the slightest degree drunk; I've never seen any man on whom liquor had less obvious effect. But when a man who is quick-tempered by nature has had a few… Well, you know what I mean.

Be that as it may – the fat was in the fire. Blake controlled himself – he didn't say anything. But I saw the look that flashed into his eyes as he stared at the back of Jefferson's head. And there was no mistaking it. I remember it crossed my mind at the time that it would be better for all concerned if they weren't at the same table.

As a matter of fact they were at opposite ends of the saloon, but there was always the smoking-room as a common meeting ground. And as they were both good sailors the foul passage we had as far as Gibraltar didn't affect them. But it affected most other people, which was a pity. For after dinner that night there were only five of us who were taking an interest in things and one of those didn't play bridge.

I confess that I very nearly refused to play myself. I am accounted a good player: I love the game. But I play it for pleasure. And after the little episode before dinner it struck me as problematical if much pleasure would be gained from a table which contained Jefferson and Blake.

I was right: the trouble started at once. I sat with Blake, against Jefferson and a man called Murgatroyd. Tea in Ceylon – he was. And the first thing naturally was how much we played for. I said, "Half-a-crown" straight away, and Murgatroyd agreed. But that wouldn't do for Jefferson. He looked at Blake and suggested a ten pound corner. And Blake shrugged his shoulders and agreed.

"Provided," he said, "we always have it through the trip, Mr Jefferson."

The point of which remark became obvious as the evening went on. Jefferson was a player above the average: but Stanton Blake was easily the best bridge player I have ever sat down to a rubber with. His card sense was simply uncanny. And just once or twice the faintest suspicion of a smile would twitch round his lips – one hand, for instance, when Jefferson did quite obviously throw away a trick he should have made.

It wasn't until the last rubber that they cut together and by then Blake was thirty pounds up on Jefferson apart from ordinary stake money. And it was during this last rubber that the buttons really came off the foils. Bridge, as we all know, can cease to be a pleasant pastime and become the vehicle of more concentrated rudeness and unpleasant back-chat than almost any other game. And though there was no actual rudeness on this occasion Blake got a thrust in that, for sheer malignant venom, was hard to beat.

Jefferson again made a mistake: I forget exactly what it was. He placed the king on his left when quite obviously it lay on his right, or something of that sort. And when the hand was over Blake picked out the trick containing the king in question. He spread it out on the table in front of him, and then he spoke.

"I suppose you wouldn't care to make our little arrangement a twenty pound corner, Mr Jefferson?"

Jefferson's face went purple.

"Thirty if you like," he said thickly.

"The limit is in your hands, Mr Jefferson," said Blake. "However, thirty will suit me admirably."

You see – that was the trouble. From the very first those two men loathed one another: long before the girl came in to complicate the question. She turned the feeling between them into bitter, dangerous hatred – the hatred out of which murder arises. The night when the doctor spoke to me there was murder in the air.

But to go back again a bit. The girl was sitting at my table, and she appeared for breakfast next morning. And though it is only the very young who can work up much enthusiasm over the opposite sex in the early hours, I confess that she gave my elderly heart a very pleasant kick. Her name was Beryl Langton, and she was one of the most adorably pretty creatures I've ever seen. And since we were the sole performers at our table it was only natural that we should start talking.

The rougher it was the more she liked it, she told me – and proceeded to lower two sausages and some fat bacon. She was going to Shanghai – an uncle and aunt were there who had asked her to stay.

"It's simply too wonderful all this," she said. "Of course it's stale to you, but I've never done a longer sea trip than from Weymouth to Jersey."

Her enthusiasm was positively infectious. As far as I am concerned a sea voyage is a necessary evil to be suffered as best one can. But as we staggered up and down the deck that morning – she was doing a sort of corkscrew lurch – I found myself actually looking forward to the present one. I told her stories about the East, and she clung on to my arm and looked up into my face with eyes that shone with excitement.

"I think it's glorious," she said. "The sea is glorious, and life is glorious, and all the things I'm going to see are glorious."

"You might change your mind about the sea," I laughed, "if you were on board a boat like that."

An aged tramp was wallowing past with the waves breaking clean over her, so that she looked like a half-submerged submarine.

"'The Liner she's a lady,'" she quoted, her eyes fixed on the other boat. "But it's fine, you know – fine. That life... Clean and fine."

And for a moment there was a strange expression on her face.

"What about a dish of soup?" I said, and she clapped her hands.

"Splendid," she cried. "I'm beginning to feel positively ashamed of my appetite."

We battled our way to the saloon and sat down. Two or three rather wan-looking individuals looked up in an aggrieved way as we entered, and the girl's thoroughly audible remark – "Good Lord! what an unholy frowst!" was received without enthusiasm. Then the soup came, and she concentrated on that. In fact she was concentrating on the second cup when a man's voice hailed me through the open port-hole behind us.

"Care to make up a rubber?"

Somewhat naturally the girl glanced round to see who it was. It was Jefferson, and for a moment I saw his eyes fixed on her face with that sudden gleam which is unmistakable.

"No thanks," I said curtly. "I don't care about playing in the forenoon."

"Pity," he said, but made no movement to go. "This sea seems to have defeated nearly everybody."

He was including us both in the conversation, and I felt a quick unreasonable annoyance. I knew, of course, that it was quite impossible to prevent him making the girl's acquaintance if he wished to: you can get to know anybody on board ship.

Besides it was most certainly no affair of mine. At the same time – though I had nothing against him – he wasn't the type of man I'd have chosen for my daughter, had I possessed one, to have much to do with.

Then the matter was taken out of my hands.

"I simply adore it," she said to him. "Don't you?"

"I wouldn't go so far as to say that," he smiled. "Having to hold on by one's eyebrows whenever one moves gets a bit monotonous after a time. But luckily it doesn't affect me otherwise. You look very comfy in there. May I come and join you?"

And so the second phase started. Jefferson sat with us till lunch, and it was obvious to the meanest capacity that he was immensely attracted by her. I didn't blame the man – I was attracted myself. And in his full-blooded, boisterous way he wasn't a bad fellow I decided after a while.

Then ten minutes before the bugle went, the first danger rock suddenly showed its head above water. Stanton Blake came in, and nodded good-morning to me. And as he did so he saw the girl and paused close by us. Jefferson beckoned the steward, pointedly ordered "*Three* cocktails," and continued his story to Miss Langton. A more blatant request to move on could hardly have been given, and I saw Blake's face as he did so.

Of course it was only the first point in a long game. Jefferson couldn't sit permanently in the girl's pocket, even had she evinced the smallest desire that he should. And that very afternoon, happening to glance out of the smoking-room, I saw Blake and her walking up and down the deck. Jefferson saw them too, and I noticed *his* face as he did so.

From then on the situation developed rapidly. There was nothing novel about it, and had the circumstances been ordinary doubtless one would have watched with a certain amount of amusement. But Mark Jefferson and Stanton Blake were not ordinary, and from the very first there was a substratum of fear in my mind as to how it was going to end.

The girl seemed supremely unconscious of what was happening, though being a woman I don't suppose she was so in reality. But she certainly did not seem to realise that there was any difference between them and half a dozen others of us who saw a good deal of her. Moreover she never showed – openly at any rate – the smallest preference for one man over the other. She went ashore at Gib with Jefferson: it was Blake who took her up to Citra Vecchia when we anchored at Malta. And in the intervals she played deck games, and danced, and laughed, and won everybody's heart – while the strain in the smoking-room whenever those two were there at the same time grew almost unbearable. In fact there was only one point on which they agreed, and that was too trifling to ease matters.

There are I suppose on board every ship a certain number of women who prefer the smoking-room to the other saloons. And we had two of them. They appeared first just before we reached Gib with a nondescript sort of man in tow.

One of them was a harmless little thing who continually giggled: the other – well, the other I should imagine was not quite so harmless. Her name as shown on the ship's list was Delmorton – Mrs Delmorton. She was invariably most beautifully dressed: she was an extremely good-looking woman: but – that terrible but to the man who has lived much abroad – there was an undoubted touch of the tar-brush. That she had pots of money was obvious: her jewellery was simply magnificent. But she was undoubtedly one of those women into whose past it is inadvisable to inquire too closely.

From the very first she was obviously attracted by Mark Jefferson. Their total dissimilarity of appearance probably accounted for it. And from the very first Jefferson was equally obviously not attracted by her. Which brings me to the one point on which the two men agreed.

They were playing bridge as usual – I had cut out for that rubber – and Mrs Delmorton was standing behind Jefferson. At last she turned and left the room, and quite deliberately Jefferson addressed the players in a low voice.

"If that — nigger stands behind me any more I shall play bridge in my cabin."

And the epithet I regret to state was one which is more applicable to underdone roast beef.

"I agree," said Stanton Blake quietly, and tears came into the eyes of all who heard. Blake and Jefferson had agreed.

I tottered to a corner with the purser: such a moment had to be commemorated. And it was only after a solemn two minutes' silence that I asked him about the woman.

It seemed that she'd travelled in the boat before, and always haunted the smoking-room.

"Who or what Mr Delmorton is, I don't know," said the purser. "I don't even know if there is one. But he must have been a pretty wealthy gentleman."

"Marvellous pearls she has," I said idly.

"They are," he agreed. "But by far her most marvellous piece of jewellery is a thing you haven't seen. She'll wear it before the voyage is out – probably on the night of the fancy dress ball. Made that way, you know: black blood, I suppose. Loves barbaric display."

"What kind of a thing is it?"

"It's a sort of hair-slide effect," he answered. "Diamonds and emeralds. Personally I think it's appallingly vulgar – but its value must be enormous. I keep all her stuff, of course, locked up, and she sends for it as she wants it. And I examined the thing the other day. In fact I showed it to one of the passengers who happened to be in my office, who is a bit of an expert. He valued it at forty thousand pounds. She'll show it to you if you ask her. She adores parading the things."

But I did not trouble Mrs Delmorton: I continued to avoid the lady like the plague. Any interest that the voyage held for me lay in the human drama – not jewels. And the human drama continued to develop in a way that nobody liked. I even noticed the skipper who had happened to come into the smoking-room one night, staring at them a bit hard. Because – though I've said it before, I'll repeat it again – there were times when there was murder abroad in that ship. And murder it might have come to on the night of the fancy dress ball, but for Mrs Delmorton's diamond and emerald hair-slide.

As the purser had prophesied, she wore it. She came in some Oriental costume, and I must admit she looked magnificent in it. And it was the hair-slide that put the finishing touch on it. It was such a magnificent piece of jewellery, in fact, that I overcame my dislike of the lady and asked her to allow me to examine it. There was no doubt about it – if anything, forty thousand was an underestimate. Beryl Langton was with me at the time, and she gave a little gasp of awed envy. A dozen or more large flawless diamonds: the same number of magnificent emeralds, and a quantity of smaller stones in an old-fashioned setting. Barbaric: probably at one time it had belonged to some Eastern potentate. And the net result was that I fully agreed with the purser, though naturally I did not tell the lady so. The final effect was vulgar, unless it was worn with some fancy costume such as she had on that night.

Beryl Langton agreed with me.

"If that belonged to me," she said, in a sort of ecstatic whisper, "I'd have the whole thing reset into a dozen different pieces. Brooches, rings – and imagine a bracelet made of those smaller stones."

Then she laughed. "And to think that when I went to the purser today to get my poor little pearl necklace she was getting *that* out at the same time."

And we are not concerned in any way with the fatuous answer I made. Three pink gins before dinner can be responsible for a lot... We are merely concerned with the extraordinary happenings in the smoking-room which took place after dinner that night. And though for reasons that will appear later it is now two years since the events I am about to describe took place, I think my memory is fairly clear on the matter. At any rate I have forgotten nothing of importance.

It was about ten o'clock when I went in there, and a glance at the card table indicated trouble. Blake and Jefferson were partners, and the sneer on Blake's face was ugly. Mrs Delmorton and the lady who giggled were there, and about half a dozen others.

Just as I came in the rubber ended, and Blake leaned across the table.

"Why in God's name, Mr Jefferson," he snarled, "don't you have lessons in the game? Or else stick to snap with the curate?"

Jefferson half rose in his seat – the back of his neck a dull purple.

"Steady," said Murgatroyd, who was playing. "Ladies present."

"I tell you what I will do, Mr Blake," said Jefferson thickly. "I'll play you one hand of show poker for a monkey."

"A monkey." Blake seemed a bit taken aback.

"Afraid of a real gamble," sneered Jefferson.

And suddenly a grim smile flickered round Blake's lips.

"I agree," he said.

We drew round and watched with bated breath. Everyone seemed to realise that there was more than a monkey at stake.

They cut and Jefferson won. Being show poker he dealt the cards face upwards from a new pack. And when they each had four cards in front of them Blake had a pair of sevens, and Jefferson wanted a nine for a straight.

I looked at the two men, and Blake's fingers were twitching. But Jefferson was absolutely calm. He flicked the card across the table to Blake – another seven. Three – and a little gasp ran round the circle of onlookers.

"It would seem that I want a nine," he said quietly.

He held up the card with its back towards him, so that Blake could see. And Blake's face turned livid.

"It would seem from your appearance that I've got one," he added.

He had: it was the nine of clubs.

"A monkey, I believe, Mr Blake, was the bet," he remarked suavely.

And once again Blake smiled sardonically.

"I'll get it," he said abruptly and left the room.

"What the devil does he mean?" said Jefferson, staring after him. "Get it? Get what?"

"I'm so glad you won, Mr Jefferson," said Mrs Delmorton, leaning over him.

"Thanks," said Jefferson abruptly, his eyes still fixed on the door.

And the next moment I thought the man was going to have an apoplectic fit. Moreover, I didn't blame him. Stanton Blake re-entered the smoking-room carrying in his arms a live monkey.

"What's this damned foolery?" said Jefferson thickly.

"We were playing for a monkey, I believe," remarked Blake calmly. "Here it is – and a very nice one, too."

"You…you…blasted sharper!" roared Jefferson. "I suppose if we'd been playing for a pony you'd have given me a cab-horse. We were playing for five hundred pounds – and you know it."

"We were playing for a monkey," repeated Blake. "I presume I am allowed to put my own interpretation on the word."

It was at that moment that Jefferson picked up the heavy water-bottle that stood on the table, and lifted it above his head.

Somebody – the first officer, I think – shouted – "Steady, for God's sake…" – *and all the lights went out.*

"You swine – you…"

Jefferson's voice came out of the darkness – and the lady who giggled gave a scream. Then after an interval the lights went on again, and we saw that Jefferson had got Blake by the throat. Mrs Delmorton was cowering back against a chair: the monkey was gibbering in the open porthole.

"Get the skipper," shouted the first officer, and flung himself on Jefferson, with three more of us to help. And it took us all we could do to pull him off.

The skipper came rushing in, and he was in a towering rage.

"If you two men give any further trouble," he roared, "I'll clap you both in irons."

Jefferson was still struggling furiously, when there came the diversion. Mrs Delmorton raised her hands to her hair, and gave one horrified scream.

"My slide. It's gone."

An instant silence settled on the room.

"Gone," said the skipper. "What do you mean – gone?"

"It was in my hair. You saw it, didn't you?" She turned to me.

"I certainly saw it before dinner," I said. "I can't say I've noticed it since."

"Close the doors," ordered the skipper curtly. "No one is to leave the room. Now let's get at the bottom of all this. You, sir" – he turned to me – "will you kindly tell me what happened?"

I told him, while Blake and Jefferson sat in opposite corners glaring at one another.

"Who turned off the lights?" he said curtly as I finished.

And no one spoke.

"Did you?" He turned to the steward.

"No, sir. The switch is over there by the door. And I was the other side of the room."

"Please," came a frightened little voice through the porthole, "I did."

We all looked up: Beryl Langton – her face as white as a sheet – was looking in.

"Come in, Miss Langton," said the skipper more gently. "We'd like to know why you did it."

She came in, casting frightened glances at the two men.

"I was passing the door," she stammered, "and I saw Mr Jefferson with a water-bottle in his hand. And I thought he was going to kill Stanton – Mr Blake, I mean. And without thinking I switched out the light. Was it terribly wrong?"

"The point is this, Miss Langton," said the skipper gravely. "Mrs Delmorton has lost her diamond and emerald hair-slide."

"Lost it!" cried the girl. "But I thought you'd taken it off, Mrs Delmorton – and put it in your cabin or something..."

"Taken it off!" echoed the other. "Nothing of the sort."

"Why did you think Mrs Delmorton had taken it off?" asked the skipper.

"Because when I passed you twenty minutes or so ago – you were dancing with Mr Norris, I think – I'm sure you hadn't got it in your hair then. I looked specially to see."

"When was the last occasion, Mrs Delmorton," said the skipper, "that you definitely remember feeling that the slide was there?"

And that was exactly what Mrs Delmorton could not say. In fact when pressed the last time that she could remember with certainty was at dinner, when I gave it back to her.

"Does anybody here remember seeing it before Miss Langton turned the lights out?" asked Murgatroyd.

And once again no one could say with certainty: we had all been far too occupied with the quarrel between the two men.

"Well, Mrs Delmorton," said the skipper, "unless it's fallen overboard it must be on board the ship. And if it's on board the ship we'll find it for you."

"My goodness! Captain Brownlow," she almost wailed. "I've suddenly remembered too that I did lean over the rail for quite a time…"

"You'd have probably noticed if it had fallen off then," he said reassuringly. "We'll find it, Mrs Delmorton. First we'll start with this room."

We were all of us searched, and naturally no one objected. Every seat was minutely examined – even the spittoons were inspected. And there was no trace of that slide. One thing at any rate was certain: it was not in the smoking-room.

At last the skipper gave it up: even Mrs Delmorton was satisfied. But as he left he turned once more to Jefferson and Blake.

"And as for you two gentlemen," he continued, "I meant what I said. If you can't behave yourselves I'll put you both in irons."

But the kick seemed to have gone out of them. In fact they seemed thoroughly ashamed of themselves.

"Confound it, Jefferson," said Blake, "it was only a jest. I'll write you out a cheque in the morning…"

"Sorry if I was a bit hasty," said the other sheepishly. "Look here, we'd better go and join in this search. Why the cursed woman wants to wear valuable jewels in her head at all for I don't know! What's it look like anyway?"

They went out together, Blake with the monkey on his shoulder.

"Do *you* think it was a jest?" said Murgatroyd to me as we followed them.

"I'm not a thought reader," I laughed. "Ask me another."

Well, that ship was searched with a fine toothcomb, but no trace of Mrs Delmorton's hair-slide was ever discovered. And after a while the excitement died down. It was insured anyway, so she would suffer no financial loss. And the finally accepted verdict was that it had probably fallen overboard when she was leaning over the rail.

In fact, after three days the incident was almost forgotten. And the only effect of it that remained was on Jefferson and Blake. It seemed to have sobered them up, and though by no stretch of fancy could it be said that they were friendly, one at any rate no longer feared violence when they met.

Indeed, I was told that the night before Jefferson got off at Colombo, Blake stood him a drink. I didn't see this amazing occurrence, but that the rumour of such a thing could have been received without derisive laughter showed the change of affairs.

Blake went on to Singapore, and mindful of Beryl Langton's slip when she had called him Stanton, I watched them fairly closely. I should have been very sorry if anything had come of it: Blake wasn't the type of man for her. But nothing happened: obviously it had just been a mild board ship flirtation.

And finally, in the fullness of time, I saw her off at Shanghai. Moreover, up on the boat deck the night before we got in, I – well… However, that is altogether another story…

It is at this point that I can imagine the intelligent reader saying with a bewildered air – "What the deuce is all this about? What's the point of it?"

Sir, you are justified in your query. And if it hadn't been that my doctor ordered me to Carlsbad a week ago, I should not have wasted my own time and yours in writing it down. But he did, and the first night I was there I noticed an elderly man of unprepossessing appearance around whom the staff buzzed like bluebottles. It was Guggenheimer – the German millionaire.

I was watching him idly, when suddenly a flutter of excitement ran through the lounge. And the cause of it was a girl with a monkey perched on her shoulder. I gazed at her speechlessly – a perfectly gowned, *soigné*, cosmopolitan woman. I gazed at her speechlessly – Guggenheimer's latest. I gazed at her speechlessly – Beryl Langton. And as she passed close to me I noticed she was wearing a lovely diamond and emerald bracelet.

But so dense can the human brain be at times that even when a biggish red-faced man came up and spoke to Guggenheimer I didn't realise anything was amiss. In fact I didn't realise it until I saw the German introduce him to the girl.

Then the brain did begin to function. For why it was necessary to introduce Mark Jefferson to Beryl Langton was a thing no feller could understand…

My mind went back to that voyage out East, and from a totally new angle I set out to consider the things that had happened.

That Mark Jefferson and Beryl Langton could have forgotten one another was obviously absurd: therefore they were playing a game: therefore they were in collusion.

If they were in collusion now, there was no inherent reason why they shouldn't have been in collusion then. With Stanton Blake as the third member of the gang.

And if that was so the three of them had fooled us all from the very first.

I lit a cigar: the thing wanted thought. They had fooled us with only one idea – to lead up to that culminating moment in the smoking-room when they stole Mrs Delmorton's hair-slide.

I ran over things from the beginning. They knew Mrs Delmorton would be travelling by the boat: they knew her habits – and they laid their plans accordingly. And then when the two men of the gang had got the attention of everyone in the smoking-room riveted on themselves, the girl switched off the lights.

One of them – Blake probably: he had the touch of a conjuror – had whipped it out of her head in the darkness. But the point was – what the deuce had he done with it? It hadn't been on him or in that room when the search took place. That I could swear to.

And then suddenly it dawned on me, in all its rich genius. The monkey. The whole bet about the monkey became pointless if they were members of the same gang, unless the object was to introduce the animal into the room in a perfectly natural way.

It was the monkey that had passed the slide to the girl through the open porthole – it had been sitting there chattering when the lights went on. And if the lights had gone on the fraction of a second too soon, it would merely have been taken as a mischievous trick.

Clever – you know: deuced clever. Of course, I may be wrong: possibly that slide is at the bottom of the Indian Ocean.

But Beryl Langton, who now calls herself Louise van Dyck, cannot have completely forgotten Mark Jefferson, who now calls himself John P Mellon, in two years. And she does wear a lovely diamond and emerald bracelet. And she did give a start of unfeigned amazement when we found ourselves drinking the water at neighbouring tables. And she did look a bit nonplussed when I asked her about Stanton Blake and her uncle in Shanghai.

Of course, I suppose I ought by rights to warn the police or old Guggenheimer.

But I shan't. He's an unpleasant-looking man. And she *was* perfectly adorable on the boat deck that night. Moreover, I may be wrong, but I have a sort of idea that she might…

No – damn it! I came here to drink the waters.

THE BLACK MONK

1

When Jack Tennant got engaged to Mary Darnley, their world at large decided that it was good. And it would have been difficult to decide otherwise. Jack was one of the dearest fellows imaginable: Mary was a darling. They each had looks: and – a detail which cannot be ignored in these prosaic days – there was a sufficiency of money on both sides to ensure comfort.

They both came from the same part of the county, so that their friends were mutual. So, too, were their tastes. They both went well to hounds – in fact, there was a considerable section of the hunt who would have liked to see Jack as Master: they both played tennis and golf above the average. So that, in a nutshell, the world's decision in their case could be pronounced correct.

We had all seen the drift of affairs during the hunting season, but it was not till May that the engagement was definitely announced. And, funnily enough, the man who actually told me was Laurence Trent. Which necessitates another peep into our little corner of England. It had been common knowledge for two or three years that nothing would have pleased him better than that Mary should take the name of Trent, and when he told me the news I glanced at him curiously to see if he was at all upset. But not a bit of it.

"Of course," he said, as he stuffed tobacco into his pipe, "it would be idle to pretend that I wouldn't have preferred Mary to choose someone else, but since she hasn't there is no one I'd sooner see her married to than old Jack. They ought to make a thundering good pair."

I agreed, and felt pleasantly surprised. Not that Trent wasn't a very good fellow: he was. But somehow I didn't expect him to take it *quite* so well. I'd always felt that there was something about him, something I couldn't define, which just spoiled an otherwise first-class sportsman. Perhaps it was that he didn't lose very well at games. True, he rarely lost at all – he was easily the best tennis player round about. But if by chance he did, though he kept himself under perfect control, and to all outward appearances took his defeat quite pleasantly, I'd seen a glint in his eyes that seemed to prove the old tag about appearances being deceptive. However, here he was taking his loss in the biggest game of all as well as Jack Tennant would have taken it himself.

"When are they going to be married?" I asked.

"Fairly shortly I gather," he answered. "There can't be anything to wait for."

And sure enough when the announcement appeared two or three days later in *The Times*, it stated that "a marriage had been arranged and would shortly take place."

They were inundated, of course, with congratulations. And I, being old enough to be their father, felt specially honoured when they both came to dine with me quietly.

"A dull evening, my children," I said. "It was good of you to come."

"Go to blazes, Bill," said Jack. "It was damned sporting of you as a confirmed old bachelor to run the risk of asking us. You are probably proposing to retire to your study after dinner, on the pretence of writing letters, and then herald your return with a coughing fit in the hall. I warn you that if you do we shall come too, and bonnet you with your own paper basket."

"It is true," I murmured guiltily, "that some such idea had entered my brain, but in view of your threat it shall be abandoned."

And, by Jove! they stopped till one. Just once or twice his hand would touch her arm: just once or twice a look would pass between them that made even a confirmed old bachelor wonder if he wasn't really a confirmed old fool. They were two of the best, and it did one's eyes good to see them together. Certainly if any couple ever seemed to have been smiled on by Fate, it was this one. Which made the tragedy all the more dreadful when it occurred.

However I will take things in their proper sequence. It was on the 15th of June, so I see from my diary, that a party of us went for a picnic. Jack and his girl were there, and Laurence Trent, and several others whose names are immaterial. We went in three cars, starting after lunch, and our destination was an old ruined Priory some forty miles away which was reputed to be haunted. The ghost was said to be the black cowled figure of a monk, and if it came to a man it meant death. There was a good deal of ragging and chaff, and one of the men, I remember, covered himself with a tablecloth and stalked about amongst the ruins. In fact the whole atmosphere of the party was what you would have expected when a bunch of healthy normal people find themselves in such a locality in broad daylight.

Laurence Trent was particularly scathing on things ghostly, and roared with laughter at the usual stories of people's aunts who had woken up in the middle of the night to feel a spectral hand clutching the bedclothes.

"It's always somebody's aunt," he jeered. "What I want to know is if any one of you personally have ever felt this clutching hand. It's rot – the whole thing. Due to indigestion. For all that I'm glad we came, because it's a beautiful old place. I'm going to take some photographs."

He set up his camera – photography was his great hobby – and took several exposures from different angles.

"Perhaps we'll see the black monk in one of them," he laughed. "Come on, Jack – I've got one film left. You and Mary go and pose in the foreground."

Now I was standing at his side at the moment, and the rest of the party were fooling about behind us.

"That's right," he said, with his hand on the bulb. And even as I heard the click of the shutter, he muttered "My God!" under his breath. I glanced at him: his face was as white as a sheet, and he was staring with dilated eyes in front of him. Jack and Mary had turned away: no one had seen his agitation except myself.

"What's the matter, Trent?" I asked quickly.

"Nothing," he said at length, "nothing."

The colour was coming back to his cheeks, though his hands shook a little as he dismantled his camera.

"You didn't see anything, did you, Mercer? Standing by Jack?"

"Nothing at all," I said brusquely. "Did you?"

"I thought," he began, and then he shook himself suddenly. "Of course not," he laughed. "A trick of the light."

But it seemed to me that his laughter didn't ring quite true, and I watched him curiously.

"Did you think you saw the black monk?" I said jocularly.

"Go to Hell," he snapped. And then, "Sorry, Mercer. But it's best not to chaff about these things."

Which coming from the person who had chaffed about them more than anyone else struck me as a little cool. However I thought no more about it. We drove home in different cars, and when, two or three mornings later, I saw him walking up my drive I had completely dismissed the matter from my mind. In fact I merely wondered what had brought him: Trent was not a frequent visitor of mine.

"Can you give me a few minutes, Mercer?" he said gravely, and I wondered still more at his tone of voice. "I want to ask your advice."

"Of course," I said. "Come indoors."

I led the way, and he followed in silence.

"You remember our picnic at the old Priory," he remarked when I had closed the study door.

"Perfectly," I answered, suddenly recalling his strange agitation.

"You remember that when I took a photograph of Jack and Mary, you pulled my leg and asked me if I thought I'd seen the black monk?"

"I do," I said. "You seemed so upset."

"I was," he answered quietly. "Because that is exactly what I had seen."

"My dear Trent," I laughed. "You! The most scathing cynic of us all!"

But he wasn't to be drawn.

"I admit it," he said gravely. "I admit that up to that moment I regarded anything of that sort as old women's foolishness. All the way home in the car: all that night I endeavoured to persuade myself that what I had seen was a trick of the light as I said to you. And I almost succeeded. Now I know it wasn't!"

"You know it wasn't!" I echoed incredulously. "But how?"

"You may remember that I took the photograph," he said. "And, Mercer, the camera cannot lie."

He was taking a print out of his pocket as he spoke, and I stared at him wonderingly. In silence he handed it across to me, and, as I looked at it the hair at the back of my scalp began to prick. In the background stood the ruins of the Priory: in front were Jack and Mary. But it was not at them that I was looking. Standing by Jack was a black cowled figure, with one arm outstretched towards him. The face was concealed: the hand could not be seen. But the whole effect was so incredibly menacing that I felt my throat go dry.

"A defect in the film," I stammered after a while.

"Then it's a very peculiar one," he said gravely. "I tried to think it was that, Mercer, but it was no good. That's not a defect. You see" – he paused a minute – "I saw it myself."

"Then why didn't I?" I demanded.

"God knows," he said, and for a while we fell silent.

"But this is impossible," I said at length. "Things like that don't happen."

"Exactly what I've been saying to myself," he remarked. "Things like that don't happen. And in your hands you hold the proof that in this case it has. And to me of all people. I, who have always ridiculed anything of the sort. I've heard – who hasn't? – of spirit photographs, and I've always regarded them as a not very clever type of fraud."

"You've got the film?" I said.

"No," he answered. "I haven't. I made two prints of it, and then I got into a sort of panic. Damned foolish of me, but 'pon my soul, Mercer, I've hardly been able to think straight since I developed that roll. Anyway I put a match to it and burnt it. However that's not the point, is it? The point is, what are we going to do?"

"Do," I repeated stupidly. "What can we do?"

"Well, ought we to warn Jack? You know the legend. Heaven knows I do. No one jeered at it as much as I did, and now I can't get it out of my mind. If the black monk goes to a man it means death. And that afternoon it went to Jack."

"Confound it, Trent," I cried irritably, "this is the twentieth century. We're talking drivel."

"Go on," he said wearily. "Say again all the things I've said already to myself. Say we're two grown men, and not hysterical children. Say that the whole thing is absurd. Say everything you darned well please. I have – several times. And then, Mercer, look at the photograph you hold in your hand."

He got up and began pacing up and down the room.

"I tell you," he went on, "I've thought of this thing from every angle. And the more I've thought of it the more utterly nonplussed have I become."

"Even granted," I said slowly, "that this – this thing was there that afternoon…"

"Damn it," he almost shouted, "is there any doubt about it?"

"Very well then," I said, "I'll put it a different way. Although this thing was there that afternoon, it doesn't follow that the rest of the legend is correct. That it means – death."

"I know it doesn't," he cried eagerly. "That's the one straw at which I'm clutching."

"And most emphatically," I went on, "nothing must be said about it to Jack. If – Great Scott! you know, it seems too ridiculous to be even discussing it in the broad light of day – if it does portend death then death will come whatever we do. And if it doesn't – if there's nothing in it – there's no earthly use making Jack's life a burden to him. Wondering what's going to happen. Why, he might even break off the engagement."

He nodded two or three times.

"You're right," he said. "Perhaps I ought to have torn up the whole thing and said nothing about it. But to tell you the truth it's given me such an appalling shock that I felt I simply must talk to somebody about it. And as you were with me when it happened, I naturally thought of you. I wish to Heavens I'd never suggested going to the beastly place."

"Was it your suggestion?" I said. "I thought it was Lady Taunton's."

"I suggested it to her," he said moodily. "Anyway it's done now, and we went. Look here, Mercer, don't think me an ass. And I shall quite understand if you would rather not. But I'd be most awfully grateful to you if you'd keep that print. Lock it away in your safe. I sort of feel," he went on apologetically, "that it would help me considerably if I could know that there was somebody else – You know..."

"Morbid," I said. "Let's tear it up, and try and forget it."

"Isn't that tantamount to confessing that we're frightened?" he said. "You can tear it up easily enough, but that isn't going to wipe it off our minds. However I leave it to you: do as you like."

He nodded abruptly, and stepped through the open window.

"So long," he grunted, and for a while I watched him striding down the drive. Then I went back to my desk and again picked up the print. The whole thing seemed so utterly incredible that my brain felt dazed. The average Englishman who leads an outdoor life doesn't worry his head as a general rule about the so-called supernatural, and I had certainly been no exception to the rule. If I had been asked to sum up my ideas on the subject, I suppose I should have said that though I was quite prepared to believe that strange things happened outside our ken, I had never come across them and I didn't want to. And here I found myself confronted with this astounding photograph. Back and forth, this way and that did I argue it out in my mind. And I got no further forward. If it was a defect in the film, then in view of what Trent had seen, it was the most amazing coincidence that had ever happened. And if it wasn't.

The lunch gong roused me, and for a moment or two I hesitated. My hand went out towards a box of matches: should I burn it? And then Trent's remark came back to me – "Isn't it tantamount to confessing that we're frightened?" I went to my safe and opened it. I thrust the print far into the back. Time would tell. And as the days passed, and the weeks, gradually the thing faded from my mind. When I thought of it at all, I regarded it as one of those strange inexplicable things which are insoluble.

2

The wedding was fixed for the end of September. On the 31st of August Jack Tennant was killed. To this day I remember the blank feeling of numbed shock I experienced when I heard the news. I had almost forgotten the photograph, and I just sat staring speechlessly at my butler as he told me.

It appeared that he had fallen over the edge of Draxton Quarry, and had broken his neck on the rocks below. I knew the place as well as I knew my own garden – but so did Jack Tennant. It was an old disused chalk quarry, and for years people had been agitating to have railings put round the top. And because it was everybody's business, no one had attended to it. To a stranger it was a dangerous place, but it was extraordinary that a man who knew the quarry as well as he did should have ventured so near the edge. As always when the soil is small landslips were frequent.

"It was Mr Trent who found him, sir," concluded my butler, and instantly my thoughts reverted to the photograph. So the legend of the black monk had not proved false.

I ordered my car, and went round to see Trent. He was in a terrible state of distress, and it appeared that not only had he found Jack's body but he had seen the whole thing happen.

"I was walking back from Oxshott Farm," he said, "and when I got level with the quarry, I saw old Jack away to the left close by the top. So I started to stroll towards him. I hadn't gone more than about twenty yards, when he suddenly threw up his arms, gave a great shout and disappeared. The ground had crumbled under his feet, but what I can't understand is why he should have been standing so close to the edge. I got down to the bottom as quickly as I could, but the poor old chap was stone dead."

"What a ghastly thing," I muttered.

We looked at one another, the same thought in both our minds.

"Did you tear up that photograph?" he said at length.

"No, I kept it. It is in my pocket now. Have you got yours?"

He nodded. "Yes, I have. Look here, Mercer, what are we going to do about them?"

"I don't see that there's anything to be done," I said. "The poor old chap is dead, and nothing can alter the fact."

"I know that," he answered. "But there will be an inquest, and of course I shall be called. In fact, as far as I know, I'm the only witness: the place was absolutely deserted when it happened. Oughtn't I to say something about it?"

"What on earth is the use?" I cried. "As the thing stands at the moment it is merely a ghastly accident. There's nothing to tickle the public fancy over it, and it will be dismissed by the Press in a few lines. But if you mention those photographs, you will immediately start a first-class sensation. You'll have every reporter in England buzzing round, and it will be most unpleasant for all of us."

"I suppose you're right," he said slowly. "And yet – I don't know. It's all so extraordinary, isn't it? I almost feel as if I was suppressing a piece of vitally important evidence."

A shadow fell across the room, and I looked up quickly. A man was standing in the open window – a man who bore a marked resemblance to Jack Tennant.

"Forgive my intrusion," he said gravely, "but I heard that Mr Trent was on the lawn and…" He paused, looking from one to the other of us…

"That's me," said Trent, and the other bowed. "And this is Mercer."

"I'm Jack's brother," he remarked. "I gather it was you who found him."

"Not only that, but I saw the whole thing," said Trent. "I've just been telling Mercer about it."

Once again he told the story, and the other listened in silence.

"Is that all?" he said when Trent had finished.

"Everything. Why?"

"Because I could not help overhearing, as I came in, a remark you made to Mr Mercer. You said you felt as if you were suppressing a piece of vitally important evidence."

Trent glanced at me, question in his eyes.

"I think," I said at length, "that Mr Tennant at any rate should be told. And then he, as Jack's brother, had better decide."

And so Trent told him the other story too, whilst Tennant listened with ever-growing amazement on his face.

"You feel," said Trent, "just as I felt: just as Mercer felt when I first told him. I don't believe there was a man in England more profoundly sceptical on psychic matters than I was. But there you are: look at it."

He took his copy from his pocket and handed it to the other.

"The film I destroyed, and have never ceased regretting that I did so. But I am as convinced in my own mind that poor old Jack was under sentence of death from that day, as I am that we three are in this room. We talked it over, Mercer and I, and rightly or wrongly we came to the conclusion that it would be worse than useless to tell him. If there was nothing in it we should only be upsetting him needlessly: if the reverse then it would do no good."

"Most extraordinary," said Tennant. "A pity you destroyed the film. You have kept your copy, Mr Mercer?"

"As a matter of fact, I have it on me now," I said, taking it from my pocket.

"They are exactly the same," cried Trent. 'Two prints of the same film. Good Lord! I'm sorry. How infernally clumsy of me."

A stream of ink had shot across his desk soaking one of the prints that Tennant was examining side by side.

"My dear sir – ten thousand apologies." He dashed round with blotting paper. "It's not on your clothes, is it?"

"Luckily not," said Tennant. "But I'm afraid one of your prints is ruined."

"That doesn't matter. Anyway one is all right. And that brings us to the point we've got to decide – whether or not anything shall be said about this at the inquest. Mercer thinks it will bring a swarm of journalists about our heads, and he is probably right. I, on the other hand – well, you overheard my remark. Ought we to suppress it?"

"It's certainly most strange," said Tennant thoughtfully. "You say, Mr Trent, that you actually saw this apparition?"

"I did. And it shook me badly at the moment, as Mercer will tell you."

The other rose and went to the window, where he stood looking down the drive.

"And you didn't see it, Mr Mercer?"

"No," I said, "I didn't. But I can vouch for Trent's agitation."

"Which was quite understandable," agreed Jack's brother. "However the point on which you apparently want my advice is whether or not this photograph should be produced at the inquest. I unhesitatingly agree with Mr Mercer. To produce it can do no good, and will inevitably throw us all into the limelight."

"Very good," said Trent, "I will say nothing about it."

He picked up his copy and replaced it in his pocket.

"Not much good keeping yours, Mercer, I'm afraid."

"I don't want it," I said. "Tear it up and throw it away."

"Well then it's understood," he said as he dropped the pieces in his waste-paper basket, "that nothing should be said about this. On second thoughts I think you're right."

He paused for a moment, and then turned to Tennant.

"May I tender you my sincere sympathy in your great loss?"

"Thank you," said the other. "Jack was a dear boy. Well, Mr Mercer, if that is your car outside I wonder if you would give me a lift back. I'm staying at the Boar's Head."

"Of course," I cried, and Trent followed us through the hall.

"Will you be at the inquest?" he said as we got in.

"I certainly shall," said Tennant, and with that we drove off.

"How is Mary taking it?" I said, as we turned into the road.

Instead of answering he made a remark which seemed to be in the most questionable taste.

"I believe I'm right in thinking that Mr Trent was – shall we say – a runner up for Mary?"

"Really, Mr Tennant," I said stiffly, "I am not in his confidence to that extent. And anyway this is hardly the time to discuss it."

"I think I remember Jack mentioning the fact to me in a letter last winter. They were getting up some amateur theatricals, and Trent was acting."

"He is a very good actor," I remarked. "In fact I believe for a while he was on the stage in London. Before he came into money."

"I thought he must be," was his somewhat surprising reply. "It's strange that a man who is presumably neat with his fingers should be so clumsy with his hands."

"I don't know that I should have called Trent particularly neat with his fingers," I said.

"That makes it even stranger," he remarked. "People who are not neat with their fingers – men especially – generally dislike sewing."

For a moment or two I stared at him blankly, but his face was expressionless.

"What on earth?" I began.

"Though of course," he continued, "occupation of some sort is a great help if one is upset. But sewing a button on a coat is hardly one I should have expected a man to select. You didn't notice that? Well – it's not surprising. Like the majority of people you see – but you don't observe. Now on Mr Trent's desk was a reel of black cotton and a needle – a sufficiently unusual thing to find on a man's desk to make one wonder why it was there.

When one further notices that the bottom leather button of his shooting coat is sewn on very crudely with black cotton the connection becomes obvious."

I confess I found myself disliking the man intensely. Within a few hours of his brother's death, that he should callously discuss little deductions and inferences struck me as absolutely indecent.

"Of course I may be wrong," I said coldly. "But the death of a boy who was almost like a son to me, seems of more importance to my mind than the sewing on of fifty buttons."

He turned to me with a sudden very charming smile – a smile that brought back Jack irresistibly.

"Forgive me, Mr Mercer," he said. "Believe me, I am not as callous as you think."

And with that he relapsed into a silence that continued till we reached the Boar's Head.

3

The inquest revealed nothing that we did not know already. The jury returned a verdict of Accidental Death, tendered their sympathy to the deceased man's family, and added a rider to the effect that steps should be taken immediately to erect a suitable fence round the top of Draxton Quarry. Trent gave his evidence with considerable emotion – as the jury well knew he and Tennant had been friends – and true to what we had arranged he said nothing about the black monk. It was therefore with some surprise that when I went into the Boar's Head for luncheon I was at once tackled on the subject by the landlord.

"It's all over the place, Mr Mercer," he said. "Not as how I holds with that sort of stuff, but you know what folks be round here."

I made some non-committal reply and sought out Tennant.

"Are you surprised?" he said quietly, "I'm not."

"But who started it?" I cried. "You say you've said nothing, and it wasn't me."

"Which narrows the field somewhat – doesn't it?"

And at that moment Trent came in, and I tackled him.

"Good Heavens!" he muttered, "it's spread as quick as that, has it? It was my gross carelessness. Like a fool last night, I forgot to take the papers out of the pocket of my coat when I changed for dinner. And my man must have seen it. Damn the fellow! I'll sack him."

He went out fuming angrily, and I turned a little curiously to Tennant.

"Why did you say you weren't surprised?" I said.

He smiled enigmatically.

"Those sort of things have a way of coming out," he remarked. "Shall we lunch together?"

And, as we were going in, a page brought him a telegram. He opened it and gave a grunt of satisfaction as he read the contents. Then he turned to me.

"Would you be good enough to ask me to dinner tonight? And a friend of mine too – a lady."

I stared at him blankly.

"I am aware it sounds a little strange, and my next request will sound stranger still. Does Trent know your family intimately? Your relations, I mean."

"Far from it," I said.

"So you could quite easily invent a niece, shall we say, without him suspecting anything."

"What the devil are you driving at, Tennant?" I cried.

"Because I would like this friend of mine to be your niece. And I shall meet her for the first time at your house. And so will Trent, who I want you to ask to dinner also. Incidentally here he is. Ask him now, please" – his voice was low and urgent – "and mention your niece."

There was something compelling about the man, and I found myself doing as he said.

"Dine," said Trent. "Thanks, Mercer, I'd like to. Eight, I suppose."

"There will be a niece of mine there," I remarked. "I don't think you've ever met her. I suppose you wouldn't care to come, Tennant."

"Will it be quite quiet?" he said doubtfully.

"Just us," I answered. "And my niece."

"Thanks very much," he said, "I'll come."

At that moment I happened to glance at Trent, and it seemed to me that he gave a tiny frown. It was gone in an instant, but the impression that he wasn't too well pleased at my inviting Tennant, lingered in my mind. And it was still there when Tennant and the lady arrived at a quarter to eight. All the afternoon I'd been racking my brains trying to think what all the mystery was about, and the instant they came I turned eagerly to Tennant.

He cut short my questions immediately.

"Listen, Mr Mercer," he said curtly, "we haven't got too much time. This is Miss Greyson. You will call her Monica. You are her uncle: so she will call you uncle – what?"

"Most people call me Bill," I said.

"Very good. She will call you Uncle Bill. She is staying in the house: but that fact must not be alluded to in front of the servants, or they may give it away."

"But," I cried, "what is it all about?"

"With luck you'll know before the evening is out," he said gravely. "Take your cues from us, and if it's urgent – for God's sake jump to it, or it may be too late."

"What may be too late?" I said blankly.

"Monica is taking her life in her hands tonight," was his astounding reply. "Perhaps we all are. Above all – don't forget – not a word to Trent."

And at that moment Trent was announced. In a sort of dream I heard a voice introducing him to Miss Greyson – and realised the voice was my own. In a sort of dream I went in to dinner, and found myself eating what was put in front of me mechanically. Taking her life in her hands. Was I mad – or was he?

After a while I pulled myself together – as host I had to make some pretence at talking – and found they were discussing the photograph.

"If I were you, Trent," Tennant was saying, "I would send that photograph to the Society for Psychical Research."

"Dash it, man," answered Trent, "I couldn't. I've cursed my man's head off for speaking about it at all, and I don't want any more publicity. I mean Mary is in the photo too, as well as poor old Jack. It's incredible how it's spread all over the place so quickly."

"It is without exception the most wonderful spirit photograph I have ever seen," said Tennant. "And it's a thing I'm extremely interested in."

"Are you?" said Trent in surprise. "Somehow I should never have thought it of you."

"Only, of course, as an amateur." He glanced across at the girl. "Forgive the impertinence, Miss Greyson, but surely you are clairvoyante?"

She looked at me with a smile.

"I don't know what Uncle Bill will say about it," she said, "but you're quite right, Mr Tennant. Only I don't want it talked about in the family, Uncle Bill."

"My dear, I'll say nothing," I said.

"How did you know?" asked Trent curiously.

"My dear fellow," said Tennant, "when you've dabbled in it even as little as I have, you'll recognise it at a glance. There is something in the face – something indefinable and yet quite obvious. I should imagine that Miss Greyson was possessed of remarkable powers."

The girl laughed.

"That, I'm afraid, I don't know. I've not done much of it, and, of course, when one is in a trance one knows nothing."

"It would be interesting to try tonight," said Tennant. "That is to say if Miss Greyson doesn't mind."

Trent fidgeted in his chair.

"I don't know that I'm particularly keen," he muttered. "The black monk is enough for me – at any rate for the present."

And then for one moment, Tennant stared straight at me, and the unspoken message might have been shouted aloud, so clear was it.

"I think it might be quite amusing," I said. "But of course Monica must decide."

"I don't mind," cried the girl. "If Mr Trent would sooner not..."

"Oh! I don't mind," he said sullenly.

"I can't guarantee anything," went on the girl. "Sometimes I'm told I simply talk gibberish."

"Naturally," said Tennant quietly. "No medium can ever be certain of getting results."

For a while we stopped on at the dinner table, but the atmosphere was not congenial. Trent sat in moody silence, looking every now and then from under his eyebrows at the girl. And at length Tennant gave me an almost imperceptible movement of the head.

"Shall we go into the other room?" I said. "And then Monica shall take charge."

"Mind you," she repeated with a smile, "I don't guarantee anything."

"I suppose we put out the lights?" I said.

"It's always better," she answered. "Now if you three just sit down, anywhere you like, and keep quite still I'll see what I can do."

And the last thing I noticed as I switched off the lights was Trent's sullen, scowling face. For a while we sat in silence, and I know that my nerves were far from being as steady as I would have liked. That one remark of Tennant's kept ringing in my head – taking her life in her hands. But how? And why the secrecy over Trent?

Suddenly a long shuddering sigh came from the girl, and I sat up tensely.

"She's under," said Tennant in a low voice. "Be careful."

Again silence – and then a man's loud voice – "Peter."

"Good God!" I muttered, "it's Jack."

I could hear Trent's breath come in a quick hiss.

"Peter! Peter!"

"Is that you, Jack?" said Tennant quietly.

"Peter! The button. Proof from the button."

"What button, Jack?"

"Proof. Proof." The voice was far away. "He came down to get it."

"Jack, come back, Jack. How are you, old chap?"

"Proof. Peter – no accident. That devil – that devil…"

"Who, Jack – who. Did someone murder you?"

"That devil – that devil – Laurence…"

There came a shrill piercing scream, and a dreadful worrying noise.

"Lights," roared Tennant, and I dashed for the switch. In the room behind, a voice I didn't recognise was muttering harshly again and again: "Yes – damn you, I did it. I did it, you swine." On her back, on the floor was Monica Greyson and kneeling over her with his hands clutching her throat was Trent. His face was distorted with fury: there was murder in every line of it. And even as I watched, fascinated with horror, Tennant and another man hurled themselves on him.

"Sand-bag him, Simpson," shouted Tennant. "He'll kill her."

And the next instant Trent lay still, and Tennant with his arms round the girl was calling for brandy.

"Good enough, Simpson, I think," he said curtly, and the other nodded. "By the way, Mercer – this is Inspector Simpson of Scotland Yard."

"But what does it all mean," I said feebly.

"That that devil murdered Jack in cold blood," he said grimly. "And he's going to swing for it."

Trent, handcuffed by now, had come to, and lay glaring at the speaker.

"You wouldn't have got me but for that cursed girl," he snarled. "A man can't compete against that."

And Tennant laughed.

"It may interest you to know, Laurence Trent, that the whole thing tonight has been a fake from beginning to end. Just as your photograph of the black monk was a fake."

4

"Has it ever occurred to you, Mercer, that by far the best way of stopping people talking about a thing, is to present them with a ready-made solution which accounts for that thing? If in addition that solution can be substantiated by an unbiased witness its value is greatly increased."

Trent had gone in the custody of Inspector Simpson, and Tennant and I and the girl – little the worse now for her rough handling – were sitting in my study.

"There is nothing so fatal," he continued calmly, "to arriving at the truth as to start with a preconceived theory. And a ready-made solution in nine cases out of ten causes just such a start. If a man is perfectly satisfied with his solution he has no incentive to try and find another.

"The preconceived theory in this case was that Jack had met his death accidentally. I was perfectly prepared to believe it: at the same time I was equally prepared to disbelieve it. And when I arrived here, I endeavoured to make my mind a blank except for three facts, none of which were conclusive and all of which were perfectly consistent with the accident theory.

"The first was that it was strange that Jack should have been standing so near the edge. Not impossible – but strange.

"The second was that it was Laurence Trent who found him.

"And the third was – that *if* it wasn't an accident – Trent is, as far as I know, the only man who had any motive for killing Jack – namely Mary.

"That was my state of mind when I first saw Trent. I had no proof whatever that it wasn't an accident: but I had no proof that it was. And then I noticed the button. To you it conveyed nothing: to me it was a most significant thing. To a man who was in the condition of agitation that he was in to set to work to sew a button on his coat struck me as most peculiar. Unless he was afraid of such a thing as finger-marks: unless, perhaps – it was still only perhaps – there had been a struggle, a button had been wrenched off his coat, and he had decided to sew it on to prevent questions.

"Then you started the black monk question. Well, Mercer, I frankly admit I'm sceptical. But I am old enough now to realise that just because I don't happen to believe in a thing, that that is no proof of its falseness. Men of brains, men of intellect have assured me that they have indisputable proof that spirit photographs have been taken. And when Trent showed me his copy I was still prepared to believe in the possibility of its being genuine. Until you showed me yours. Did you ever see the two prints side by side?"

"Never," I said.

"And Trent never intended that anyone should. It was his one great mistake. In your copy the outstretched arm of the black monk just reached a corner of the priory behind it: in his copy there was at least the sixteenth of an inch overlap. Which proved instantly that it was merely an ordinary fake done by superimposing one film on another. It also proved instantly that we were dealing with a singularly dangerous man – and a singularly clever one."

"For the life of me I don't quite see the object," I said.

"You go to the theatre, don't you, Mercer? And you know the effect of concentrating the limelight on one figure. The audience doesn't worry about the others. Now if you were to walk into any public house within a radius of five miles at this moment, you would find that the black monk is the sole topic of conversation. The sceptical ones will say it's coincidence, and the superstitious that it's fate. But it would have served its purpose with both parties – and that was to occupy the front of the stage leaving the rest in darkness.

"You were there to give an air of truth to the whole thing. Why – you believed it yourself: you vouched for his agitation when he took the photo."

"I can hardly believe that the man had planned the whole thing then," I said. "It seems too monstrous."

Tennant shrugged his shoulders.

"Who knows? Perhaps it was a whim of the moment: perhaps he really did think some trick of the light was the black monk. And then the idea grew until it obsessed him. He was committed to nothing: all he had to do was to wait his chance. But the point is that when I left with you in the car I knew Trent had murdered Jack. Which is a totally different thing to proving it. He had destroyed the main evidence by tipping the ink over it: and even if the police arrested him – which was most unlikely – there wasn't a hope of his being convicted on the evidence I had."

He mixed himself a drink.

"Theatrical, perhaps. And yet I don't know. On the face of it it seemed so theatrical that it must be true. Wherein lay his cleverness. However, Monica proved tonight that other people could act too."

And then came the strangest thing of that strange night.

"I suppose you realise, Peter, don't you," she said quietly, "that I was completely off?"

He stared at her blankly.

"You were what?" he stammered. "You say you were – off. Good God!"

THE HIDDEN WITNESS

I don't know exactly when it was that I first realised that Miles Standish was in love with Mary Somerville. As a general rule men are very unobservant on such matters, and I suppose I was no exception. All I know is that when I mentioned the matter guardedly to Phyllis Dankerton she observed brightly that the next great discovery I should make was that the earth was round. So I suppose it must have been fairly obvious.

Anyway it doesn't much matter, except that I'd like to get it accurate. The house party was all there when I arrived. To take them in order there were, first of all, our host and hostess – John Somerville and his wife. He was a wealthy man – something in cotton – who had reached such a position of affluence at a comparatively early age that he could, had he wanted to, have given up business altogether. But he preferred to have something to do, and now, at the age of forty-five, he still went up to London five days a week. A smallish man, thin and spare, with shrewd thoughtful eyes that missed very little that went on around him.

It was through Mary, his wife, that I had got to know him. She was fifteen years his junior, and if ever there was a case of wondering why two people had got married, this was it. She was one of the most lovely creatures I have ever seen – the sort of girl who could have married literally anyone she chose. And then quite suddenly five years ago she had married John.

Personally I have always thought that money had a good deal to do with it. Not that John wasn't quite a decent fellow, but having said that you'd said all. By no possible stretch of imagination could he be regarded as the sort of man to inspire romance in a girl's heart. He was far too self-centred: far too much the business man to the exclusion of everything else. And yet, Mary, with numerous men at her feet, had selected him.

My own impression was that she had begun to regret it. They got on very well together, but it was a very restrained relationship. She liked him and he was inordinately proud of her – and that was the end of it. So much for our host and hostess.

There was a married couple – Peter Dankerton and his wife. He was a bridge fiend with the tongue of an adder – but distinctly good-looking and very amusing company.

The younger element consisted of Tony Merrick, a subaltern in the Gunners, and a jolly little kid called Marjorie Stanway, who spent most of their time practising new steps in the hall to a gramophone.

And finally there was a man called Miles Standish, who was the only one I had never met before. He was a planter of sorts out in the FMS. About thirty years old, he seemed to have been everywhere and done everything. He had rather a lazy, pleasant voice, and a trick of raising his eyebrows when he spoke that made the most ordinary remark seem amusing: and little Marjorie, to the fury of young Merrick, adored him openly. In fact, the outstanding personality of the party, Mary always excepted.

She introduced me to him as soon as I arrived.

"The only one you don't know, Bill," she said. "Miles – this is Bill Canford, who is almost a fixture about the house."

"A very pleasant occupation," he remarked lightly, and I got the impression that his eyes were very observant. "If I could afford to become a fixture, I should choose an English country house to do it in."

We talked on casually for a while, and he was certainly a most interesting man. And an efficient one. His knowledge, obviously acquired on the spot, of rubber and its future showed him as a man who could observe and think for himself.

"And where," I said, after a while, "is our worthy host?"

"My dear Bill," laughed Mary, looking up from the tea table, "John has got a new toy. His present secretary's face is so frightful that he can't bear her in the same room with him. So he has got a sort of phonograph machine – a super-dictaphone I think he calls it – and he dictates his letters into it. You don't have to talk into a trumpet like you do with most of them. It stands in a corner, and looks just like an ordinary box. Then each morning she comes and takes off the records and writes down what he has said."

"It might almost have been worthwhile to change his secretary," said Standish lazily. "Still he is doubtless very happy."

He leant over to light her cigarette, and I was struck by the atmosphere of physical fitness that seemed to radiate from the man. Hard as nails: without an ounce of superfluous flesh on him. In fact a pretty tough customer in a rough house.

I suppose a woman would have spotted the lie of the land that night after dinner. In the light of subsequent events I now realise that the tension was already there, though I didn't get it personally. It was just a little thing – a casual scrap of conversation between two rubbers. Standish was shuffling the cards, and Phyllis Dankerton, who had been his partner, made some remark about the excellence of his bridge not having been impaired by his living in the back of beyond.

He grinned and said, "We're not all savages, Mrs Dankerton. Even though there aren't no Ten Commandments, and a man can raise a thirst."

"At the moment," remarked John Somerville quietly, "we don't happen to be East of Suez."

The faintest of smiles flickered for an instant round Phyllis Dankerton's lips. Then –

"How marvellously Kipling gets human nature, doesn't he?" she murmured. "You and I, Bill – and an original no trumper of mine is open to the gravest suspicion."

Yes – the tension had begun. To what extent it had grown I don't know: but it was there. As I say, I realised that afterwards. John Somerville suspected his wife and Standish. Not that he said anything, or even hinted at anything that night, with the exception of that one remark. As always he was the courteous perfect host – at least so it seemed to me. Though when a couple of days later I was discussing things with Phyllis Dankerton she regarded me pityingly when I said so.

"My dear man," she said, "you must be partially wanting. There is an atmosphere in this house you could cut with a knife. Our worthy John is watching those two like a cat watches a mouse. It's all excessively amusing."

"Do you think Mary is in love with Standish?" I said.

"Wasn't it Maugham who said in one of his plays that a lot of unnecessary fuss is made about the word love? Quite obviously she is immensely attracted by him – who wouldn't be? I'm crazy about him myself. And, my dear Bill, I might be eighty-one with false teeth for all the notice he takes of me. It's cruel hard on a deserving girl. There's poor old Peter who wouldn't notice the Alps unless they were covered with Stock Exchange quotations, and yet I throw myself at that brute's head in vain."

"I wonder how Mary met him," I said.

"Really, Bill," she cried impatiently, "you're intolerably dull today. She met him in the same way that everybody does meet people presumably. Anyway what does it matter? The beginning has nothing to do with it: it's the end that interests me."

"You really think that it's serious," I said.

She shrugged her shoulders.

"With a woman like Mary, you never know. I don't believe she would ever have a real affair with a man if she was still living in her husband's house. But she's quite capable of bolting for good and all if she loved the man sufficiently. Cheer up, Bill," she laughed, "it's not your palaver. By the look on your face Mary might be *your* wife."

"I'm very fond of Mary," I said stiffly. "We've known one another since we were kids."

And at that moment young Merrick came in and the conversation dropped. But I couldn't get it out of my mind. That there should be even the bare possibility of Mary running away with another man seemed to knock the bottom out of my universe. And soon I found myself watching them too, and trying to gauge the state of the affair. Was Mary in love with him? That was the question I asked myself a dozen times a day. That he should be in love with her was only natural. But was the converse true? I studied her expression when she didn't know I was looking at her, and I had to admit that there was a change. For a few moments, perhaps, she would sit sunk in her thoughts, and then she would make an effort to pull herself together and be laughing and bright as she always used to be. But it was forced, and I knew it: she couldn't deceive me. And sometimes when she came out of her reverie, if Standish was in the room her eyes would rest on him for a second, as if she was trying to find the answer to some unspoken question.

Then I started to watch him. But there wasn't much to be got from Miles Standish's face. Years of poker playing had turned it into an expressionless mask when he wished to make it so. But I managed to catch him unawares once or twice. After lunch one day, for instance. He was holding a match for her cigarette, and over the flame their eyes had met. And in his was a look of such concentrated love and passion as I have never seen before. Then, in an instant it was gone, and he made some commonplace remark. But to me it seemed as if the truth had been proclaimed through a megaphone.

And another time it was even more obvious. Without thinking I went into the billiard-room, and they were alone there. They were standing very close together by the fireplace talking earnestly, and as I opened the door they moved apart quickly. In fact it was so obvious that I almost committed the appalling solecism of apologising for intruding. Standish picked up a paper; Mary smiled and said, "Why don't you two men have a game?" But once again the truth had been shouted to high Heaven: these two were in love with one another. What was going to be the end of it? Was Mary going to bolt with him, or would the whole thing die a natural death when he went out East again?

I believe it might have been the latter, had John Somerville not brought matters to a head. It was after dinner, on the same day that I had surprised them in the billiard-room.

"By the way, Standish," he said as we were beginning to form up for bridge, "when are you going back again?"

"I haven't quite decided yet," said Standish, lighting a cigarette. "Not for some little while, I think."

"Want to pay a round of visits, I suppose, and see all your friends. I've just remembered, my dear," he turned to his wife, "Henry Longstaffe is very anxious to come for a few days, as soon as we can put him up. He and I have a rather considerable business deal to discuss."

I glanced at Phyllis Dankerton: a smile was hovering on her lips.

I glanced at Miles Standish: his face was expressionless. I glanced at Mary: she was staring at her husband. Because all three of them knew, as I knew, that there was no spare room in the house. If Henry Longstaffe came to stay, somebody had to go.

"I'm afraid I shall have to fold up my tent and fade away very soon," said Standish easily. "Would the day after tomorrow do for Mr Longstaffe, or would you sooner he came tomorrow?"

"The day after tomorrow will do perfectly," said Somerville. "Sorry you can't stop longer."

And then we sat down to bridge in an atmosphere, as Phyllis Dankerton afterwards described it, which would have frozen a furnace. Nothing more, of course, was said – but words were unnecessary. The gloves were off, and everyone knew it. Miles Standish had been kicked out of the house as blatantly as if he had been shown the door. Moreover it had been done in the presence of all of us, which made the matter worse.

"I think John is a fool," said Phyllis Dankerton to me just before we went to bed. "And a vulgar fool at that. One doesn't do that sort of thing in front of other people. If I was Mary I'd give him such a telling off as he would never forget."

"He's an extremely angry man," I remarked. "And that accounts for it."

"Then it oughtn't to," she retorted. "It simply isn't done. To have said it to him privately would have been a very different matter. And you mark my words, Bill. Unless I'm much mistaken friend John will have achieved the exact opposite to what he intended. He has simply forced their hands."

"You think she'll run away with him?" I said.

"I think she is far more likely to now than she was before. And if she does John will be very largely to blame. Tomorrow is going to be the crucial day, while he is in London. The great decision will be made then."

She gave a little bitter laugh and her eyes were very sad.

"God! what fools women are," she said under her breath. "What damned fools!"

Then she went to bed, leaving me to a final nightcap. And when I had followed her example, and lay tossing and turning, unable to sleep, there was one picture I couldn't get out of my mind. It was the picture of Mary and Miles Standish together, leaning over the stern of an East-bound liner. And at last they turn and look at one another, as man and woman look at one another when they love. Then they go below.

I must get the events of the next day straight in my mind. Phyllis Dankerton was right: it was the crucial day. But somehow or other things seem a little blurred in my head. I'm not quite certain of the order in which they happened.

First of all there came the interview between Mary and Miles Standish. I overheard part of it – deliberately. They were in the billiard-room once more, and I happened to stroll past the little window, at one end of the room which is high up in the wall. It was open, and I could hear what they said distinctly, though they couldn't see me.

"My dear," Standish was saying, "it's a big decision that will alter your life completely and irrevocably. It's a decision that cannot be come to lightly. Divorce and that sort of thing seem a comparatively small matter when applied to other people. But when it's applied to oneself it doesn't seem quite so small. Wait, my darling, wait: let me have my say first. You are going to be the one who has to make the big sacrifice. It's not going to affect me: it never does affect the man. And in my case even less so than usual. My home is out East: it doesn't matter the snap of a finger what I do. But with you it's different. You're giving up all this: you're running away with a man who is considerably poorer than your husband. You are coming to a strange life, amid strange surroundings – a life you may not like. But a life, which, if you do leave your husband you will have to stick to."

Yes: he put it very fairly, did Miles Standish. There was no trace of pleading or emotion in his voice: he seemed to be at pains to keep everything matter of fact. And because of that the force of the appeal was doubled.

"We are neither of us children, Mary." The quiet, measured words went on. "We know enough to disregard catch-phrases like the world being well lost for love. It isn't, and nobody but a fool would think it was. And if you come with me it won't be – it will be changed, that's all. But it's going to be a big change: that's what I want you to get into your head."

And then, at last, Mary spoke.

"I realise that it's going to be a big change, Miles. Do you really think that matters? I realise that life out there will be different to this. Do you really think I care? My dear, it's not any material alteration in surroundings that has made me hesitate – it's been something far more important and fundamental. I'm not going to mince words: you attracted me from the first time we met. But my great problem was – was it only attraction? If so, I'd have been a fool to go. It is a big decision as you say – an irrevocable one, and to take it because of a passing whim would be folly. Last night – when John said what he did to you – I knew with absolute certainty. Every single instinct and thought of mine ranged themselves on your side. I've never loved John: now I positively dislike him."

"That's not quite enough, Mary," said Standish gravely. "I don't want you to come with me because you dislike John: I want you to come with me because you love me."

"Miles – my darling."

I scarcely heard the words, so softly were they spoken. And then came silence. In my mind I could see them there staring into one another's eyes: staring down the unknown path that they were to take together. A little blindly I turned and walked away. The matter was decided: the choice had been made. For good or ill Mary was going with Miles Standish.

"Bill, what is the matter with you? Are you ill?"

With an effort I pulled myself together: Phyllis Dankerton was looking at me with amazement on her face.

"Not a bit," I answered. "Why should I be?"

"My dear man," she said lightly, "I am partially responsible for Peter's tummy, but I hold no brief for yours. I don't know why you should be ill, but you certainly look it. Incidentally I saw our two turtledoves making tracks for the billiard-room. I wonder if the momentous decision has yet been reached."

I said nothing: I felt I couldn't stand the worry any more. Phyllis Dankerton is all right in small doses, but there are times when she drives one positively insane. So I made some fatuous remark and left her, vaguely conscious that the surprised look had returned to her face. What the devil did it matter? What did anything matter except that Mary was going with Miles Standish?

Nothing could alter that fact now: they were neither of them the type of people who change their mind once it is made up. And at dinner that night I found myself watching them curiously. They were both more silent than usual, which was hardly to be wondered at. And John Somerville, who obviously had not yet been told kept glancing from one to the other.

That he would be told I felt sure. The idea of bolting on the sly would not appeal to either Mary or Standish: they weren't that sort. But would it be done after dinner, or postponed to the following day? Or would Standish go in the ordinary course of events, leaving Mary to break the news to John?

The point was settled after dinner. John Somerville had gone to his room to write some letters, and suddenly I saw Standish glance at Mary significantly. Then with a quick little nod he left the room.

"What about a stroll, Canford?" said young Merrick, and automatically I got up. Why not?

"It strikes me," he remarked confidentially when we were out of earshot, "that there's a bit of an air of gloom and despondency brooding over the old ancestral hall. Somerville's face at dinner was enough to turn the butter rancid. And Standish seems quite different these last few days."

"When a man," I remarked, "is in love with another man's wife and the other man finds it out, it doesn't make for conviviality in the house."

He stopped dead and stared at me.

"Good Lord!" he muttered, "that's the worry, is it? Well, I'm damned. I never spotted it. But I jolly well know which of the two I'd choose. Mine host, even though I'm eating his salt is not much to my liking."

"Perhaps not," I said curtly. "But he happens to be your hostess's husband."

"You mean to say," he began, and then suddenly he gripped my arm.

"My God! Canford – look there."

We were about a hundred yards from the house. From one of the downstairs rooms the light was streaming out through the open French windows. And the room was John Somerville's study. He was standing up with his back to the desk facing Miles Standish, and it was evident that a bitter quarrel was in progress. We could hear no actual words, but the attitude of the two men told its own tale.

"Damn it – let's clear out," muttered Merrick. "Rather rotten, don't you think? Seems like spying on them. I'm going back to the house anyway."

He strolled off, and I watched the glow of his cigarette fading away in the darkness. Then once again I riveted my eyes on the study window: on that grim, fierce, age-old struggle of two males for a female: the struggle that brings murder into the air.

And when ten minutes later I went back into the drawing-room the atmosphere was not much better. Mary glanced up quickly as I came through the window, and her face fell when she saw who it was. Merrick made a grimace at me, and Phyllis

Dankerton went on playing patience religiously. Even little Marjorie Stanway seemed to feel there was something the matter, and was fidgeting about the room.

Then, suddenly, it happened. The door was flung open and Somerville's secretary dashed into the room. Her face was ashen white, and she was gasping for breath.

"Mrs Somerville," she almost screamed, "he's dead. There's a knife in his back. He's been stabbed."

For a moment no one spoke. Then Dankerton said a little dazedly: "Who is dead?"

"Mr Somerville," sobbed the woman. "At his desk."

And again, for what seemed an eternity, there was silence. Mary, her face as white as a sheet, was staring at the secretary, as if she couldn't grasp what had happened: young Merrick was saying "Good God!" under his breath over and over again and watching me. And at last I heard a voice say: "We must get the police." It was my own.

"Don't you think that we ought to go and make certain?" muttered Dankerton. "He may not be dead. Not the women, of course."

And then, at last, Mary spoke.

"Where is Miles?"

It was hardly more than a whisper, but it sounded as if it had been shouted through a megaphone in the deathly silence. And at that moment he appeared in the window. For a second or two he stood there looking from one to the other of us: then he spoke.

"What on earth is the matter?"

It was Dankerton who answered him.

"Somerville has been stabbed in the back," he said gravely. "His secretary says he is dead. We were just going along to see."

"Stabbed in the back!" cried Standish in amazement. "But who by?"

"We don't know," I said, and once again Merrick's eye met mine. "Let's go and see if there is anything to be done."

But there wasn't: that was obvious at the first glance. He lay there huddled over his desk, his eyes glazed and staring. And thrust into his back up to the hilt was a knife I had often seen lying on the mantelpiece. For a long while no one spoke: then Dankerton pulled himself together.

"Look here, you fellows, this is a pretty ghastly business. We must get the police at once. I'll tell the butler to ring up."

"Yes," agreed Standish quietly. "We must get the police."

His eyes were riveted on the knife: then with an effort he turned and looked at us each in turn.

"He and I had a frightful row tonight." He spoke with intense deliberation, and once again Merrick looked at me. "A frightful row."

"My dear fellow," muttered Dankerton awkwardly. "Look here, I'll see about the police."

He bustled out of the room, and suddenly Merrick took the bull by the horns.

"This is a pretty grim affair, Standish. You see Canford and I were outside there, and we saw you having words with – with him."

"Then you must have seen who did this," said Standish eagerly.

"Unfortunately I didn't," said Merrick. "It seemed to me to be a private affair, and I went back to the drawing-room."

"And I followed shortly after," I remarked.

Once more silence fell, while Standish stared at the dead man.

"I had a frightful row," he repeated mechanically, "and then I went out into the garden through the window. Damn it," he exploded suddenly, "you don't think I did it, do you?"

"Of course not, my dear chap," I cried. "Of course not."

He walked a little stiffly out of the room, and I turned to Merrick.

"What's your opinion?" I said at length.

"What's yours?" he answered. "Damn it, Canford, if he didn't do it somebody else did. And if it was anybody in the garden we'd have seen him."

"We might not," I said. "If he was hiding."

"In the back too," he muttered. "A dirty business. God! I wish the police would come."

And in about half an hour they did. An Inspector and a sergeant arrived and with them the doctor. The cause of death was clear: the knife had penetrated the heart. Somerville had died instantaneously. Then came the turn of the police, and it soon became evident in what direction their suspicions lay. Standish made no attempt to hide the fact of his quarrel with the dead man: incidentally it would have been futile in view of the fact that Merrick and I had seen it. But he flatly refused to say what it was about, and he denied absolutely that he was the man who had done it.

"Nobody said you were, sir," said the Inspector sternly. "You go too fast!"

"Rot," said Standish curtly. "I'm not a damned fool. If I have a violent row with a man, and a few minutes later he is found dead, there's no good telling me that suspicion doesn't fall on me. Of course it does."

And the next day suspicion became certainty. A fingerprint expert arrived from Scotland Yard, and the marks of Standish's fingers were found on the hilt of the knife. It was proof irrefutable, and the only explanation he could give was that in the heat of the argument he had snatched up the knife from the mantelpiece. But he still denied that it was he who had struck the blow.

"Then how comes it that yours are the *only* prints on the knife?" said the Inspector quietly.

I think the only person who believed in his innocence through the days that followed was Mary. To us it was painfully, terribly clear. As I said to Merrick the night before the trial it was the most obvious case, short of having an eyewitness, that could be put before a jury. And he agreed. He and I, of course, were two of the principal witnesses for the prosecution, but our evidence was really unnecessary. Standish had never denied the fact that he and the murdered man had had a bitter quarrel. And that and the fingerprints on the knife formed the evidence against him.

He still refused to say what the quarrel was about, though we all of us knew it concerned Mary. And from the point of view of his innocence or guilt it didn't really matter. He and the murdered man had quarrelled over something, and in a fit of ungovernable rage Standish had picked up the knife and stabbed him. That was all there was to it.

And that was all there was to it when Counsel for the Crown had finished his final speech. The members of the jury had obviously made up their minds already: it was difficult to see how they could have done otherwise. And Sir John Gordon – Standish's Counsel – was just rising to commence his hopeless task, when there occurred an amazing interruption. A strange, distraught-looking woman carrying a big brown box forced her way into court and shouted out: "Wait. Wait. Don't go on." Her face seemed vaguely familiar to me, and suddenly I placed her. She was John Somerville's secretary.

Everybody was so astounded that she had reached Sir John before anyone could stop her. And by the time ushers and attendants had rushed up to her, she had said enough to Sir John to cause him to wave them away.

"My Lord," he said, "this woman has just made a most important statement to me. In spite of the irregularity of the proceedings I propose to put her in the witness box."

And so Emily Turner was duly sworn, and made her statement. And when she had finished you could have heard a pin drop in the court.

"I understand," said the Judge, "that the position is as follows. The box in front of Sir John is the instrument which the murdered man used for dictating his letters into. This morning, not having thought of it since the night of the tragedy, you opened the box. And you found that a record had been made. You thereupon played that record, if that is the correct phrase, and you discovered that the conversation between prisoner at the bar and the murdered man was what was recorded. Is that correct?"

"Yes, my Lord."

And then came a harsh voice from the dock, "Smash the thing, I tell you. Smash it."

"Silence," said the Judge sternly, and Miles Standish faced him steadily.

"My Lord," he remarked, "I give you my solemn word of honour that my conversation with Somerville that night had nothing to do with it. Moreover it affects a third person. Therefore need that record be given?"

"It must certainly be given," said the Judge. "If what this witness says is correct, a vital piece of evidence has just come to light. Turn on the machine."

I can still see that scene. Miles Standish, impassive and erect: the jury tense and expectant: the public craning forward in their seats. And the centre of everything – that plain little woman bending over the box.

There came a faint scraping like a gramophone: then it started.

"Sir. With reference to your last quotation, I beg to state – "

John Somerville's voice: God! it was uncanny. Things began to blur a bit before my eyes. John Somerville dictating a letter.

"May I have a few words with you, Somerville?"

A gasp ran through the court – instantly quelled. Miles Standish had spoken. The living and the dead – reproduced before us.

"Certainly, Standish."

"There is not much good beating about the bush, Somerville. Your wife and I are in love with one another."

"How excessively interesting."

How well I knew that cold sneering tone of Somerville's. I could see now the slight rise of his upper lip. I could see the man himself again, as I hadn't seen him since that night: as I'd never expected to see him. He was dead, damn it, dead: and that cursed instrument had brought him to life again. What was he saying now?

"I certainly can't prevent my wife going away with you, Standish. But it's going to be a little awkward for you both. Divorce proceedings bore me, and I hate being bored."

"You mean you won't divorce her, Somerville?"

"You damned swine. You utterly damned swine."

There came a pause, then Somerville's voice with fear in it.

"Put down that knife, you fool. Put down that knife."

I hadn't told them that: I'd kept that dark. I'd seen Standish pick up the knife – seen it myself. Just as he said.

"And now clear out, blast you."

Somerville's voice again – icy, contemptuous. How I'd hated his voice, the thin-lipped swine...

And it was then I remembered.

"Stop it," I screamed. "Stop it."

People stared at me in amazement, and suddenly I felt icy calm. The machine scraped on, then, "Hullo! Canford. What do you want? I'm busy."

Somerville's voice: he'd said it to me as I entered the room.

"What the devil – Oh! my God!"

Followed a little sobbing grunt: then silence. The record was over.

Yes: I did it. I'd always loathed him, and I loathed Standish worse. Because Mary loved Standish, and I loved Mary. And when Standish rushed out past me into the night I saw my chance to get them both. I wrapped a handkerchief round the hilt of the knife to prevent fingerprints: I'd thought of everything.

Everything except that cursed machine.

THE TWO-WAY SWITCH

As a winter sports resort Dalzenburg is known only to the select. Not the rich, clothes-changing select of St Moritz: not the stiff-backed, skating select who pirouette round the homely orange of Morgins: not even the ski-mad select of Mürren – but just the Dalzenburg select. Year after year the same people go back to the same rooms in the same hotels, so that Christmas is like a reunion of a cheery house-party, the members of which all know one another intimately.

Ski-ing, somewhat naturally, is the main topic of conversation, though bobs may be mentioned, and skating alluded to. Curling – well curling is more or less taboo. A few wild-eyed Scotchmen are wont to mutter dark things nightly in a corner of the bar, concerning handles and crampits, but as Jim Weatherby said, when people spent the day throwing a brick along the ice and pursuing it with oaths and curses they must be humoured at night.

There are advantages, many advantages, in a clientele which continues unchanged, but there are disadvantages also: particularly for a stranger arriving for the first time. With the best will in the world cliques are apt to form, and the new arrival finds himself out of it, at any rate to start with. And this is especially the case if the hotel is not a large one. I will say, however, that at the Hotel Victoria there is less of it than in many places. All the old *habitués* ask is that the newcomer should prove him or herself a good fellow, and then after a short period of probation the body corporate opens and the stranger is absorbed. Then all is well unless perchance the morsel proves indigestible...

It was on the Tuesday before Christmas that I arrived there accompanied by Geoffrey Sinclair. He it is true was a stranger, but since he was vouched for by me as a fully qualified member of the assembly to be the goods, he was accepted on the spot. And we found ourselves up to the neck in an indignation meeting.

"Peter," said Jim Weatherby, "a thing of vile aspect has arrived!"

"A black slimy slug," remarked Johnny Laidlaw.

"An inhabitant of the Solomon Islands," added Daisy Farebrace.

"Who eats his young," said Tom Kirton with commendable originality. "Hist! it comes."

I glanced up as the subject of these eulogies came through the bar. He was certainly not a prepossessing specimen, but I'd seen many worse. That he was a Dago was obvious: that his smile when he saw us was of the type oleaginous was also obvious. But he made no attempt to butt in and join our party, and frankly I thought their remarks exaggerated and said so.

"You wait," said Daisy darkly. "He's the sort of man who would murder his mother."

"In that case," laughed Geoffrey Sinclair, "send for me. I promise to bring the crime home to him."

"My poor friend," I explained to the crowd, "labours under the delusion that he is a detective. He goes about with magnifying glasses, and sleuths."

"But how perfectly thrilling," cried a girl. "Do sleuth him, Mr Sinclair. You can start with his name – Pedro Gonsalvez de Silvo."

And as the days went by it was certainly a little difficult to see what had brought Pedro Gonsalvez to such a spot as

Dalzenburg. His sole method of amusing himself as far as could be seen was to sit on a luge and go down twice a day to the pâtisserie in the village, where he consumed inordinate quantities of sickly cakes. He loathed the cold, and he frankly admitted the fact.

"Then why not drift gently to the warmth, Mr de Silvo," said Jim Weatherby hopefully.

But Pedro Gonsalvez only smiled his smile and stayed. And the reason of his staying soon became obvious – Beryl Carpenter.

Beryl Carpenter was the uncrowned queen of the hotel. As a ski runner she was miles in advance of any other girl: in fact, in open races there were only two men who could be relied on to beat her. One was young Laidlaw: the other was Hilton Blake – of whom, more anon.

She was adorably pretty, danced like an angel, and was quite unspoiled. Moreover – and I think it was in this that lay much of her charm – she had a delightfully intent way of listening to whoever was talking to her. It wasn't a pose: she really did listen, and listen intelligently. And even if she was bored she never showed it.

One other characteristic she had – she never said unkind things about people. In every hotel, comment of a terse nature, to put it mildly, is apt to fly round concerning one's fellow guests, but Beryl Carpenter always went out of her way to find a good point in the accused. Or if she couldn't do that she said nothing at all.

Admittedly in the case of Pedro Gonsalvez it was difficult. And had it not been that everybody united in damning him, I think even she would have drawn the line at dancing with him. But it was the old story of the underdog, and Beryl Carpenter fell for that every time.

"Poor little blighter," she said when arraigned before a rag court-martial, "he can't help being what he is. And you people are giving him such a putrid time."

It was on New Year's Eve that Milton Blake arrived. Personally I had never cared about the fellow very much, though he was quite popular with both men and women. He was a man of about forty, with a clean-shaven, rather aquiline face. He had a fund of amusing stories which he told extremely well, and to all outward appearances he was a very nice chap. And yet...

I asked Geoffrey Sinclair – than whom no better judge of human nature exists – what he thought of him.

"The same as you, Peter," he remarked. "An amusing club acquaintance, but I don't know that I would trust the gentleman very far. By the way, is there anything between him and that nice Carpenter girl?"

"Nothing at all as far as I know," I said. "I believe she is more or less engaged to some boy at home, who hasn't got a bean. What makes you ask?"

"Idle curiosity," he answered. "I saw 'em together in the bar before dinner, and it struck me he seemed a bit intense. Has he got any money?"

"He always behaves as if he had," I said. "He's something in the City."

But Geoffrey's question stuck in my mind, and during the next two or three days I found myself watching them when they were together. And once or twice it struck me that the word intense was very apt. He was a man who never showed his feelings on his face – one had only to play bridge with him to realise that – but it was obvious that the topic of discussion was not of the usual hotel chatter order. And yet it didn't seem to me that he was making love to her.

It was Tom Kirton who supplied a possible solution.

"Pity Tony Carruthers doesn't come out," he remarked. "I suppose he can't manage it while his boss is away."

"What's that?" I said. "Tony Carruthers. You mean the fellow Beryl ran round with a year or two ago?"

"That's the bloke. He's in Blake's firm. I expect it's concerning him that they are always pow-wowing in a corner."

Then he lowered his voice confidentially.

"I don't know what you think, Peter, but it doesn't strike me that Beryl is quite herself this year. Not these last few days at any rate. Seems a bit pensive and worried."

"The course of true love, I suppose," I answered.

"Good Lord! old boy," he said, "if you mean Tony, there was never much chance of that going smooth. They haven't a bob between them."

He drifted away, and, as I say, it struck me as a possible solution, Milton Blake, perhaps, feeling it his duty as a business man to tell the girl that young Tony was never likely to become a Rothschild. Then someone roped me in for a rubber of bridge, and I dismissed the matter from my mind. And it was during that rubber that the first act of the tragedy occurred.

It was obvious something had taken place before we had finished. The room where we were playing was next to the bar, and during the last two hands we could hardly hear ourselves think. The whole hotel seemed to have gathered there, and everybody was talking at once.

"No more bridge for me," I said. "It's like Bedlam. What on earth is the excitement, Geoffrey?"

He was sitting inside the door of the bar as I went in.

"A most unpleasant scene," he answered, "has just taken place in the ballroom between our Mr Pedro Gonsalvez and Blake. I can't quite tell you what the beginning of it was, because I don't know, but it terminated in Blake knocking him down in the middle of the floor. Then Pedro Gonsalvez – who has more guts than I gave him credit for – went for him like a wild cat. The band stopped, and some fool woman began to scream, and I tell you, Peter, we had hell's own job to separate them. Finally we got 'em apart, but it interfered somewhat with the harmony of the evening."

"Something to do with Beryl Carpenter, presumably," I said.

"It was," remarked Jim Weatherby, who had joined us. "But, dash it all, Peter, Blake has only got himself to blame. You know what I think of Pedro Gonsalvez, but in this case it's only common fairness to say that it wasn't his fault. I mean if Beryl chooses to dance with him, it's nobody's affair but her own."

"What happened exactly?" I asked.

"Pedro and she had just finished a dance," he said. "Beryl left the room, and Pedro was crossing the floor to get back to his table, when Blake walked up to him and stopped him. What he said to him, I don't know, but Pedro turned a bright olive green with rage.

" 'Go to hell, Mr Blake,' he said in a thick sort of voice.

" 'So don't dare to do it again, you blasted Dago,' was Blake's next remark.

"It was obvious, of course, then that Blake had been ticking him off for dancing with Beryl.

" 'I shall do exactly what I like, you damned Englishman,' answered Pedro, at which Blake knocked him down. Then they went at it hammer and tongs. Oscar," he called to the barman, "give me a whisky and soda. I admit," he went on, "that to be called a damned Englishman by Pedro Gonsalvez is a bit over the odds, but for all that the bald fact remains that Blake started it. And my own personal opinion is that Master Milton had had just one over the eight."

"That's possible," said Johnny Laidlaw, who had caught the last remark, "but the real trouble was that he and Beryl had had words. I couldn't help hearing – I was sitting at the next table to her before her dance with Pedro. Blake asked her for it, and she refused. Said she was booked for it to the Dago. Blake said something I couldn't catch, and then Beryl quite distinctly and clearly remarked, 'I would sooner dance with Mr de Silvo than you.' By Jove! our Milton's face was a study as he walked away. He was wild with rage: looked as if he could have murdered her."

"Well," said Geoffrey, getting up, "it was an unpleasant scene, but it is over. And in view of the fact that there is a race tomorrow, I'm for bed."

"I'm with you," I said, and we strolled together towards the lift.

"Young Weatherby is right," remarked Geoffrey, "Blake had no right whatever to do what he did."

"It's going to make it a little unpleasant in the hotel," I said, "unless one of them goes."

"Well, old boy," answered Geoffrey, "as far as I am concerned I don't mind which of them departs. I like that fellow Blake less and less every day."

It was about three o'clock that I awakened suddenly with the sound of a woman's scream ringing in my ears. For a moment I thought it was a dream: then footsteps in the corridor outside, and agitated voices told me it was reality. I scrambled into a dressing-gown and opened the door.

The first person I saw was Geoffrey. He was talking to little Mrs Purefroy, who from her agitated condition I guessed was the giver of the scream.

"I happened to turn on the light, Mr Sinclair," she said, "and I saw it. Oh! go and look: go and look for yourself."

She was shuddering violently, and with a reassuring word Geoffrey left her and went into her room.

"My God!" he muttered. "It must have been a bit of a shock."

There was a table near the bed, and in the centre of it was a big red pool. It had spread nearly to the edge, and even as we looked at it a big drop splashed into it from the ceiling.

"Quick, Peter," he cried. "Up to the room above. Somebody has had a hæmorrhage. That's blood."

We raced upstairs to find that the occupants of that floor had also been aroused by the scream. All the doors were open save one, and Geoffrey darted for it. The room was in darkness, and at first when he switched on the light we could see no one. The bed had been slept in, but the occupant was no longer there. And then we saw him. He was lying on the floor, with his knees doubled up, and his face so distorted that it was hard to recognise him as Milton Blake. And driven up to the hilt in his heart was a fine pointed dagger. No hæmorrhage this: just plain murder.

"Keep all the women out of the room," said Geoffrey quietly. "Rouse the manager: get the police and a doctor. And don't go trampling all over the place, you fellows: stay still, if you want to stay at all."

The quiet authority in his voice had an instantaneous effect. Gone was the pleasant, genial, skiing Geoffrey: in his place was a man absorbed and intent on the thing that was his job in life – the detection of crime.

"Is he really a detective?" whispered someone in my ear.

"Probably the most brilliant in England," I answered. "Keep quiet."

I had seen him at work once or twice before, and his procedure was invariably the same. He stood motionless in the centre of the room, his eyes slowly travelling round it so that he seemed to soak in every detail. In fact he once told me that after two minutes' study he could so visualise the position of everything in the room that he would know at once if even the smallest ornament was moved later.

After a while he knelt down by the dead man and carefully examined the knife without touching it. Then with a little shrug of the shoulders he got up.

"On the face of it, the thing seems fairly obvious," he remarked. "The poor devil has been murdered, and the murderer is the owner of this dagger."

"It's not quite as easy as that, Sinclair," said Jim Weatherby, "I happen to know that dagger belonged to Blake himself. I've often seen it lying on the table. He used it as a paper cutter."

But Geoffrey seemed hardly to have heard. He was staring at the switches by the head of the bed with a curiously intent expression. There was the ordinary light switch, a contrivance for summoning either the valet or the *femme de chambre*, and an electrical gadget by which the door of the room could be bolted or unbolted from the bed. It was a two-way switch and it was this that seemed to be absorbing him.

"Just close the door," he said curtly.

Someone did so, and he moved the switch backwards and forwards thereby bolting and unbolting the door.

"Very peculiar," he remarked. "Very peculiar indeed. Get the importance of it, Peter?"

"I can't say I do," I answered. "They've got them in every room."

"That is why I should have thought you would have studied their working," he said.

"Good Lord! Sinclair," said Weatherby gravely, "surely it's obvious what has happened. I know one oughtn't to prejudge a case, but this seems clear. I mean after that row this evening, the whole thing is plain."

"You mean that de Silvo did it," said Geoffrey. "I confess that on the face of it that seemed the most likely conclusion."

"Seemed," echoed Weatherby. "Doesn't it seem so now?"

"There are one or two little points of detail which are of interest," answered the other. "However, the fingerprint test will settle it conclusively."

He walked to the balcony and stood looking out. The room was on the third floor, and the balcony was a small one, affording but little more room than would enable one to stand on it. There were similar ones on each side about six feet away, and he stood there for so long staring at them that even I began to get bored, whilst the others were frankly derisive.

"Confound it all, it's obvious, as I said," cried Weatherby. "The swab came up here: they had another quarrel. Then in a blind rage he snatched up that dagger and stabbed Blake."

"Strange that in a wooden hotel like this, where you can hear every sound, no one heard the quarrel."

Geoffrey had come back into the room, and was once again staring at the switch.

"My God! What is this I hear? Mr Blake dead!"

A sudden silence settled on the group: de Silvo himself was standing in the doorway, still dressed in evening clothes.

"Murdered," said someone curtly.

"Murdered! But who by? Who would want to murder him?"

He glanced round the room, and suddenly he realised.

"Holy Mother! Gentlemen. You do not suspect me?"

"We suspect no one, Mr de Silvo," said Geoffrey quietly. "At the same time, in view of what took place in the ballroom last night, you will understand the position. I see you have not been to bed."

"No." He hesitated a moment: then finished lamely. "I have been sitting up."

"Sitting up, Mr de Silvo," said Weatherby incredulously. "Till four o'clock. Where? In your bedroom?"

"That is my affair," said de Silvo, and turning on his heel he left them.

"What did I say," cried Weatherby. "The fellow must be mad to expect us to believe such a yarn."

"I quite agree," said Geoffrey with a short laugh. "And since whatever else he may be he is not mad it makes the thing even more perplexing."

He turned to the manager who had just appeared and was wringing his hands in a corner.

"Who have got the rooms on each side of this one?" he demanded.

"Miss Carpenter on that side, Monsieur, and Mrs Denton on the other."

"Thank you. I shall be in my room if I'm wanted."

He beckoned to me and I followed him downstairs. Little groups of people were standing about discussing the thing, and as we passed them de Silvo's name was on everybody's lips.

"No, no, no, Peter," he said as he closed the door. "It screams to high heaven that it wasn't de Silvo. Though unless he can establish a thundering good alibi they'll arrest him for a certainty."

"What makes you so sure that he is innocent?" I asked, but I got no answer. He was pacing up and down the room, with his hands behind his back and I doubt if he even heard my question. And after a while I left him, and went to my own room.

Further sleep was impossible, and having dressed, I went downstairs to find that practically everybody else had done the same thing. And since as far as Oscar, the barman, was concerned business was business, murder or no murder, bacon and eggs were the order of the day.

"Hullo! Peter," said Jim Weatherby as he saw me, "come and join us. Your pal may be the hell of a detective but he's gone off the deep end a bit this time. Who could it be but de Silvo?"

"Where is he now?" I asked.

"I think the police are on to him. They are upstairs."

"Mr de Silvo, sir!" Oscar was staring at Jim in amazement from the other side of the table. "You mean it was Mr de Silvo who did it? Oh! no, sir: that is impossible."

"Impossible! Why impossible?" Jim was staring at him blankly.

"Come on, Oscar," I said as he hesitated. "It will have to come out sooner or later. Why do you say it is impossible?"

"Because, sir – only I would prefer that it should not be known to the manager – Mr de Silvo has been playing cards with me all the night."

"Well, I'm damned," muttered Jim. "That's a fair knock out."

"Deep end not quite so deep as you thought, Jim," I chaffed.

"But does he often do that, Oscar?" said someone.

"Almost every night, sir. He loves to gamble, and I think he knows that you gentlemen do not care to play with him. And so I take his money, because he cannot play cards – how do you say it – for nuts."

And once again Jim muttered, "Well I'm damned," which I think expressed everyone's feelings. It had seemed such an absolute certainty, and in a second the bottom had been knocked out of the whole thing. It explained his being in evening clothes and his hesitation when asked where he had been. And it conclusively proved his innocence just as it conclusively proved someone else's guilt.

Who? Who had murdered Milton Blake? And now that Geoffrey's opinion had been so triumphantly vindicated over de Silvo, everyone was eagerly demanding that he should be produced. As the expert it was felt that it was hardly decent of him to be absent at such a moment, so I volunteered to go and try and get him.

I found him dressing, and he listened to Oscar's bombshell almost with impatience.

"I'm glad for de Silvo's sake," he said. "Otherwise all that fool chatter would certainly have ended in his arrest. What is far more important, Peter, is that there are no fingerprints on that dagger. With the permission of the police I went up and examined it with powder and a powerful glass. The murderer therefore was wearing gloves. Why?"

"To prevent fingerprints," I said brightly.

"A very pithy answer," he remarked. "For all that I wonder if you're right. Let's go downstairs. I could do with a cup of tea."

His appearance was hailed with volleys of questions, but he shook his head gravely.

"You heard nothing, I gather, Mrs Denton," he said, halting in front of her.

"Absolutely nothing," she answered. "I was very tired, and was asleep by eleven."

"And you bolted your door?"

"Yes. I always do."

"And you, Miss Carpenter?"

Beryl Carpenter shook her head.

"Not a sound. I was waxing my skis till about midnight and then I went to bed."

"And you also bolted your door?"

She nodded, and Jim Weatherby turned to me.

"What's he driving at now, Peter?" he muttered. "What does it matter if they bolted their doors or not?"

"Ask me another, Jim," I said. "He's beyond me at times."

And certainly for the next two hours he was in his most unapproachable mood. After drinking his tea, he retired to his room again, and when I went up at eight o'clock ostensibly to find if he wanted breakfast, but in reality to see if he'd got on any further, he bit me good and hearty.

"Sorry, Peter," he apologised, "but I feel I'm being a fool. And a damned fool at that. There's a link missing somewhere, and yet there oughtn't to be. Or am I all wrong?"

"But if you've got to that point," I cried, "you must suspect somebody. Who is it? Now that de Silvo is out of it, as far as I can see it might be anybody."

"I hope to heaven you're right, Peter," was his amazing answer. "But I can't let it go at this: I must know the truth. Let's go up to Blake's room again: I've missed something – I must have."

The *gendarme* on guard made no demur about us entering. The dead man, covered with a sheet, was lying on the bed; nothing else in the room had been moved. But Geoffrey went straight to the balcony, where for a long time he stood motionless.

Suddenly he leaned forward, a curiously intent look on his face. Then he whipped out his magnifying glass. He was examining the balcony side rail, and I saw him scratch the wood with his fingernail. And after what seemed an intolerable time he straightened himself up.

"So that's it, is it?" he said gravely. "Stupid of me not to have thought of it before. But you can take it from me, Peter, I wish I hadn't thought of it now. Still there must be some good reason."

He opened the door, and to my utter amazement instead of going downstairs he walked the other way towards Beryl Carpenter's room. He knocked, and receiving no answer walked straight in. Again he went straight to the balcony, and scratched the side rail nearest Blake's room.

"The pluck of it," he remarked quietly. "The astounding pluck."

"What on earth are you doing in my room?"

Beryl was standing in the doorway regarding us with the utmost astonishment.

"Come in, Miss Carpenter," said Geoffrey gently, "and please regard me as your friend, as well as Peter. Now – why did you do it?"

"Good God!" I almost shouted, "you're mad." But I looked at Beryl and the words died on my lips, for every vestige of colour had left her face and she was staring at Geoffrey as if hypnotised.

"Let me tell you just what happened," went on Geoffrey, still in the same gentle voice. "For some reason or other you decided to go into Blake's room. You guessed his door would be bolted: possibly you tried it and found it was. Then you thought of the balcony. It was possible you might have jumped from one to the other, but if you failed you would be killed by the fall and even if you succeeded the noise would have awakened Blake. Suddenly you thought of your skis. You laid them side by side between the two balconies, having put on gloves because it was cold. Then you walked across the gap on the skis, and got into his room. Then something happened, and you stabbed him. Then you unbolted the door, returned to your own room, and replaced the skis. Am I right?"

The colour had returned to her cheeks, and she faced Geoffrey steadily.

"Perfectly right, Mr Sinclair," she said. "Though how you've found out I don't know."

"Don't let's worry about that at the moment," said Geoffrey gravely. "I want to hear why you did this thing."

"In the first place I didn't go to the room to kill him," she began.

"Of that I am sure," agreed Geoffrey.

"I went to get a paper out of his pocket-book – what it was doesn't matter."

"Excuse me," he interrupted, "it does matter. This is a very serious affair, Miss Carpenter, and if we are to help you we must know the truth."

"Very well," she said. "I will tell you. I am more or less engaged, as Peter knows, to a man at home, Tony Carruthers – Tony is in Milton Blake's office. To cut a long story short Tony has been playing the fool over money – the firm's money – and Milton Blake found it out. Of course he could have sacked him, but Milton Blake wasn't that sort of man. He forced Tony to sign a confession and armed with that he came out here to present an ultimatum to me."

"The damned swine," I cried, but Geoffrey signed to me to be silent.

"The ultimatum he gave me," she continued, "was either prison for Tony, or my marriage to *him*. In the past I'd looked on him as a friend: since he has been out here this time I've got to know him in his true colours. I told him I didn't love him and never could love him: he said he didn't care, and that he would chance that. Then last night it suddenly came to me that if I could get the paper, it would at any rate be something. I could prevent Tony signing another and it might be some help. So, just as you described, Mr Sinclair, I went to his room. And I'd just found his pocket book when I felt his arms round me. He" – for a moment she hesitated, then continued in the same steady voice – "he left no doubt as to his intentions. I think perhaps he'd been a little drunk earlier. He kissed me, and went on kissing me though I tried to beat him off: then – then he started forcing me towards the bed. And without thought I picked up the first thing that came to my hand and struck him with it. His grip suddenly relaxed, and he slipped to the floor. For a moment or two I couldn't make out what had happened: then I realised. I seized the paper, and flew to the door and unbolted it. And that's all. Except one thing. If Mr de Silvo had been arrested I should have told the police what I've told you now."

For a while there was silence: then Geoffrey rose and held out his hand.

"In the event of the police arresting anyone else, Miss Carpenter, it may be necessary for what you have told us to become public. Otherwise I think Peter agrees with me that you have just advanced a remarkably ingenious theory to account for the death of Milton Blake, but one which we do not see our way to accepting. My own belief is that the thing was accidental. Blake was reading late, using the dagger as a paper cutter. He fell asleep and in turning over the dagger penetrated his heart."

For a moment she swayed and his steadying arm went round her: then she pulled herself together.

"It is good of you, Mr Sinclair," she said quietly. "And you too, Peter."

"But there is just one thing you must do, Miss Carpenter," he told her. "Scrub the wax off the rail of your balcony."

"So that was how you spotted it," I said as we went downstairs.

"That was the final link, Peter: I'd spotted it before then. At the very first I admit I thought it was de Silvo. The door was open, and after the row last night suspicion naturally fell on him.

And then suddenly I saw the one vital thing which you all missed though I alluded to it specifically – the switch for the door bolt. *The bolt was unfastened, but the switch was set for the bolt to be fastened.* I at once tried the switch and found that it worked perfectly, and the immense significance of the point struck me at once. Of course, you see it yourself now."

"I may be dense, old boy," I confessed, "but I can't say I do."

"With those little bolts," he explained, "the current is very small. And though they shut and open as actuated by the switch, it is perfectly simple to shut and open them by hand. That is to say, that even if the switch points to shut, you can move the bolt by hand to open. Which was exactly the state of things in Blake's room. Now was it even remotely likely that Blake having bolted his door by the switch, then got up and unbolted it by hand?

"Frankly it didn't seem so to me. And once that was granted it altered everything, because it proved conclusively that the person who had killed Blake had not come in through the door. Therefore entry had been through the window.

"I'd advanced so far when de Silvo appeared on the scene, and any lingering doubts I might have had as to his innocence were dispelled. The mere fact that he was in evening clothes and admitted not having been to bed was enough to acquit him. No man could be such a complete half-wit as that if he had done it.

"So back I went to the window, and then came the next difficulty. As I said upstairs, jumping would have been too great a risk – so how had access been obtained to Blake's balcony? That was the link that was missing, and a damned important one it was. That it was done with the knowledge of either Miss Carpenter or Mrs Denton was clear. But how?

"Mrs Denton I had dismissed from my mind – she is one of those people one would always dismiss from everything. But Beryl Carpenter was a very different proposition. That there had been something in the wind between them ever since he arrived was obvious to us all. What was it? Now we know: then I didn't.

Moreover, Beryl Carpenter was a girl with a head like ice, and nerve above the average. So that in my own mind I was already convinced that she knew a great deal more about the matter than she said.

"Then we went up to Blake's room again, and I saw marks on the balcony railing. I scratched them with my nail and found they were wax. And like a flash her remark came back to me – 'I was waxing my skis till about midnight.'

"Normally of course the wax wouldn't have come off; but the skis weren't being used normally. Her weight on them as she crossed the gap made them bend up and down and consequently rub against the wood of the railing. Also the wax had just been put on.

"And that I think is all, Peter. It just shows the vital importance of tiny points of detail. Because had the door bolt been opened by using the switch near the bed, it could never have been found out."

"I hope to heaven it never will be," I said fervently.

"Not if I can help it," he answered. "She's a great girl – that. In fact I am now going to begin the rumour of it having been an accident. The stout Swiss official will probably jump at it."

WILL YOU WALK INTO
MY PARLOUR?

Jimmy Sefton sat outside the Angler's Rest at Drayminster with a puzzled look on his good-natured freckled face. On the table by his side was a tankard of ale, and an opened packet of Virginian cigarettes. It was five o'clock in the afternoon, and save for him the place was deserted. Soon it would fill up, when the mystic hour arrived which allowed unfortunate mortals who were not staying in the house to get a drink, but until then he would have the place to himself – a fact for which he was thankful. He wanted to think.

No one would have called Jimmy a brainy young man, but he had a certain shrewd common sense which often serves better than a quicker and cleverer brain. He might take longer in arriving at a conclusion, but when he did get there he was generally fairly near the mark. And now he once again proceeded to run over the chain of events that was directly responsible for his presence in Drayminster.

The first had been a dinner at the "Cheshire Cheese" some three weeks previously. At it were present Teddie Morgan and Bob Durrant, two journalistic pals of his, though Teddie Morgan, to be correct, was more than a pal. He and Jimmy had been at school together, and they had joined the staff of the *Daily Leader* at the same time. And that was five years ago – five years during which acquaintanceship had grown into real friendship. The fourth member of the party was a man called Spencer, who was more or less the stranger at the board. He, too, was a writing man, but his speciality was crime. And the principal interest he had for the other three was an intimate knowledge of Scotland Yard, an institution with which they had only a bowing acquaintance.

He could recall quite clearly the gist of Spencer's remarks. Dinner was over, coffee and port were on the table. And he could still see Spencer's thin aquiline features through the thick haze of tobacco smoke, as he recounted some of the cases he had had first hand knowledge of.

"You may take it from me," he said, "that there is not much wrong with our police system. It is the custom of lots of people to deride them as men of small brains and large feet, but nothing is farther from the truth. The local village constable may not be a particularly bright specimen, but for the matter of that the local French gendarme is not a second Newton as a general rule. And there's another thing too which lots of people are apt to forget – the difference between our legal code and those of other countries. With us the onus of proving a man guilty lies on the police: in France, for instance, the onus lies on the man proving himself *not* guilty. And the difference is enormous. There are half a dozen men at large in London today whom the police *know* to be criminals. But they can't arrest them because they can't *prove* it. In France they would be under lock and key in no time, and it would be up to them to prove that they weren't."

Spencer had talked on in this strain for some time, and then had come the information which had proved the first link in the chain of events that had since taken place.

"But they are up against it at the moment," he had said thoughtfully, "up against it good and strong. And have been for some weeks. Forged notes – on a scale never hitherto attempted."

His audience had pricked up their ears: this was something better than vague generalisations about police methods.

"They're not very chatty about it at the Yard, but I have my own channels of information," he had continued. "And this is the biggest thing of its kind they have struck yet. The headquarters of the gang are in this country, but they are not dealing with English notes. Which makes it so very much harder to track them. French and Belgian notes of fairly large denomination: American five and ten dollar notes are what they are making. And that is where the complication occurs. You see the usual method of running the headquarters of a gang of this sort to earth is by getting on the line of the men who pass the notes. A fiver, let us say, comes into a bank. That fiver is never again issued, but is destroyed. The bank people find it is a forgery. Scotland Yard then sets to work to trace the movements of that fiver back to the first person who handled it. And thus, if there are several, in time the man who originally passed it is found. From him, they go still farther back, because it is not the passer they want but the utterer – the forger himself. Now in this case there is a very grave difficulty. The forger is in this country: the men who are passing the notes work in other countries. And not only that, they are mixing up the currencies. They are getting rid of American notes in Belgium, we'll say, and French notes in Italy."

"How long has it been going on for?" someone had asked.

"The Yard has been down to it for about six months now," was the answer. "And though they won't admit the fact they are no nearer the solution now than when they started. As I said it is a very big thing. Two or three of the smaller fry have been caught abroad, and though they have been subjected to foreign methods of examination nothing has been found out. Probably because they none of them knew anything to pass on. The only vague clue, which may not even be a clue at all, is that two of these men bought their forged notes in Brighton, and the other at Bognor."

"Bought!" Teddie Morgan had cried.

"That is the usual method," Spencer had explained. "A thousand franc French note is worth roughly eight pounds. The man buys it – say for five. If he passes it he is three pounds to the good: if he doesn't he is jugged. But whichever happens the big man is a fiver in pocket. But to go back. The fact that Brighton and Bognor were selected as rendezvous for the transactions points to the possibility of the headquarters being in Sussex. But it is only a possibility."

And then Teddie Morgan had laughed.

"I will attend to the matter," he had said. "Tomorrow I leave for a well-earned fortnight's holiday. The earth is mine to roam in: I shall select Sussex. And if anyone offers to sell me thousand franc notes for a fiver, I shall dot him one with a beer mug and summon the police."

Thus the first link in the chain. The party had broken up shortly after, and no one had thought any more about it. In fact until three days previously Jimmy Sefton had not known that Morgan had even gone to Sussex. And then had come the second link. It consisted of a picture postcard showing the village of Drayminster. It contained the pointed information that that village had been classified fifth in order of beauty in England. It also contained the following message written in Morgan's sprawling handwriting:

"Tell Spencer that there is many a true word spoken in jest."

Jimmy had been busy at the time, and having put the card in his pocket had forgotten all about it, until that very morning, when the third grim link appeared in the form of a paragraph in the paper. He took it out of his pocket book now as he sat at his table and reread it for the twentieth time.

"The body of a well-dressed young man was found in the river Dray yesterday afternoon by two farm labourers. It was discovered in the weeds some three miles from the picturesque old country village of Drayminster, one of the famous beauty spots of England. An empty fishing creel was slung round his shoulder. It is assumed that the unfortunate gentleman, who has been identified as Mr Edward Morgan, a well-known London journalist, and who was staying at the Angler's Rest, must have slipped in one of the deep and treacherous pools of the river and been drowned. The current then carried the body to the spot where it was found. No trace of his rod has been discovered. The inquest will be held today."

And Jimmy Sefton had just returned from that very inquest. No difficulty about identifying the body; it was poor old Teddie right enough. From the medical evidence he had been dead about two days, and the verdict was a foregone conclusion. The landlord of the Angler's Rest, who had done the identification, had been asked by the Coroner as to whether he had not been a little alarmed when the days had passed by with no sign of his guest.

"No, sir," he had answered. "Mr Morgan took the room for a week, and he told me that he might frequently sleep out. He was very fond of walking, and, as the weather was fine, he would very likely get a shake-down in a barn or under a hayrick."

Jimmy Sefton, who had explained to the coroner that he was a brother journalist on the same paper, and who was sitting at the back of the room, had listened to this piece of evidence in silent amazement. Not that he disbelieved the landlord – for a more transparently honest and upright man he had seldom seen – but for a very different reason. If there was one form of exercise which Teddie loathed with a superlative loathing, it was walking. He would take a bus to go half the length of Fleet Street rather than walk the distance. So that for some reason or other Teddie had deliberately lied to the worthy man whose naturally cheerful voice could even now be heard, suitably lowered for the occasion, recounting the details of the tragedy for every new arrival at the bar. Why had he lied?

Then Mr Purley, who sold rods and flies and all the other paraphernalia of the angler's craft, had identified the deceased as the gentleman who had come to his shop to be completely fitted out four days previously – on Tuesday last. He had admitted he did not know much about it, but having been told of the marvellous trout fishing which could be got in the river Dray he had determined to try his hand at it. To this evidence also, Jimmy Sefton had listened in some surprise. Not, it is true, with that utter bewilderment which the landlord's story had produced in his mind, but still with considerable doubt. He could not picture Teddie being suddenly seized with a desire to become an angler. He knew his tastes – none better. He had loved all games, but except for an occasional ride he had never gone in for what are known as the sports. Shooting and fishing he had had no opportunity to try his hand at. So why this sudden craving to become a fisherman?

Jimmy Sefton called for another pint of ale.

"Do you remember," he asked, "when it was that Mr Morgan told you he might be going on a walking tour?"

The landlord scratched his head.

"Let me see, sir," he said. "Today is Saturday. He was out, I remember, last Sunday night, but took his meals here Monday. And Monday night he was out too. And after that I never saw him again. Perhaps a week ago he told me."

"I see," said Jimmy. "Thank you."

The landlord returned to the bar, and Jimmy lit a cigarette. According to Mr Purley it was Tuesday when Teddie had bought his tackle. It was also on Tuesday that he had sent the postcard to Jimmy. So that presumably either on Monday night or on Tuesday morning he had discovered something which had caused him to alter the blind of a walking tour to that of becoming a fisherman. What was it that he had discovered? And where? Was it really as his postcard suggested, that he had by some extraordinary stroke of chance stumbled on the headquarters of the forgers? And if that was so – Jimmy Sefton's jaw tightened a little at this point in his reflections – if that was so, was the verdict of "Accidentally drowned," correct? Or had Teddie Morgan been murdered?

Jimmy was not at all an imaginative young man, and his first impulse was to call himself several sorts of an ass. Murders and gangs of forgers he told himself were part of the stock in trade of the sensational novelist. In fact he used every single argument he could think of to prove to himself that he was wrong. But it was no use: try as he would his mind kept reverting to that one big question. Had Teddie Morgan found out too much and been murdered?

After a while he made a sort of mental table of points for and against.

For.

Number One. Teddie's remark to the landlord concerning a walking tour was so obviously a lie that it was clear he had been doing something which he did not wish to talk about.

Number Two. If there was any meaning at all in his postcard, and it was highly improbable he would send a card without any reason, that something had to do with the gang of forgers.

Number Three. If he had discovered them was it likely that a gang of such a formidable nature would allow the life of a stray journalist to stand in its way? They would undoubtedly murder him, and dispose of the body in such a way as to make it appear an accident.

Against.

Jimmy scratched his head: he could think of no point against, which could be summarised as tersely as his three points for. In fact the only other alternative to his theory was that Teddie had thought at one time that he had stumbled on traces of the gang, *vide* the fact of his postcard and his absence from the hotel on two nights. Then he had decided not to go on with it, had genuinely decided to try his hand at fishing, and had, as the verdict said, been accidentally drowned.

Jimmy finished his beer in a gulp, and stood up abruptly. The frown on his face had gone: his mind was made up. Because he knew the great fallacy that underlay his alternative theory. Teddie was not the type of man to decide not to go on with a thing. Once he had his jaws into a job nothing could shake him off: it had been a characteristic of his ever since he was a boy. Therefore Teddie was still on it when he was posing as a fisherman. So that even if the verdict was right, and he had been drowned, the accident had not occurred because of his devotion to fishing, but because he was following up some trail. And once that was settled, the next step was obvious. Mr Purley would receive a second order for a fishing outfit complete: Jimmy Sefton was going to take over from his pal. And the first thing to do was to get on the 'phone to his editor, because he had intended returning to London that night. He knew there would be no difficulty, especially if he gave a hint over the wire that he was on a scoop. So he went into the hotel to find the instrument. It was situated, as is so frequently the case in small hotels, in the office, which rendered any private conversation impossible. However he knew the editor sufficiently well to realise that the merest veiled hint would be all that was required. He put through the number and sat down to wait in the hall. Opposite him were a man and woman drinking a cocktail, and he glanced at them idly. They were both well dressed, and the woman, who was little more than a girl, was extremely pretty. And Jimmy, who was no more and no less susceptible than the average young man of his age, found his glance ceasing to be idle as far as she was concerned. Once she looked up and caught his eye, and it seemed to him there was just that perceptible addition of time before she looked away, that would constitute grounds for hope. Then the telephone bell rang, and he took the call.

"*Daily Leader*?" he said. "Put me through to the Editor. Sefton speaking."

With his elbow on the table, and the receiver in his hand, he was staring out of the window. Suddenly his eyes narrowed. The lower part of the window was shut, and served sufficiently well as a mirror for him to see that the man had risen abruptly, and was now standing close to the door of the office, studying the announcement of a local cattle show. There was, he reflected, nothing inherently suspicious in such an action, but he was in the mood when the most commonplace thing took on a certain significance. Was it interest in the cattle show, or the mention of the *Daily Leader*, that had inspired the sudden movement? Then he heard the Editor's voice at the other end of the wire.

"Hullo! Is that Mr Jameson? Look here, sir: it is urgent that I should stop at Drayminster for two or three days. Things to arrange about poor old Morgan. Yes; urgent. I can't be more explicit: this machine is specially placed for the maximum of publicity. Right – thank – you, sir."

He put back the receiver, and for a moment or two he stood there motionless. The man had returned to his seat as abruptly as he had left it. And his return had coincided with the end of the call. Once again it was not impossible that that had been the exact time necessary to allow him to study the details of the show. Not impossible: but… And Jimmy was thinking of all that lay behind that 'but' as he turned to the girl in the office and made inquiries about a room. There proved to be no difficulty, and having fixed the details, he returned to his seat. He, too, would have a cocktail, and during its consumption he would continue the good work of finding out if his grounds for hope were justified. Also he might find out other things.

After a moment or two, the man rose and, picking up his hat, left the hotel.

"I'll be back in about twenty minutes," he said, as he stepped into the road.

"Don't hurry," answered the girl. "I shan't be dull."

She picked up a copy of *The Tatler*, and Jimmy lit a cigarette and waited. Had he made a complete boss shot, or had he, by a most astounding bit of luck, stumbled on a clue? In either case, he reflected, he was perfectly safe in carrying out his plan. Further he would soon know. If his suspicions were correct, within the next twenty minutes the girl would start a conversation with him. As he read it, that was the reason of the man's departure. And he wondered by which of the time-honoured methods she would dispense with the formality of an introduction.

She was displaying a considerable amount of extremely attractive leg – a spectacle to which he took no exception. And it was with almost a start that he averted his eyes from it to realise that the method to be used was the well-known old favourite of no matches.

"Allow me," he murmured, as she looked round despairingly.

"Thank you so much," she said with a charming smile. "I ought to have a box chained to me; I lose them so invariably."

They fell into a light conversation, and he studied her covertly. From a closer range he saw that she was older than he had at first thought, saw, too, with the discerning eye of a man who in, the course of his trade has rubbed shoulders with all the types that go to make up a world, that indefinable something in her face that no art can conceal. It lies principally in the eyes and in the mouth, and it spells danger. This girl was as hard as nails. But no trace of his thoughts showed in his face: no one could act the part of a guileless youth better than he, as many people he had interviewed had discovered in the past.

The man he gathered was her Uncle Arthur and she was motoring with him on a tour. Jimmy, whose face had brightened at the first piece of news, became perceptibly depressed at the second.

"I'd hoped you were staying here," he said gloomily.

"Are you stopping in the hotel?" she asked.

"For a few days," he answered. "A great pal of mine has just been drowned here, poor old chap."

"How dreadful," she said sympathetically. "I heard something about it this afternoon."

"The inquest was this morning," he went on. "Verdict of accidentally drowned. But I wonder."

For the fraction of a second the mask slipped. Had he not been looking for it he would have missed it, so instantaneously was it replaced. But in that moment of time he saw what confirmed his suspicions – he saw fear.

"How do you mean, you wonder?" she asked, and her voice was quite normal. "Is there any doubt about it?"

"Not in the Coroner's mind," he answered mysteriously. "But there is in mine. I believe," he lowered his voice, and glanced round the hall, "I believe he was murdered."

"Good Heavens!" she cried. "But who by? You sound so deliciously mysterious."

"I am going to let you into a great secret," he said. "And I am the only person in the world who knows it. Promise you won't say anything to a soul."

"Fingers crossed," she answered.

Jimmy leaned even closer to her.

"I believe," he said, "that Teddie Morgan was murdered by a gang of forgers whose headquarters are near here. I believe that somehow or other he did what the police so far have been unable to do – he located this gang. He wrote me a letter, in which he hinted at it, and from one or two things I've heard since I've been here I'm sure he was on their track. Now I'm a journalist," he went on with engaging candour, "and it will be a tremendous scoop for me if I can nab them."

"But how will you set about it?" she asked. "Because if what you suspect is true they might kill you."

Jimmy looked at her knowingly.

"I'm going to become a fisherman also," he said. "That's where the clue lies – near the river. Only I shall be more careful than he was. And when I've found these people I shall give the information to the police. But it will be a *Daily Leader* sensation, and I shall have the writing up of it."

"How splendid!" she cried. "Here is my uncle returning, but I'm thrilled to death. I shall simply be dying to know how you get on. When I get back to Town I must ring you up at your office, and you must come and tell me all about it."

"I'd love to," said Jimmy fervently. "But you must promise you won't say a word to a soul."

"It's our secret," she whispered softly. "I do hope you succeed."

She rose, and giving him a delicious little smile, joined her uncle in the car. One little wave of the hand, eagerly returned by Jimmy, and then they disappeared down the road.

"Do you know who those people were who have just left?" he asked the girl in the office.

"Never seen either of them before," she told him, and Jimmy returned to his chair. Three points in all, he reflected, to go on. The sudden movement of the man, the reflecting expression on the woman's face, and lastly the fact that people who tour in motor cars generally carry luggage. On the one that had just driven off there had been none. In fact, he felt convinced that the arrow he had drawn at a venture had hit the mark. Those two people had something to do with it; he knew it. But, as Spencer had said, between knowing and proving there was a great gulf fixed.

He had acted deliberately in talking as he had. No harm was done if she was innocent: if on the contrary he was right, the next move would have to come from their side. Obviously they could not leave matters as they were. Though he had impressed on the girl that he wanted the whole thing kept a secret, he felt that in their position they could not bank on his doing so. They would feel that at any moment he might tell the police. And so it seemed to him that there were only two alternatives open to them. The first was to pack up and go: the second was to deal with him as they had dealt with Teddie Morgan. And of the two the second seemed the more probable.

For another ten minutes or so he sat on thinking: then a grin slowly appeared on his face. For a very amazing plan had suddenly dawned on Jimmy Sefton's brain – a plan which seemed to him quite unique in its simplicity. He looked at it this way and that, and in it he could see no flaw. A little acting: a little luck, and then, as he had quite truthfully said to the woman, the scoop of the year. And possibly some damned swine swinging for Teddie. Humming gently to himself he rose and left the hotel bound for Mr Purley's shop. What the tune was is immaterial, but the words he had put to it had a certain significance.

" 'Will you walk into my parlour?' said the spider to the fly!"

The invitation of the spider came earlier than he had expected, to be exact, at ten o'clock the following morning. The previous night he had been acutely aware of two men who had sat drinking in the bar until the hotel shut, and who had seemed to betray a more than passing interest in his movements. So much more than passing, in fact, that Jimmy Sefton had done a thing which he could never remember having done before: he had slept with his window bolted and his door locked. But nothing had happened, and, as he came down the stairs encased in his newly acquired fishing outfit, it came as almost a relief to realise that the game was starting in earnest. For the girl herself was sitting in the hall.

"Hullo!" he cried joyfully. "This is an unexpected bit of luck."

"I oughtn't to be here," she confessed. "But Uncle Arthur found a wire waiting for him at Worthing, and had to go up to London. And I had nothing to do. Please let me come with you. As I told you I'm just thrilled to death."

She clasped her hands together, and looked at him appealingly.

"I promise not to get in the way, and I'd just adore to see what you are going to do."

"I don't know myself," he admitted. "You see, I haven't a notion where the gang is."

"Look here," she said after thinking deeply for a moment, "I've got an idea. You know where your poor friend's body was found, don't you?"

"I do," said Jimmy.

"Well, if you are right, and he was murdered, the brutes probably threw him into the water above that spot, and the river carried him down."

"By Jove! that's quick," said Jimmy admiringly.

"So let us get into my car and go by road to where he was found, and then explore the river upstream from there."

"You're a marvel," cried Jimmy, giving her a soulful glance. "An absolute fizzer. Let's start."

He deposited his creel and rod in the back of the car, and climbed in beside her. Up to date he reflected the fly was playing its part very creditably; moreover that intelligent little insect was becoming increasingly anxious to see the parlour the owner of which chattered unceasingly as they drove along.

"There's the spot," said Jimmy suddenly, and she gave a little shudder.

"Poor fellow," she whispered. "However, what do we do now?"

But it seemed that the fly's brain was unequal to the task of deciding, and after a while the spider had another idea.

"About a mile further on," she said, "is one of Lord Cragmouth's places – Denton Hall. He is away, but I know him – and I know his butler. What about going there and asking the man whether he knows of any strangers who have arrived in these parts lately?"

For a moment Jimmy's brain spun round. What a headquarters – Denton Hall: one of the historic places of

England. That it was the parlour at last he had no doubt, but for a second or two he was lost in admiration at the calm audacity of renting such a place for such a purpose.

"A marvellous idea," he said humbly. "What I should have done without you..."

His hand went to his forehead suddenly.

"Good God!" he muttered. "I'm going to faint. Could you – a little water – from the river..."

She sprang out solicitously and hurried down to the stream. But when she came back he had so far recovered as to be standing by the back of the car.

"I'm so sorry," he said. "I'm better now. Damned silly of me."

"Are you sure?" she cried. "Why not rest a little? Or if we go on to Denton Hall, I'm sure the butler would give you some brandy."

"That sounds good to me," he said. "But really I'm quite all right now."

He got in beside her again, and a few minutes later the car swung right-handed past an old lodge into the huge grounds of Denton Hall. In the distance was the house with its broad terraces running down to the big ornamental lake, with its celebrated pagoda on the little island in the middle. Further on a line of weeping willows marked the banks of the river Dray, which passed right through the property.

The car drew up at the front door, and Jimmy's heart began to beat a trifle quicker. A glance at the butler did not inspire him with confidence. And as the door closed behind him he understood the feelings of the fly.

He looked up as three men came down the stairs, and the centre one was Uncle Arthur.

"Here he is," laughed the girl. "It was almost too easy."

"My God!" stammered Jimmy. "I don't understand... I... This is a trap."

The girl had lit a cigarette and was laughing softly to herself, but the three men had stood looking at him in silence.

"You are a very foolish young man," said Uncle Arthur at length.

"Let us come in here." He led the way into what was evidently the smoking-room.

"You are going to murder me, are you?" said Jimmy. "Like you murdered Teddie Morgan. But awkward, won't it be – having dead journalists lying about all over the place?"

"They are a tribe who can well be thinned out," answered the other genially. "Yes, Mr Sefton, owing to your reprehensible curiosity, you are, as they say, for it. You see you left us with no alternative."

He lit a cigarette.

"I assure you I have given the matter deep and earnest thought," he continued. "I don't want to kill you, any more than I wanted to kill that other young ass. But I have to weigh in the balance your life against my future peace of mind. I should hate to think that at any moment I might meet you, and you might say – 'That charming well-dressed gentleman is a forger.' "

"And murderer," said Jimmy, lighting a cigarette in his turn.

"Have it your own way," conceded the other. "But you see my difficulty. Supposing I let you continue your hunt for my poor person – for the headquarters of the gang as you so realistically put it. In the course of a week you might have stumbled on something – just as your friend Morgan did. Will you believe it, what put him on to us was the fact that he happened to see my butler's face one day as he passed the lodge gates?"

"Any judge would convict on that alone," agreed Jimmy affably.

"We have not all got your classical beauty of features, Mr Sefton. Still the point is a small one: the result was what mattered. He became most intrusive: he even trespassed on my property. In fact we actually discovered him concealed by the edge of the lake watching that charming pagoda through field-glasses. He pretended he was fishing, Mr Sefton – even as I gather you were going to do. Yet his rod was not put together, and his basket was empty."

Jimmy strolled over to the window and looked out. "And so you propose to kill me!" he said thoughtfully. "Will it be done with your own fair hands, dear Uncle Arthur?"

He swung round, and suddenly the room grew strangely silent. For there was a look on his face that none of them could understand.

"Admirable things – windows, aren't they," he continued. "Without curtains you can see through them: with curtains you can't. Then they act as mirrors, uncle dear. Are you going to the cattle show you were studying the notice of when I was telephoning?"

Jimmy began to laugh softly.

"And you, my dear lady, should really learn to control your face. And you shouldn't say you are touring when you haven't any luggage."

With a sudden movement he flung open the window, and waved his hand.

"My God! It is the police." Uncle Arthur had sprung to his side. "The young swine has fooled us. There are a dozen of them. Quick – bolt."

"Not this time," said a deep voice at the door, and Jimmy recognised the speaker as Superintendent Naylor of the Yard, with Spencer and half-a-dozen men behind him. "So it's you, is it, Verriker? There have been times when I suspected it must be. Where's the plant?"

"I should think a visit to the pagoda might help," said Jimmy mildly, and Verriker began to curse.

"Good work, Sefton," cried Spencer. "But it gave us a bit of a shock when we got the address."

"So it did me," said Jimmy. "In fact I almost fainted in the car."

Verriker ceased cursing and stared at him.

"Do you mean to say you only found out where you were coming when you were in the car?" he said.

"Sure thing," answered Jimmy. "My dear Uncle Arthur, we have been playing a little game of the spider and the fly. And knowing the usual fate of the fly, this one decided to take a few precautions. The only trouble was that he hadn't any idea as to where the parlour was. That he was going to be invited in he felt sure, but he felt a little dubious as to the hospitality that would be extended to him there. So he invited down a few friends" – he waved his hand at the police – "to remain at hand, in case they were wanted. He thought it better that they shouldn't follow him, in case they were seen, and the spider should leave the parlour hurriedly. Besides he wanted the spider to tell him all that was in his heart. And then when he had found out his destination – he pretended to throw a faint. And being left alone for half a minute, he wrote a little message. And he put the message in a little tube. And he fastened the tube to a little leg."

"What the devil do you mean?" snarled Verriker.

"Why, just that this particular fly had taken your advice in advance about empty fishing baskets. You see – his wasn't empty. Inside it was a carrier pigeon."

A HOPELESS CASE

1

Through the open window came the ceaseless noise of the tree beetles. Occasionally it would be drowned by the coughing grunt of a lion in the distance, or the shrill scream of some animal nearby – a scream that showed that death was, as ever, abroad in the land outside. But these were only interludes; life to the man who sat at the table seemed to consist of that eternal, damnable noise.

He was not a very pleasant sight – the sole occupant of the room. His chin required the attentions of a razor; his shirt, which was opened at the neck, would have done with a wash. His riding breeches were threadbare; his boots caked in mud. And yet for anyone with eyes to see one fact would have struck home. Those breeches and boots bore the unmistakable stamp of the West End.

The room was in confusion. Dust lay thick in the corners; a few odd letters littered the table. The lamp had smoked, and half the funnel was black with soot. Against one wall a cupboard minus its doors leaned drunkenly – a cupboard in which unwashed plates and an old teapot without a handle were jumbled together. And, ranged in rows along the opposite wall, empty bottles.

A full one stood on the table by his side, and after a while he picked it up and half filled his glass with whisky. Then he resumed his study of the book that lay in front of him. A strange book to find in such surroundings, and yet one which helped to explain the riddle of the riding breeches. It was a book of snapshots and odd cuttings from newspapers. A few groups cut from *The Tatler* and *The Sketch* were pasted in and it was at one of these that he was staring.

Bridesmaids; bride and bridegroom; best man – particularly the best man. He was in the uniform of the 10th Lancers, and for a long while the man sat there motionless, studying the face on the paper. Good-looking, with clear-cut features; a magnificent specimen of manhood, showing off the gorgeous uniform of the regiment to perfection. Then very deliberately he got up and crossed the room to the broken bit of mirror that served as a shaving glass. Dispassionately he studied his own face, not sparing himself in the examination. And at length he turned away.

"Great God!" he said, very slowly. "How did it happen?"

And the line of bottles gave answer.

He went back to the table, and started turning over the pages of the book. The regiment on parade; a stately home set in wonderful trees; groups on the moors with keepers and dogs; groups with the women he had known… And at last a simple snapshot of two people – himself and a girl. Pat and self – thus ran the inscription underneath it, and for perhaps a quarter of an hour he sat there motionless, staring at it. Some big insect fussed angrily against the mosquito netting, trying to get at the light; ceaselessly the beetles droned on – but the man at the table heard nothing. He was back in the might-have-been; back at Henley – three years before the war.

Pat! What was she doing now? She'd stuck to him loyally; stuck to him as only a woman can stick to the thing she loves. For it had started even then. The curse was on him: the soul-rotting, hellish curse that had brought him to this. But at last it had had to end: the thing had become impossible.

He had fought. God! how he'd fought! But it had beaten him. No excuse, of course: to be beaten is no excuse for a man. And he could still hear Pat's voice that last time – could still see her sweet face with the tears pouring down it.

"Jim – if you can beat it – come back to me."

And that was after he had had to send in his papers.

He hadn't beaten it; it had beaten him. And now Pat was married; two children – or was it three? And he – what was he? His family said he was farming in Africa. A pleasant fiction which deceived no one. Least of all himself. He was not farming in Africa; he was a drunken remittance man living on a farm in Africa.

He closed the book, and stared with haggard eyes into the darkness. Why had this girl come to stop at Merrick's farm, and opened all these old wounds? Why had he seen her that afternoon?

She'd reminded him of Pat a little. Cool and dressed in white – riding Merrick's chestnut cob in a way that showed she was used to horses. What the devil did she want to bring all that back to him for? Girls and horses were all part of the life he'd lived a hundred years ago.

"Yes, a trooper of the forces, who has owned his own six horses…"

And he wasn't even that. Just a drunken down-and-outer, with a father in the House of Lords who paid him five hundred a year on condition that he never set foot in England again.

Cool and dressed in white! Lord! but it was something to see a girl of his own class again. She'd stared at him in faint surprise when he'd spoken; drink doesn't kill a man's accent. And by now she'd know all about him: the Merricks would see to that.

They didn't know who he was: he'd given his name out here as Brown. But they did know *what* he was, and that was all that mattered.

"A drunkard, my dear; a hopeless case."

He could hear Mrs Merrick saying it. Not that she was a bad sort; quite the reverse, in fact. But she was the wife of a settler who had made good, and she loathed weakness. At first she had tried to pull him round – to make him take an interest in his property. For months she had persevered, and it wasn't until she found out that he wouldn't help himself that she gave up trying. Contemptuously.

And he deserved it: he was under no delusions. But now – He stood up suddenly, and instinctively his shoulders squared. Supposing he took a pull at himself; it wasn't too late. Supposing he, too, made good. Supposing that girl dressed in white –

And suddenly he laughed a little bitterly. Girls dressed in white were outside his scheme of things altogether. Quite deliberately he reached out for the bottle, and tipped what was left into his glass. Then he performed his nightly rite. With meticulous attention to dressing he placed it in line with the others; called the squadron to attention, and then dismissed them.

And ten minutes later the man who called himself Jim Brown, having kicked off his boots, lay sleeping heavily on his bed.

2

He'd shaved when he next saw the girl, and his shirt was clean. She was riding, as before, and he stood waiting for her to come up.

"Good morning," she said, cheerily. "What a heavenly day!"

"The one compensation of this God-forsaken country," he remarked, "is that the days generally are heavenly."

She looked at him steadily.

"Why do you stay if you don't like it?"

"Entirely my duty towards my neighbour," he answered. "Think of all the grief and sorrow I should cause if I departed."

"Is that your bungalow up there?" she said suddenly.

"It is," he remarked. "And dilapidated though it looks from the outside, I can assure you the interior is much worse."

"That's good," she cried. "And as I can hardly believe it possible, I'm coming up to see."

For a moment he hesitated.

"It really isn't in a fit condition – " he began.

"Bunkum," she answered. "Do you suppose I've never seen an untidy room before?"

"It isn't altogether that," he said, slowly.

Then he gave a short laugh.

"Right-ho!" he cried. "Your sins be upon your own head."

He led the way in silence, and having tethered her horse flung open the door.

"Behold the ancestral hall," he announced gravely.

Her eyes travelled round the room, resting for a moment on the array of bottles, while he watched her with a faint smile. What was she going to say?

"Get out," she remarked. "This is going to be no place for a man for the next hour or two."

It was so completely unexpected that for a moment or two he could only stare at her.

"Go on – get out," she repeated, peeling off her gloves. "You'll only be in the way."

"You topper," he said under his breath. "You absolute topper."

Then he swung on his heel and left her, not knowing if she'd heard what he'd said – and not caring.

Two hours later he returned to find her sitting on the table smoking a cigarette. And the first thing he noticed was that the empty bottles had disappeared.

"I see you've removed my squadron," he said. "It was very nearly full strength except for the officers."

"You mean those dirty old bottles," she remarked. "I've buried them outside."

"Didn't you admire their perfect dressing on parade?" he asked. "I used to call them to attention every time a new recruit joined."

She stared at him through the smoke of her cigarette.

"I've been looking at this scrap-book of yours," she said, calmly. "I hope you don't mind."

"Not at all. I fear my library is somewhat deficient. But I need hardly perhaps say that Brown still remains a very good name."

He glanced round the room; everything was spotless. The shelves of the cupboard were adorned with paper; the plates were washed and neatly stacked; even the teapot seemed to have taken on a new dignity.

"You seem to have been most thorough," he said gravely. "Thank you."

"So you won the Grand Military, did you?" she remarked.

"I believe that in some former existence of mine I had that honour. Incidentally speaking," he continued, "I trust that you haven't buried the quick and the dead together."

"There are a dozen full bottles in there," she said, pointing to his bedroom. "I thought they would be more convenient for you if you woke in the night."

He stood motionless, staring at her. His face was expressionless; her eyes met his calmly and frankly.

"I deserve that," he said in a low voice.

"My dear man," she remarked. "I don't think you *deserve* anything at all. It's the wrong word. It's not for me to judge. All I say is that I think it's a pity that being who you are you should be what you are. It seems such a ghastly waste."

"Some such idea occurred to me when I took the name of Brown," he answered, thoughtfully.

She shook herself a little impatiently.

"How you can have that book here – be reminded day in, day out, of everything that might be yours – and not go mad, absolutely beats me."

"Sometimes it beats me, too," he said, quietly.

"Good God! man," she cried, "can't you try?"

"Good God! girl," he answered, "do you suppose I haven't?"

And for a space they were silent, staring at one another. At last she slipped from the table and went up to him.

"Sorry," she said, gently, "I shouldn't have said that. Look here – can I help? Julia Merrick told me she had done her best – but Julia is married and busy. I'm neither. Shall we have a dip at it together? No slop and slush about it. If you want a drink, have one. I shan't look at you reprovingly. But if we pull together we might be able to keep whisky as a drink – not as a permanent diet."

He turned suddenly and walked over to the open window. And she being a girl of much understanding lit another cigarette and waited. In her eyes was a look of wonderful pity, but she didn't want him to see it. Something told her that she had started on the right note: that any trace of sentimentality would be fatal. For perhaps five minutes he stood there with his back to her, and only the pawing of the pony on the ground outside broke the silence. Then he swung round.

"Damned sporting offer," he said, curtly. "Afraid you'll find it a bit boring, though."

"I'll chance it," she said. "Come over and dine tonight."

3

And so the man who called himself Brown began to fight again. For hours he would sit in his bungalow sweating with the agony of it, and with every nerve in his body screaming for the stuff.

And sometimes the girl would sit opposite him, holding his two hands across the table and watching him with cool, steady eyes.

His face was haggard; his hands shook uncontrollably when she released them. But he fought on with every gun and rifle he possessed, and the girl fought at his side.

It happened unexpectedly as such things will – in his bungalow one evening. For three hours the girl had been with him, and that particular crisis had passed. They were sitting side by side on the stoep, watching the sun go down behind the distant Drakensburg, and without thought she put her hand on his knee.

"Jim," she whispered. "How utterly marvellous!"

And his hand closed over hers in the way there is no mistaking. She turned slowly and stared at him, and then caught her breath at the look in his eyes. She knew instantly what was coming: knew there was no way of stopping it. He was down on his knees beside her, his arms flung round her waist, his face buried in her lap. And for a space he went mad.

Hardly hearing – almost numbed with the suddenness of this new complication – she sat listening to the wild dreams of the man who called himself Brown. He was cured – with her help he had fought and won.

"For God's sake, don't leave me, Beryl!" he said, again and again. "Listen, dear – we'll get married. And now that I'm all right, we'll go back to England under my proper name. I'll get a job – I've got influence. And when they know I'm cured there won't be any difficulty."

He raised his face, and with blinding clearness she saw him for what he was. Before he had just been a case – a mission; now he was very much a man. A man grown old before his time, with the ineffaceable ravages of drink plain to see; a man with bloodshot, puffy eyes and trembling limbs; a travesty.

And yet, ghastly in its mercilessness though the picture was, in some strange way she seemed to see another one. Shining through this terrible mask she saw the man as he had been – clear-eyed, firm-lipped, with the pride of youth in every line of his body. And a pity that was almost divine took hold of her. She leaned forward and put her hand on his hair – and it was the hair of the man who had been that she touched. She kissed him on the forehead, and it was the forehead of the man in uniform – the man who had won the Grand Military – that she kissed.

And then he, with a little gasp of wonder, seized her hungrily and kissed her on the mouth. And Beryl Kingswood sat rigid: the dream had gone – reality had come back. The man who had kissed her lips was the man who called himself Jim Brown – the drunkard.

He was mad – incoherent with joy. He couldn't believe it: he went on pacing up and down the veranda, painting wild dreams of the future. And every now and then he would stop and kiss the back of her neck – and touch her arm almost humbly.

"Stop and have dinner with me, dear," he said, "on this wonderful night of nights. I'll take you back afterwards."

And because she was incapable of clear thought – because she was dazed by the result of what she had done in that one instant – she stayed to dinner. What was she going to do? How was she ever going to tell him? And gradually as the hours passed the thing began to get clearer. Dinner was over – a meal at which he had proudly drunk orange-juice and water. And now, sitting once again on the stoep in the darkness, her hand in his, it didn't seem so very terrible. She would go through with it; she would marry him, and bring him back to what he had been. She had put her hand to the plough – she would not turn back.

"We'll make good, my dear," she whispered, impulsively. "We'll make good between us."

Very tenderly and reverently he bent and kissed her hand.

"You utterly marvellous girl," he said.

And for a space there was silence, broken only by the ceaseless noise of the tree beetles.

4

Thus did the man who called himself Brown struggle to the foothills from which a glimpse of Heaven may be got. And Fate ordained that he should remain there for just one week – a week during which only one person mattered, the wonderful girl who had promised to marry him. He got a tablecloth from the neighbouring store, and carefully mended the broken teapot handle with seccotine, so as to be able to give her tea when she came over to see him. He laid in stocks of grub, and got bowls in which he arranged flowers for her benefit. And, perhaps, greatest wonder of all, the twelve full bottles under his bed remained full.

Of the other side of the case he knew nothing – how should he? He had not been in the Merricks' bedroom on the night they had learned what had happened – the night he had walked over with Beryl after she had dined with him. He had not seen Julia Merrick positively seize her husband as he came in, and almost shake him in her excitement.

"Tom – it's too horrible!"

"It's pretty grim, I admit," he remarked. "Still I don't see what's to be done about it. She seems to have made up her mind."

"It isn't as if she loved him even."

"What's that?" said her husband. "Doesn't she love him?"

"Of course she doesn't. How could she?"

"I dunno. Women do same damned funny things at times. Has she told you she doesn't?"

"Don't be an absolute idiot," cried Julia Merrick. "Do you suppose another woman wants to be told a thing like that? You've only got to see them together. Why, he – he almost repels her."

Tom Merrick yawned hugely.

"Well, my dear – it's beyond me. If he repels her, why the deuce has she gone and got engaged to him?"

"Because she's sorry for him. Because she thinks it her job. Because she thinks she's cured him. Because – oh! a thousand reasons – and not one of them the right one. And from what I know of Beryl, she'll carry the thing through."

Her husband turned over sleepily.

"We'd better talk it over, my dear. In the morning," he added, hopefully.

"There's nothing to talk over," said his wife. "The thing's unnatural. It's – it's ghastly. Are you asleep?"

"More or less, my dear."

"Well, become a little less for a moment. Do you honestly and conscientiously believe that that man is cured?"

"Difficult to say," he grunted. "Personally, I wouldn't trust him a yard. Think he's a hopeless case. Still, you never can tell."

"Tom, if Beryl were your daughter – would you allow it?"

"Good God! no!" he cried. "What an idea!"

"All right," said his wife, quietly. "You can go to sleep now."

And lay awake herself staring into the darkness. Dimly she had feared during the past few weeks that some such complications might occur, but never had she dreamed that Beryl would go to the length of promising to marry the man. That he might fall in love with her she had realised was more than likely: many men did fall in love with Beryl Kingswood. But that she would accept him seemed so staggeringly outrageous that she could still hardly believe it.

What to do? That was the problem.

And as the days passed by it became more acute. She was almost frightened of mentioning the matter to Beryl, because it seemed to make her shut up like an oyster. Obviously she didn't want to discuss it; just as obviously her nerves were strung up to the danger point. And Julia Merrick could have screamed with the futility of it.

Her husband was no help.

"What can I do, my dear?" he said, continually. "They're both of age. If Beryl chooses to marry the man I don't see how we can prevent her. She's her own mistress. She knows the danger she is running as well as we do. He certainly seems to have kept off the drink these last few weeks."

"Couldn't you have a talk with him as man to man?" she urged. "Say to him that it isn't fair to marry her until he is *sure*. That he ought to give it a year at least."

"I'll have a try," he said, doubtfully. "But I tell you frankly, Julia, that fellow Brown is a queer customer to tackle. He's got a way of looking at you which says 'Go to the devil', plainer than any language. Drunkard though he is, I give you my word that there are times when he makes me feel like a boy in front of a master."

"He's coming over tonight," said his wife. "Get him alone and try."

But it wasn't necessary; as I have said. Fate ordained that Jim Brown should stay on the foothills for just one week. And that night the week was up. Why he should have approached the Merricks' bungalow from behind instead of going to the front door is just one of those things that happen without reason. But he did – and found himself looking into the room that Julia Merrick called the work-room. Beryl was sitting at the table, and her name was trembling on the tip of his tongue when she looked up and he saw her face. And it seemed as if the world stood still.

He stood there rooted to the spot, staring at hopeless, abject misery and despair. Just for one moment he clutched at the wild hope that she had had bad news. But only for a moment; it wasn't mail day. There could be only one cause – and he knew it. Standing motionless in the darkness he watched this girl who meant salvation to him – watched her as some stranger might have watched her – impersonally. He felt conscious of only one dominant thought – to find out the truth.

Suddenly the door opened and Julia Merrick came in. He saw her pause for a moment, staring at Beryl; then he heard her speak with a sudden rush.

"My dear, now I know. You *can't* do this thing."

And heard the other answer.

"I *must!*"

He crept nearer the window; he had to hear everything now.

"Why did you do it, Beryl?"

He listened to the girl's puzzled – almost halting – explanation. And because the man who called himself Jim Brown had been a person of much understanding before he became a drunkard, he understood perfectly that which only exasperated Julia Merrick.

"He must be told," said that lady, decisively. "If you don't – I shall."

"If you do, Julia," said the girl, "I will never forgive you. I absolutely forbid you to tell him."

She stood up, facing the older woman squarely.

"Absolutely, you understand. I'm going through with it. I would never forgive myself if I started him off again."

"I wish to Heaven he'd have another outburst now – before it's too late," said the other. "Beryl – the risk is too ghastly. I know he's kept off it for a week or two – but he's a hopeless case. Tom says so. At least, my dear – say that you'll wait a year. Make him prove himself to that extent."

The girl shook her head.

"No, dear, I won't. I believe I can pull him through if I'm with him the whole time. And I can't be that unless I marry him. My mind is made up, Julia," she went on, quietly. "I shall marry him whatever you say. And he's got to go on believing that I'm fond of him, or half my influence will be gone."

Julia Merrick shrugged her shoulders helplessly.

"So be it, Beryl. It's your choice. But I think you're making a terrible mistake."

"Perhaps I am," said the girl. "But a mistake is better than a sin. And it would be a sin to turn him down now, when he has fought so hard. Let's go, Julia; he ought to be here soon."

The light went out; the room was empty. She would be in the drawing-room by now – sitting in the chair she usually occupied. He had only to go round to the front door and walk in, and he would see her get up with that grave little smile of hers and hold out both her hands. And she would say:

"How goes it, old lad?"

And he would answer: "Quite well, my dear – quite well."

And she would say: "Well played, partner."

Yes – just go round to the front door and walk in. Wipe these last few minutes off the slate – pretend they had never been. A grave smile flickered round his lips – half-cynical, half-tender. Then, lifting his hand to the salute, the man who called himself Brown turned and walked away into the night.

5

"I'll come with you, Beryl," said Tom.

Over the girl's shoulder he glanced significantly at his wife. It was ten o'clock, and dinner was long since over – the dinner to which Jim Brown had been bidden and failed to appear.

"All right," said Beryl, quietly. "Just as you like."

In silence they set out on their twenty-minute walk. The glorious African moon made it almost as light as day, and it wasn't until they came in sight of Jim Brown's bungalow that Tom Merrick spoke again.

"My dear," he said, gravely, "for God's sake don't be too disappointed if – if – "

"Please don't," she said, "I'd sooner not talk."

It was as they were walking up the rise to his house that they suddenly heard his voice.

"Parade! 'Shun!'"

And the girl stopped dead with a little gasp.

"Let me go first," said Tom Merrick.

"No," said Beryl, firmly. "You wait outside."

She crossed the veranda and pushed open the door. In perfect dressing on the floor stood eleven empty bottles, and on the table in front of him one that was half full. And in front of the eleven was the teapot.

"That gentleman," he said, gravely indicating the latter, "is the commanding officer. Don't you think he's rather a good-looker?"

"Jim," she said, steadily, "we were expecting you to dinner."

"The devil you were, my dear," he answered. "That's a bit of a break on my part."

"What are those doing there?" She pointed to the row of bottles.

"My soldiers, darling," he explained. "I took them out for an airing tonight. To spare your feelings, up to date, I've kept them in barracks under the bed, but the little chaps insisted on a field day tonight."

"You mean to say that you've been drinking all this time."

Her voice was unutterably weary.

"Honesty, my pet, compels me to admit the fact. It was my innate politeness which made me disguise the fact in view of your well-meant efforts on my behalf. Ah! my friend, Mr Merrick, I see. One of those honest pillars of the soil that have made our glorious Empire what it is."

"So you've lied to me," she whispered. "All this while. Oh! my God!"

And just for one brief moment did the man who had tipped eleven full bottles of whisky down the sink that night falter. Then he steadied himself and rode at the last fence.

"My dear," he said, gravely, "lie is an ugly word. Shall we say – prevaricated charmingly?"

A HOPELESS CASE

"A hopeless case, my dear," said Tom Merrick, as they neared his bungalow. "He'd gone too far."

And the hopeless case sat at his table staring with hopeless eyes into the night. The bottle in front of him was empty. At last he rose, and with meticulous attention to dressing he placed it in line with the others. He called the squadron to attention and then dismissed them.

And for a space there was silence, broken only by the ceaseless noise of the tree beetles.

THE UNDOING OF MRS CRANSBY

Mrs Cransby was a bad woman. I do not use the adjective in its strict sense: in matters of sex she was much as other women – rather less so perhaps than most. I use it in the same way as it is frequently used about a man by his fellows. And then it generally implies that the gentleman in question is a poor specimen.

Mrs Cransby was a poor specimen, though numbers of the opposite sex took a long time to find it out. She was amazing, in spite of the fact that her tongue was sharper than a serpent's tooth when she wanted it to be. She was always perfectly dressed, and her figure was divine. Moreover she was pretty. How she had maintained her complexion during years in the East only her maid and she knew. Though possibly her husband when footing the bill for face creams and lotions from England had a shrewd idea. Possibly also he wished her complexion was not quite so wonderful.

But her principal glory was her hair. It was in the days, be it known, before the shingle and the Eton crop, and Mrs Cransby's hair was undoubtedly very wonderful. Personally, needless to say, I never had the opportunity of seeing it when let down: but judging as a mere male it must have reached nearly to her knees. There were masses of it, coiled about her shapely head. In colour it was exactly the right tinge of auburn: in texture it was like the finest of gossamer silk. At least so Purvis in the Gunners assured me one night in the club, when he ought to have been at home with his wife.

And perhaps because it was so very wonderful Mrs Cransby hated to have it touched. She bit like a snapping dog if it was disturbed even accidentally. And as for anything in the nature of a caress, I understand that no man did it a second time. As a result there was never a hair out of place. At the end of a game of tennis it was still as perfectly arranged as at the beginning: at the conclusion of a dance she might just have left her coiffeur. Which is all I have to say about Mrs Cransby's hair – a very important factor in this story.

I will come therefore to a very unimportant one – her husband. Only the fact that I have already alluded to him casually justifies the poor devil's inclusion. He was a mild little individual – something in Woods and Forests – and was always alluded to as Mrs Cransby's husband. And his sole claim to notoriety was that he supplied the money which Mrs Cransby spent. Of children, needless to say, there were none: Mrs Cransby was not the type of woman to waste her time. And having got so far it occurs to me that a little more justification of my opening sentence is necessary. It shall be given in a nutshell: she was a specialist in other women's husbands. And fiancés. It was sufficient for Mrs Cransby to know that a man was engaged to a girl for her to appropriate him on the spot. And the astounding thing was that she so frequently succeeded. I think she did it to show her power. She didn't keep him permanently – two or three months perhaps, according to the value of the specimen. Then she returned him labelled "finished with", and cast round for someone else. Which made her of course, intensely popular with women.

In many cases no permanent damage was done: in some it was. Little Patricia Tennant for instance broke off her engagement to young Hill in the 10th Lancers because of her. She said she flatly refused to marry another woman's cast-off. And Hill, whose madness had completely passed, very nearly blew out his brains. Stanton, too, in a native Cavalry regiment made a very complete fool of himself over her, at a time when his wife was having her first baby. Which was not at all a good thing to do, and on that occasion even Mrs Cransby's skin was not thick enough to stand the remarks that were made. So she drifted away just before the baby arrived very much earlier than expected. And two doctors sweating through a sweltering night managed to save the mother's life.

Then there was — But why enumerate? Mrs Cransby was a bad woman, and this is the tale of her undoing at the hands of MacAndrew sometime doctor and all-time drunkard. And should anyone who reads these words ever meet Mrs Cransby – she lives in London now – let him take warning, and steer clear of mentioning any name that sounds even remotely Scotch. Because she will probably start to bite the furniture, and that would be a spectacle sufficient to shake the strongest nerve.

John MacAndrew was a character. Exactly what had caused his departure from Scotland, I never inquired into. And he was not communicative. But I do know that he was one of the most brilliant students of his year, and that when he chose to, even after twenty-five years of continuous drinking, there was practically no subject on which he could not talk far more intelligently than the majority of people.

He had a small bungalow on the Irrawaddy a few hundred miles up country. There was a branch of a teak company situated there, and originally he had gone up as doctor. And somehow or other he had stayed on, though he had long since ceased to practice. Much as we all liked him, it would have been a stout-hearted man who called in MacAndrew professionally. It was there I first met him, when I was doing Assistant-Manager.

There were ten of us whites in all, though only three others come into this story. Cooper was the Manager – a capable man and a good fellow except in the early morning when he suffered from a liver like a volcano in eruption. He was a widower and his daughter Joan lived with him. And on the subject of Joan Cooper we were all of us partially demented. It wasn't because she was the only pebble on the beach either: she would have held her own anywhere. A glorious girl – absolutely unspoilt – and radiating cheeriness and affection. But no more. I think we all proposed to her in turn: I know I did – twice. But there was nothing doing: she wouldn't dream of leaving Daddy.

Until young Jack Congleton arrived. He was a cheery youngster fresh from the Varsity, who was ultimately destined for the headquarter office in London. And he had been sent out to us to learn his job first hand.

It was after he'd been there a week, that the general drift of things became too obvious to be ignored. Even old Cooper, who as a rule saw nothing beyond matters concerning teak, sat up and took notice. Three or four times I caught him studying Jack Congleton thoughtfully in his office, when he should have been finishing important letters. But when all is said and done a prospective son-in-law is as important as any letter.

And there was nothing wrong with young Congleton. He wouldn't have won a prize in a beauty show, but he was a straight, clean, well set up boy. Moreover from a financial point of view he was eminently satisfactory. He was to be taken into partnership as soon as he returned to England. And though Cooper would have murdered the man who said so, I think the advantages of having a son-in-law as partner in the firm had not escaped him. There comes a time when Burma palls and London calls. Not – to do him justice – that he would have let such an idea influence him for a moment if Congleton had been a wrong 'un. He idolised Joan far too much for that. But it was a factor that counted in young Jack's claims to eligibility.

It came to a head after he had been there three weeks. I walked into the office one morning to find a bottle of champagne on the table, and Jack somewhat sheepishly helping Cooper to lower it.

"Hear what this young scoundrel has done, Morris?" cried Cooper. "He's had the confounded impertinence to propose to

Joan, and the child's brain is so weak that she's accepted him. Drink his health, my boy. This is damned bad for my liver, but it's not an everyday occurrence, thank God!"

I said the customary things, and then work went on as usual. And I don't believe any of us felt the faintest twinge of jealousy. They were such an admirably chosen pair: they were so idiotically in love with one another. Burma was so wonderful: and life was so wonderful: and each of them was so wonderful to the other.

And the most delighted of us all was John MacAndrew. Mac adored Joan as if she had been his daughter. And Joan adored him. Drunkard he may have been and was, but I do not believe there is a man or woman living today who could say of John MacAndrew – "That man let me down". Which is a valuation, in the big scheme of things, that is maybe of higher merit than the holding of a blue ribbon. And because Cooper was a man of understanding he had never raised any objection to his daughter knowing him.

Now it so happened that, shortly after the great event of the engagement, duty took me up country for over two months. And the night I got back found me sitting in my bungalow trying to polish off arrears of correspondence. There was a big batch of it and I was not too well pleased when I heard the Soldiers' Chorus from Faust outside, and steps ascending the veranda. It was MacAndrew's only song, and he and letter writing did not go together.

He entered, mopping his forehead with a huge red bandana, and deposited himself in a chair. Then with great solemnity he drew from his pocket a bottle of whisky, and placed it on the table beside him.

"Are you busy, laddie?" he asked.

"Never too busy to see you, Mac," I said resignedly. "But don't drink your own whisky: try some of mine."

He shook his head.

"Not on your life, my dear boy," he answered, "My consumption is so enormous that I would not run the risk of straining our friendship to that extent. But I have no objection to your drinking your own: in fact I shall regard such an action in the most favourable light."

"You old ass, Mac," I laughed. "Well, how is everything here?"

He filled his glass in silence, and suddenly a premonition took me that something was wrong. Now that I looked at him he seemed unusually grave for him.

"Water, Mac?" I said perfunctorily.

"Water, laddie," he cried. "Is your reason snapping?"

He finished half the glass, and then with the utmost deliberation he rolled himself a cigarette. From of old I knew there was no good trying to hurry him. He lit his cigarette, blew out a great cloud of smoke, and then looked at me from under his shaggy eyebrows.

"Do you by any chance ken a female called Cransby?" he said.

"Cransby," I cried. "Wife of the man in Woods and Forests?"

"Aye," he said.

"Yes I do. Why?"

"She's here," he answered, and finished the rest of his drink.

"Then as far as I am concerned the sooner she goes away from here the better I'll be pleased," I said. "She is a lady for whom I have no vestige or shadow of use."

He grunted, and mopped his forehead once again.

"Your opinion of her confirms my own diagnosis," he remarked. "I have no vestige or shadow of use for her myself. But she's here: and she's been here a week."

"Has she been trying to make you fall in love with her, Mac?" I chaffed.

"She has not," he answered gravely. "But she's been trying to make young Congleton. And she's succeeded."

"What?" I almost shouted. "But what about Joan?"

"Mon," he said, "that woman is a she devil. Listen and I'll tell you what's been happening while you've been away. You ken what those two bairns were like, with their billing and their cooing, and their this and that. You ken that each was the whole world to the other. One night – it was about a fortnight after you left – the pair of them came round to see me. And laddie it was like seeing a little bit of Heaven. Their dreams, and their hopes – and the way they looked at one another, and touched one another's hands when they thought I didn't see.

"They sat on there talking, and I let them talk and just listened. Maybe I dreamed myself a little; dreamed of Scotland and the sun turning the moors from purple to velvet black as it sets way down behind great banks of cloud."

He paused and stared into the darkness. And I waited: MacAndrew was in a strange mood tonight.

"I'm talking rot," he went on abruptly. "But I want you to get the condition I was in that night, when yon hell-cat appeared. She came out of the darkness, suddenly – and stood on the veranda smiling. And even then it was at young Jack that most of her smiles were delivered.

" 'Can you tell me where Mr Cooper's bungalow is?' said she. 'My name is Cransby, and my husband is seeing about the baggage.'

"The little girl got up, with that sweet look of hers, and went to her.

" 'But, Mrs Cransby,' she said, 'we weren't expecting you and your husband for three days. I'm so sorry neither my father nor I were there to meet you. I'll take you over to the bungalow at once.'

" 'That's sweet of you,' says the woman. 'I thought my husband had written: I'm *so* sorry if we've inconvenienced you.'

"I heard her voice dying away in the distance, and then I glanced at young Jack. And he had a funny sort of half smile, half smirk on his face.

" 'What a damned attractive woman,' he remarked.

" 'Tastes differ,' I said, and at that we left it.

"To start with, I admit, I didn't think much of it. It appeared that the husband, and maybe you know him, he looks rather like a newt with pince-nez – was here on Government business. And he was going up country."

"Good Lord," I interrupted. "I did hear there was a Government man of sorts cruising round. But I never thought it was Cransby."

"It was and is," said Mac. "He's still cruising. And his wife is still here. Cooper told her, as he naturally had to do, that she was to use his bungalow till her husband's return."

"She can't have done much damage in a week," I said, but my tone carried no conviction. Mrs Cransby could play the devil in a day.

"I would not have thought so either," he agreed, "until last night. At first there was nothing much to lay hold of – just a look here, and a glance there. But I saw from the little girl's face that she had spotted. She didn't say anything about it – she's proud is that bairn. But there was all the misery of the ages in her dear eyes when she thought no one was looking. And even now I don't know if she realises how far it has gone."

"What do you mean, Mac?" I said anxiously. "She doesn't generally go to any extreme lengths."

"I was walking down by the big plantation," he went on, "about six o'clock last night. And suddenly I heard voices. It was young Congleton speaking, and I stood there almost unable to believe my ears. 'Darling,' he was saying, 'she's only a girl – but you're the most wonderful woman in the world. Irene – my beloved.' And she answered, 'Dear, dear boy. But you mustn't forget you're engaged to her, and that I'm a married woman.' I took a step forward, and there she was stroking his face. Losh! man. I was very near sick with disgust. 'Shame on you,' I said to young Congleton, 'you miserable pup. What for are you allowing yon harpy to stroke your face, with your girl sitting at home waiting for you?' "

I grinned happily: for Mrs Cransby to be called a harpy to her face sounded almost too good to be true.

"What happened?" I cried.

"Mon," he said, "there was a terrible scene. I'm not saying that I didn't enjoy it, for I just revelled in it. The woman got to her feet, and came towards me. Her face was set like a mask, and if she'd had the power she'd have struck me dead at her feet. 'I am not in the habit,' says she, 'of being called a harpy by people – least of all by a drunken old wastrel.' 'And I,' I said, 'am not in the habit of calling a spade anything but a spade. Good God! woman, you're old enough to be his mother.' "

"Mac," I shouted delightedly, "you didn't? Why man, there must be three score women roaming this world today who would give half their worldly possessions to have heard that remark."

"I'm not denying it didn't give me a certain amount of satisfaction," he said. "But, laddie, it's serious. The boy is fairly besotted. He called round to see me this morning and asked me how I dared to say such a thing to the most perfect and wonderful woman in the world. He said that if I wasn't a drunken old swine he'd have thrashed me to within an inch of my life. Didn't I understand that it wasn't her fault that he had fallen in love with her: that she was a loyal and devoted wife and had told him all along that his duty lay with Joan? And so on. I didn't interrupt him: I let him have his say out. And then I just put my hand on his shoulder and I said 'Boy, in a moment of anger I told Mrs Cransby she was old enough to be your mother. I'm sorry. But anyway I'm old enough to be your father. And I like you. And I'm just sick to see you making such a damned fool of yourself.' "

"The rag, and the bone, and the hank of hair," I quoted without thinking. But MacAndrew looked at me intently.

"The hank of hair," he repeated. "It's curious – the hair of that woman."

"In what way," I said. "I know she is inordinately proud of it. And if you want to disillusionise young Congleton, get him to ruffle it. She'll go for him like a Billingsgate fishwife."

"It's curious," he repeated. "Verra curious."

He lapsed into silence, sunk in a train of thought of his own. And I too, sat thinking. What wretched freak of fate had brought the woman here? Not often did she accompany her husband to such out of the way places. But now that she had come, the march of events was as inexorable as day following night. Only too well did I recognise the Mrs Cransby touch. "Dear, dear boy. Don't you realise that I'm married."

Always the same. A kiss perhaps – just now and then: the pressure of a hand: the wonderful look implying how different things would have been if she wasn't married. And then the calm tossing aside like a worn-out glove. Stale to her: she'd done it so often before. But like a drug: she could no more resist doing it than stop breathing.

Only I felt furious with young Congleton. Within two months of having got engaged to a girl like Joan… The only excuse was that he *was* very young, and that other much warier game had fallen to the same gun. Anyway his punishment was coming: the pathetic thing was that another would have to share in that punishment.

"I'm afraid there's nothing to be done, Mac," I said at length. "You can't stop a man making a congenital idiot of himself if he's set on it. Mrs Cransby is the only person who could do it, and you might as well ask a tiger to leave its kill."

"Verra curious," he said, "that hair of hers."

"What the devil has her hair got to do with it," I cried irritably. I thought the old boy was getting fuddled.

"Always the same," he went on. "Verra curious."

And then quite suddenly he sat up and stared into a corner of the room.

"Mon," he cried, "look at yonder rat. As big as a rabbit."

I swung round in my chair: there was nothing in the corner at all.

"Steady, old man," I said. "I don't see any rat."

"There – running across the room." He followed its course with his finger. "Lord sakes! it's vanished into the wall."

"Look here, Mac," I said gravely, "you'd better take a pull at yourself. There wasn't any rat there at all. You're imagining things."

"No rat," he muttered. "Are you sure, Bill?"

"Perfectly sure," I answered. "You'd better go on the water wagon for a bit."

"Aye – perhaps you're right," he said. "That's what yon woman told me."

He got heavily to his feet, and put back the bottle in his pocket.

"No rat, you say. And that hair of hers. Verra curious. Well, good night, Bill. Maybe it will all turn out for the best. But it's curious – curious."

And as he stumbled down the veranda steps, I heard him still muttering that it was verra curious.

The old chap breaking up, I reflected – and then my mind came back to the far more important problem of young Congleton. Because the boy was worth saving – I felt it in my very bones. And if what MacAndrew had told me was right, he was evidently in a bad way. Of course, I could tell him what I knew of Mrs Cransby, and that he was only one of a large procession. But would he believe me – would it do the slightest good? Or I could appeal to her, an even more fatuous proceeding.

"Confound and curse the woman," I cried out loud, and at that moment I heard MacAndrew stumbling up the steps again.

"And confound and curse the man," I muttered: I'd had enough of him for one night.

"Bill," he said appearing in the window, "I'm sorry to interrupt you again. But I've been thinking. And it's occurred to me that I may have been imagining things. That rat – for instance. You say there was no rat?"

"Of course there was no rat," I cried. "You haven't come all the way back to ask me that, have you?"

"Not exactly," he answered. "But if I thought I saw a rat, and there was no rat – maybe I did yon woman an injustice when I said she was stroking the boy's face. Maybe she wasn't."

I stared at him in amazement.

"What are you driving at?" I asked. "Even if you imagined she was stroking his face and she wasn't, you can't have imagined the interview you had with young Congleton."

"That is so," he agreed. "But if I made a false accusation such as that, it would be sufficient to make them both verra angry. They have done harm to the little girl, by my blundering foolishness."

"Well?" I said. What on earth was he driving at?

"So I'm thinking I would like to apologise," he went on.

"There's nothing to prevent you," I remarked. "Though from what I know of the lady, if she wasn't stroking his face she was either just going to or just had."

"That don't matter," he said obstinately. "I would have no woman say I had done her an injustice. And the fact that I do not like her, is all the more reason that I should not be unfair. So I'm wanting you to do something for me, Bill. The night is yet young. And even if the sun has gone down on our wrath, there is no good reason why it should rise on it."

"For Heaven's sake, Mac," I cried, half angry and half amused, "get to the point. Or the sun will have risen on it."

"Go over to Cooper's bungalow," he said, "and get hold of Mrs Cransby and young Congleton. Cooper is away out tonight, and I saw a light in the little girl's room – so maybe she has gone to bed. Bring them back with you here: I saw them sitting on the veranda."

"But, good Lord! man," I cried, "it's ridiculous. What on earth excuse am I to give them?"

"Give them the real reason," he said. "Say that I'm wanting to apologise for my rudeness. You know the woman yourself, and you can say that I'm just a drunken old man with delirium tremens, who has been babbling foolishly. And that you're verra angry with me."

I hesitated, and suddenly he put his hand on my arm.

"Go, Bill, I tell you. It's important."

"Why not go over and apologise to them there?" I said.

"Because the little girl might hear," he answered. "And I would not have her know more than is absolutely necessary. Go: go, at once."

"All right," I said reluctantly. "Though why the devil you can't wait till tomorrow, I don't know."

"She'd be wearing a topee," he remarked with complete irrelevance. "Just go now, Bill."

"What's the game, Mac?" I said, staring at him.

"One on which the little girl's happiness depends," he answered. "For the boy is a good boy really. Go, Bill, and don't come back without them."

And so I went. Halfway there I very nearly turned back: the whole thing seemed so preposterously foolish. But then I realised I'd never get rid of MacAndrew if I didn't get them, and I walked on. That they would come I felt tolerably certain: Mrs Cransby would seize the opportunity with both hands of suppressing such an embarrassing piece of gossip. What I couldn't for the life of me understand was MacAndrew's attitude.

I found them alone on the veranda, and young Congleton's face did not register joy. Mrs Cransby, on the contrary, gave me one of her sweetest smiles.

"Why I declare it's Mr Morris," she said, holding out her hand. "It must be quite three years since we met."

"At Poona," I answered. "Forgive my unceremonious call," I went on, "but I have rather a peculiar mission to perform. MacAndrew is over at my bungalow..."

"Damn the drunken old sweep," exploded Congleton.

"Precisely," I agreed. "And he has been talking out of his turn. As you know I only returned today, and he came over to see me after dinner. Well to come to the point, he told me a story about you two."

"Well," said young Congleton savagely, and Mrs Cransby leaned forward in her chair with her eyes fixed on my face.

"In the middle of it," I went on, "he saw a nonexistent rat in the corner. And it shook him badly. It suddenly seemed to penetrate to his brain that if he was seeing rats that weren't there he might have imagined he'd seen things that hadn't happened."

I heard Mrs Cransby draw in her breath sharply.

"And so he is very anxious to apologise to you both for the unpardonably rude things he said."

"But, good Heavens," began young Congleton foolishly.

"I think," interrupted Mrs Cransby quietly, "that it is the least Mr MacAndrew can do. I need hardly tell you, Mr Morris, that he imagined the whole thing, and that his remarks were offensive to an insufferable degree. But I haven't lived so long in the East not to realise the devastating effect of alcohol as a permanent diet. And to learn to make excuses for the victims. We will come over with you..."

Very reluctantly young Congleton rose and followed us. To him the whole thing was an absurd waste of time, which might far more profitably have been spent with his adored one. Was he not going to tell Cransby when he returned the whole state of affairs? So what did it matter what the old fool saw or didn't see? Besides – he *had* seen it: so what was the good of pretending he hadn't? And had some supernatural power told him that his

143

adored one was already bored stiff with him, and had fully determined to leave long before her devoted spouse returned in order to prevent any such embarrassing complications, he would have dismissed the suspicion with scornful laughter. Had she not kissed him that very evening? And the fact, that even had she remembered such a great event, it sank into utter insignificance beside the vital necessity of silencing old MacAndrew's tongue, was hidden from him. Such things are hidden from those who fall to the rag and the bone and the hank of hair...

We found MacAndrew standing by the table in the centre of the room, swaying slightly. And the first thing I noticed was a large bucket of water close beside him, an article of furniture which most certainly had not been there when I left.

"I have been cooling my head," began MacAndrew gravely, "so that my words, Mrs Cransby, shall be as clear as those of an old man may ever be."

He was rolling his R's grandly, was Mac, and I pulled forward a chair for Mrs Cransby.

"I am glad to hear it, Mr MacAndrew," she said coldly. "It is a pity you didn't think of the cure sooner."

"Maybe, it is," he agreed. "But I'm an old man."

He broke off suddenly. With his eyes dilated with horror he was staring at Mrs Cransby's head, and instinctively she rose to her feet.

"What is it?" she cried.

"Lord's sake, don't move," he muttered, hoarsely. "An enormous tarantula."

He stretched out a vast hand, and seized Mrs Cransby's hair. And he pulled Mrs Cransby's hair. And with a slight sucking noise Mrs Cransby's hair came off – every atom of it. And it disappeared into the bucket of water.

Now I have seen in the course of my life perfectly bald men, but I have never seen except on that occasion a perfectly bald woman. And as a spectacle it shakes a man to the marrow. I stood gazing speechlessly at that shining cranium and conquering with the greatest difficulty, a desire to burst into screams of laughter. Then I stole a look at young Congleton. His jaw had dropped: his eyes were fixed on the same target. And his face had rather the expression of a man looking down the wrong end of a loaded gun.

Only MacAndrew who was staring into the depths of the bucket seemed unmoved. He was agitating the water gently, and whistling under his breath. And at last he spoke in a hushed voice.

"Bill," he said, "you're right. No r-rat: no enorrmous tarantula. I must go on the water wagon."

And at last Mrs Cransby spoke – not in a hushed voice. She spoke for five minutes without repeating herself. Then she happened to see her reflection in the glass. And she ceased speaking, and left.

"A terrible thing," said MacAndrew thoughtfully. "No r-rat: no enorrmous tarantula. And I have never apologised for my unworthy suspicions."

He turned to young Congleton.

"Let this be a warning to you, laddie: keep off the strong drink. And maybe you'd take the lady's wig over with you when you go. If she hangs it out to dry it should be fit to wear in the morn."

A little dazedly young Congleton took the sodden mass: then he, too, left.

"Tell her," called MacAndrew after him, "that I will come tomorrow to apologise. And if I should see another enorrmous tarantula in her hair, I will leave it there."

He looked at me and his eyes were twinkling.

"I'm thinking, Bill, he's cured. And the little girl will perhaps be merciful to him. But Lord's sake! man, have ye ever seen such a fearsome spectacle as yonder woman with a head like a billiard ball?"

"But how the devil did you know, Mac?" I asked weakly.

"I didn't," he answered. "I just thought it was verra curious – that hair of hers. I thought that if I pulled hard enough, something might happen. And all I'm feared of now is that the judgement of the Lord may come upon me. It would be a terrible thing if I really did begin to see r-rats and enorrmous tarantulas, which were not there. Terrible."

He rose to his feet.

"Ah weel – I'll be away home."

"You mean to say, Mac, that the whole thing was a put up job," I gasped. "Didn't you think you saw a tarantula in her hair? And that rat?"

"Laddie," he said majestically, "when I see rats and tarantulas there are rats and tarantulas. To hear you talk anyone might think I was addicted to strong drink. But I suppose nothing better can be expected of a mere Sassenach. I bid you goodnight."

A QUESTION OF MUD

"And who," I asked, "is the somewhat inane-looking youth with the charming girl at whom you cracked a smile?"

Jim Featherstone grinned.

"He looks most kinds of an ass, doesn't he?" he said. "And yet, Bill, not only is there a deuced quick brain behind that vacuous face of his, but his actual pose of asininity on one occasion helped him to land that girl for his wife and get one of the most notorious crooks in Europe laid by the heels. No; you can take it from me, Tommy Maunders is not such a blithering idiot as he looks."

"One is almost tempted to murmur the obvious," I remarked. "But I'll spare you that if I'm right in supposing that a story is attached."

Jim settled himself comfortably in his chair.

Well, it might amuse you (he said), though I'm not much of a hand at spinning a yarn. It happened two years ago, on the occasion of the celebrated cricket match between Robert's Rabbits and Dick's Duds. I don't suppose you'll find any account of the encounter in Wisden's – like other great things in this world, it blushed unseen. Yet for keenness, my boy, that annual match has Middlesex and Surrey beat to a frazzle. Robert's Rabbits are a team raised each year by old Bob Seymour for the express purpose of playing this match against an eleven led by Sir Richard Templeton. Heaven knows how the thing started, but today that match is the event of the season for the twenty-two warriors concerned. It always takes place at Dick Templeton's place in Warwickshire. He has a nice little cricket ground, and in the year dot was quite a good average player. Now he's got a tummy like a balloon, and stops the ball with his foot – sometimes.

His house is charming and really old. A big, rambling sort of place where Charles I hid from the Roundheads and all that sort of stuff. And since Dick, who rolls in boodle, is mercifully possessed of excellent taste, all the improvements and additions he has made fit in with the general scheme. Which is just as well, because he's almost doubled the original property.

The procedure is invariably the same. Robert's Rabbits arrive on the Wednesday; the match is played on Thursday and Friday; and the party breaks up on the Saturday or Monday according to what one's own particular plans are. The house is big enough to accommodate every one and several ladies besides, so, as you can imagine, it's a pretty jolly show.

Now, it so happened that the year before, the Duds had completely wiped the floor with the Rabbits. Defeat and utter annihilation had been our portion – I'm a Rabbit, incidentally. To such an extent, in fact, that, as Bob Seymour and I had driven off on Monday morning, Dick Templeton had pursued us with words which ate deep into our souls.

"Try and give us a game next year, you lads," he had said kindly. "It makes things so much more interesting."

Now, an insult of that sort can be wiped out only with blood, and Bob had apparently been pondering on it all through the winter. And the result of his cogitations was communicated to us as the train left Paddington.

"It was weakness in bowling," he announced. "Jim's combination of half volleys and long hops wouldn't have got a girls' school out."

"Some of your lobs bounced six times," I retorted.

"Dry up," he said; "your leader speaks. Now, Peter has not recovered from his hunting accident, so I had to find a substitute. I have; and he bowls."

"That's all right, Bob," said Huntly, the wicket-keeper, doubtfully, "but what sort of a cove is he?"

You'll understand, Bill, that in a show of that sort, however keenly you may take the cricket, it is absolutely essential to have the right type of fellow. One outsider, and the whole thing is spoilt. And since for years our two elevens had been almost the same, perhaps varying by one or two at most, Huntly's question was not irrelevant.

"All right," said Bob reassuringly. "I met him lunching with a man at the club. And he seemed a very decent fellow. By name of Carruthers. He's left-hand medium, and, in addition, I gather, is good for a few runs."

Well, it sounded all right, and I must say when we came to vet him he looked all right. It's always a bit difficult coming into a big house-party who all know one another well, but he seemed perfectly at his ease at once. He could tell a deuced good story, and the general consensus of opinion was that if his cricket was up to the rest of his form, Bob had struck oil.

So much for that end of the stick. Let's get down to Tommy Maunders.

Tommy was one of Dick Templeton's main standbys. In spite of his face he was a bat distinctly above the average – which was the sole reason why he was included in the Duds. Every year did Dick's cricketing soul war with his parental soul, as to whether Tommy should be asked, and up to date cricket had triumphed. To be a little more explicit, when Tommy was at the wicket the sun got up to shine on him, in Dick's estimation; when he was not at the wicket the sun set with extreme rapidity. And the reason of the change was the charming girl you alluded to – Dick's daughter.

THE FINGER OF FATE

As a cricketer there was much to be said for Tommy; as the man who wanted to marry Moyra – Dick's daughter – the amount to be said for him did not give Dick throat trouble. As to what was Moyra's opinion of Tommy at the time I really can't tell you; as she has since married him, presumably it was not entirely adverse. But whatever she thought, one thing was quite certain: she had no intention of marrying him until her father gave his consent. And that Dick showed no signs of doing. He was quite nice about it, but very firm.

"My dear Tommy," he was wont to say, "you're not a bad bat, and you're a good cover-point, but there you begin and end. You're a lazy young devil, with the brains of an unintelligent louse. If only that fool aunt of yours hadn't left you fifteen hundred a year you might have been some use, because you'd have had to work. True, some firm little knows what it has escaped, but that would have been their worry. This is mine, and as a husband for Moyra you don't fit the bill at all."

Dick was a widower, and Moyra, being the only child, was the apple of his eye. I think that was the main reason why she wouldn't go against his wishes. It certainly wasn't for lack of asking on Tommy's part. At morn, at midday, at sunset and midnight Tommy used to get it off his chest. Once, rumour had it, he was discovered in the act at breakfast, but that naturally could not be tolerated. So he was given six of the best with a stump in the pavilion, in case the rumour was true. However, enough of that. I will pass on to the actual party of two years ago.

There were thirty of us altogether – our eleven, six of Dick's – the rest of his team were local products – and the remainder were women. And with the exception of Bob's new find, Carruthers, and a girl whose name I completely forget, I knew everyone there. I won't weary you with their names, because, with the exception of one woman, they don't come into the story. And that woman was Lady Carrington.

I don't know if you've ever met the lady. If not, you haven't missed much. Why Dick always asked her was a bit of a mystery; personally, I always regarded her as one of the world's worst horrors. I think Dick and her husband had had some business dealings or something of that sort; I know he disliked her himself.

Lady Carrington was a woman of about forty – good-looking in a vapid sort of way, and entirely devoted to Society. She lived, in fact, for nothing else. The money she spent on clothes would have rebuilt a slum; if her jewellery had been realised, the cash obtained would have rebuilt a village. And of that the *pièce de resistance* was her pearl necklace. I am not much of a judge of these things, but even I could appreciate that necklace. It consisted of three ropes, each one graduated perfectly. It was insured, I gathered, for seventy thousand pounds, and I could well believe it.

On the Wednesday night she wore it for dinner. My own personal opinion was that it was vulgarly ostentatious to do so. That, however, is beside the point. She wore it for dinner, and it was duly admired by those of us who had seen it before and by those of us who hadn't. And the first class outnumbered the second largely. Lady Carrington was a hardy annual, and, except for Carruthers and the girl, we'd most of us seen those pearls before.

I happened to know, because he had told me so the year before, that our host would infinitely have preferred her not to bring the necklace at all. The house was an old-fashioned one – low and rambling. Even a second-rate burglar would not have had the slightest difficulty in breaking into it. And with a necklace as well known as this one, the first-class men were likely to be attracted.

"I do wish you'd allow me to put it in my safe," he said as we stood around preparatory to going to bed. "Your house in

London is one thing, Lady Carrington, but anyone could break in here."

However, she was obdurate.

"My dear man," she said, "I sleep in them. There are some eighteen good men and true in this house, and if you hear me scream in the middle of the night I shall expect a combined rush to my bedroom."

We all laughed, and the matter was left at that. Personally, I don't think any of us cared a rap if the woman lost her necklace or not, but I could quite understand Dick's point of view. If anything did happen he'd sooner it did so somewhere else. However, there was nothing to be done about it. Lady Carrington had brought her necklace; she was going to sleep in it, and that was that.

Now, though we called ourselves Rabbits and Duds we took our cricket very seriously. And it was the invariable rule that on Wednesday and Thursday we had an early bed. Afterwards nothing mattered, but on those two nights we all hit the hay before midnight. And on that night I remember there was a bit of bridge, and Carruthers did some conjuring tricks – and did them wonderfully well.

After which we all turned in. And the last thing I noticed before turning out my light at a quarter to twelve was that it had come on to rain. To me the only importance in the fact lay in its possible effect on the game next day. I little thought it was going to result in a marriage.

I suppose I fell asleep about twelve. It was at a quarter past four that I was awakened by the most appalling commotion in the house. I got up, slipped on a dressing-gown, and went into the passage. Various men were running about in different conditions of semi-sleep, and from a room at the end of the wing came Lady Carrington's agitated voice.

"What's happened?" I asked in alarm.

"The combined rush that was spoken of," was the reply. "The bally woman has lost her pearls."

Just then I saw Tommy. He was coming from Lady Carrington's room, talking to Dick Templeton, who appeared terribly worried.

"Of course, you must get the police at once, sir," I heard Tommy say, and Dick went on downstairs to telephone.

"My hat, old man!" said Tommy to me with a grin. "I've seen some fairly awe-inspiring spectacles in my life, but Lady Carrington in the light of early dawn wins in a canter."

"Has she really lost her pearls?" I said.

"Beyond a shadow of doubt," he answered. "According to her, she went to bed wearing her necklace as usual. She says she fell asleep almost at once – a most unusual thing for her to do. But last night she felt very sleepy, and so she did not have her usual read. She woke quite suddenly about ten minutes ago, and felt that there was something strange. For a moment or two she couldn't make out what it was; then she realised. Her necklace had gone. True to her promise, she let out a bellow that must have scared the rooks, and here you perceive the eighteen good men and true engaged in the combined rush. I was the first to arrive, and I regret to state that the pearls had undoubtedly gone. My tactful suggestion that she should search in the bed was unnecessary – she had already done so."

"I've 'phoned the police," said Dick, joining us. "Confound that woman," he muttered angrily. "I told her to let me lock the thing up. By Jove! you fellows, I wouldn't have had this happen for the world."

"Well, anyway," said Huntly, coming out of his room, "there's been a pretty useful trail left. Come and look out of my window."

His room was next but one to Lady Carrington's, and we all trooped in. The rain had ceased; the morning was perfect. And when Dick had peered out it seemed to me he gave a sigh of relief.

Hundy was right. The trail was more than useful – it was obvious. Lying on the ground was a ladder, and in the flower-bed under Lady Carrington's bedroom were two distinct marks of feet. The thief had placed the ladder in the earth of the bed, climbed up it, taken the pearls, laid the ladder down on the ground, and departed.

"Was that ladder there last night?" asked someone.

"As a matter of fact, it was lying on the other side of the house," said Dick. "Rogers – he's one of the gardeners – has been cutting ivy. Huntly, old boy, you couldn't have shown me a more welcome sight than that. I am very sorry she's lost her pearls, but, thank Heaven, we now know how the burglar got in! I'll just go and tell her."

I wandered back to my room with Tommy, and lit a cigarette.

"Why this profound relief on Dick's part?" I asked.

"Well, old boy, our Lady Carrington was talking a little out of her turn. I don't blame her – it's a bit disconcerting to lose a thing like that. But she was insisting on everyone in the house being searched and so on."

"But surely she didn't suspect one of us?" I cried.

He shrugged his shoulders.

"As I say, she was talking a little out of her turn," he said. "Look here," he suggested suddenly, "what about doing a bit of sleuthing? Let's go and cast an eye on the flower-bed."

"My dear Tommy," I laughed, "what do you expect to find – the burglar's visiting card?"

"You never can tell, laddie," he burbled genially. "We might see something."

So I followed him, principally because there was nothing else to do. Hideous cachinnations were still coming from the Carrington woman's room. It seemed that she was now blaming Dick for not having burglar alarms fitted on all his windows.

And this, mark you, at four-thirty in the morning, of all ungodly hours.

However, we reached, the flower-bed, and inspected clues with a professional eye. The whole thing was perfectly obvious, as I had anticipated. There were the marks of the two feet of the ladder in the wet earth perfectly clear and distinct, like a plaster cast; there was the damp mould sticking to the wood of the uprights. And if any further proof were needed as to how the thief had got in, at that moment Dick leant out of Lady Carrington's window above us.

"There are marks of mud on the sill here," he said. "Don't go putting your great flat feet all over the place, Tommy – there may be footprints about there somewhere."

I glanced at Tommy, and for a moment I thought he'd gone bughouse. He was staring first at the ladder, then at the marks in the flower-bed, and his eyes looked as if they were popping out of his head.

"What's stung you?" I asked kindly. "Is the burglar a left-handed man with a stammer and a harelip?"

"I may be several sorts of an ass, Jim," he answered, "but, dash it all, that's deuced funny!"

"What is deuced funny?" I grunted.

"Oh, things," he said airily. "Mud and stuff like that. Yes, by Jove! It's most peculiar – what?"

I took no further notice. Tommy was himself again – more so than usual, if possible. Once again his face expressed that completely vacant look which was habitual to it; his brief moment of brightness had gone.

"I'm going to have a jolly now," he cried. "Go round and see that all these lazy sons of Belial are up, and all that. Coming, old flick? No. Right ho!"

I watched him depart with profound relief. Tommy in the early morning was above my form. And shortly after, floods of blasphemy in various male voices proclaimed that he was carrying out his threat.

It was six o'clock before the police arrived, and by that time we had scratched up a bit of breakfast and were feeling better. All, that is, except Lady Carrington, whose face was reminiscent of a gargoyle on a French cathedral.

Another infamy of the miscreant had come to light. Lying on the floor by her bed had been found a handkerchief smelling strongly of chloroform.

"That's rum," burbled Tommy when he heard it. "What about the jolly old tum-tum, and all that?"

"May I ask what on earth you mean, Mr Maunders?" said Lady Carrington acidly.

"Icky-boo – or anything like that?" he persisted.

"Will no one suppress this impossible youth?" she asked resignedly. "No, Mr Maunders, thank you. The jolly old tum-tum is not icky-boo, or anything like that."

"Deuced funny," said Tommy darkly, and then, as far as I remember, someone flung him out of the window, and he was forgotten in the police examination.

It was more or less a formal affair – the whole thing was so blatantly obvious. And the main point on which the Inspector concentrated was how the burglar could have known which room was occupied by Lady Carrington. It pointed strongly, he declared, to the presence of a confederate inside the house. But at that Dick stuck in his toes. All his servants had been with him for years, he pointed out; it was incredible to suspect one of them. And as for his guests, the mere idea was farcical.

"The matter is perfectly simple," he stated. "Lady Carrington's necklace is probably known to every crook in England. It was known that she was coming here; and as the principal lady guest it would be easy to find out which room she would have."

"What about Rogers, Sir Richard? Funny thing to do, to leave that ladder lying about."

"And he's going to get his tail twisted good and strong for doing so. But there's no more to it than that, Inspector. Rogers has been with me since he was a boy. He is absolutely trustworthy; I'll vouch for that."

And so to breakfast, with nothing further discovered. The Inspector searched everywhere for finger marks, with no result.

Of clues, save the obvious ones which were plain for all to see, there were none. And so, perforce, it had to be left at the fact that some man unknown had climbed into Lady Carrington's bedroom, removed her pearls while she slept – probably with the help of a whiff of chloroform – and got away with them.

The Inspector was vaguely hopeful; he felt sure it was one of the big men. And probably Scotland Yard would be able to trace their movements. But when he left Dick's study it struck me that his optimism was more official than real.

"I wouldn't have had it happen for the world, Jim," said Dick as the door closed behind him. "I know the wretched things are insured, but that's not the same thing at all. And from all I can see of it, it's the clearest getaway I've ever heard of. What the devil do you want, Tommy?"

He swung round irritably as the door opened and Tommy came in.

"Look here, sir," said Tommy quietly, "what will you say if I get those pearls back for you?"

"You get 'em back for me?" spluttered Dick. "What under the sun are you drivelling about?"

But Tommy was very serious.

"Perhaps I'm drivelling, and perhaps I'm not," he said. "But you haven't answered my question."

"If you get 'em back," laughed Dick. "Well, if you do, Tommy, you may marry Moyra."

"Glad it was you who suggested it," grinned Tommy. "Because that was going to be my price. And it comes more gracefully from you. But there's only one thing I ask. Not a word to a soul. You both promise?"

We both did, and Tommy went out whistling.

"What's the young fool talking about?" said Dick to me with a puzzled frown. "He can't possibly know anything about it."

"If he doesn't, we'll be no worse off than we are at present," I answered. "And I wonder if – "

I broke off and lit a cigarette. I had just remembered Tommy's strange look early that morning as we had stood side by side staring at the marks in the flower-bed. Was it possible that he had noticed something we had all missed?

However, if he had, he gave no sign of it that day. He drivelled on in his usual fatuous way until threatened with death unless he desisted. And eleven o'clock found us all in the pavilion ready to start. Nothing was to be gained by putting off the match, though I think the Carrington woman thought we all ought to be scouring the country in search of the burglar.

The Duds won the toss, and Tommy went in first – I forget with whom. And he proceeded to knock up a very useful fifty, before being run out. Well, I don't know if anyone else spotted it, but it seemed to me at the time that he could have got into his crease if he'd tried. But he gave a sort of half stumble, and was out by two yards. And as he passed me on his way back to the pavilion he gave me a very deliberate wink.

"So, my young friend," I reflected, "I was right. You purposely ran yourself out. What's the game?"

That it was something to do with the pearls I was sure – but what? True to my promise, I said nothing, of course; but when we all assembled for luncheon and there was no sign of him, my curiosity increased. He arrived about ten minutes later and sat down next to me.

"Thank God! I'm out," he remarked, "so that I can eat 'earty. By Jove! Carruthers, old fish, that valet of yours is a pretty grim-looking bird. He gave me quite a turn when I met him in the passage."

"What on earth are you talking about?" said Carruthers sharply. "I haven't got a valet."

A sudden silence settled on the table. Was this some new development of the burglary?

"Not got a valet?" cried Tommy blankly. "Then who is that fellow with a face like a third-rate prize-fighter who said he was your valet? Said he hadn't been able to come with you yesterday, but had followed on today. Wanted to know, which your room was."

"Did you tell him?" snarled Carruthers.

"Of course I did," bleated Tommy. "Hang it all! I thought he was your bird, and I couldn't stand his face lying about the house."

"You fool!" Carruthers had gone white with rage. "What the devil do you mean by sending a strange man into my room?"

He had pushed back his chair and risen.

"Will you excuse me, Sir Richard, if I go to the house? I haven't got much of value, but I don't particularly want to lose my links. And what is more to the point, I should think it very likely that this so-called valet of Maunders' imagination is last night's burglar, engaged in making a complete haul of the house."

"What's that?" shouted Dick. "If you're right, Carruthers, we'd better have a general round-up. Come on, you fellows!"

"Hold hard, Sir Richard," said Carruthers. "Wary does it, if we want to catch the bird. If he sees us all making tracks for the house he'll be off like a scalded cat. Let me go in alone, while you split into four parties. Each party to keep under cover and watch one side of the house."

"Right you are, Carruthers," cried Dick. "You bolt the badger, and we'll do the rest."

And it was then I turned and looked at Tommy. His eyes were bright, and one could see he was excited.

"Tommy," I said, "is all this part of the game?"

"I dunno, Jim," he answered. "First time I've tried my hand at this sort of job. And for all I know, I may have made the most ungodly bloomer. Anyway," he added, "I'm such an ass that nobody will be surprised."

We were standing together behind a clump of bushes watching the front door. Carruthers had disappeared into the house, and old Dick, who was hopping about from one leg to the other, could hardly contain himself.

"You're a drivelling idiot, Tommy," he kept on saying. "Why the devil you didn't get hold of Perkins or one of the footmen passes man's understanding. For all that, even if you're only partially responsible for getting those pearls back, I'll forgive you."

It was ten minutes before Carruthers emerged again, and it was obvious that he had drawn blank. We were hidden, of course, and he stood for a moment or two on the drive looking round to find us.

"What luck?" said Dick, coming out into the open.

"None at all," answered Carruthers. "I saw no sign of anything being disturbed in my room, and then I took the liberty of having a quick look into all the others. But not a trace could I see of anyone. Can't you give us a bit fuller description of the fellow, Maunders? It might enable the police to place him."

Tommy, whose eyes were riveted on the front door, hardly seemed to hear.

"What's that?" he said vaguely. "Description of him? Oh! you know – a funny-looking bloke, with a face like a foot. Looked a bit of a mess and all that sort of thing. Ah-h!"

He caught his breath sharply, and we all swung round. Stalking majestically through the front door came the butler,

Perkins. In his hands he carried a tray; on the tray reposed a pair of white objects which proved, on closer inspection, to be cricket boots.

"What under the sun is Perkins doing?" said Dick feebly.

The butler continued to advance until he halted in front of Tommy.

"Mr Carruthers' cricket boots, sir," he said majestically.

There was a moment's dead silence, and then I glanced at Carruthers. And he was staring at Tommy with a look of such concentrated fury on his face that involuntarily I took a step forward.

"You little rat-faced swab," he said tensely, and the next instant the pair of them were at it hammer and tongs.

"Sit on the blighter's head," spluttered Tommy with his mouth full of grass. "He's the blinking burglar."

"The devil he is!" cried Huntly, and dotted Carruthers good and hearty on the point of the jaw.

"In the trees, sir," remarked the unperturbed Perkins, when silence reigned again. "With a further assortment lifted – I believe that is the correct word – a few minutes ago."

"Will someone elucidate?" cried Dick hopelessly. "Am I to understand that Carruthers is the burglar?"

"Of course you are," said Tommy, plucking mud out of his teeth. "And he's a rotten bad bowler too."

Carruthers looked at him venomously, and Huntly flourished a stump.

"No more thick ear work," he said curtly. "Is this a fact, Carruthers?"

"Well, there's not much good denying it," he muttered sulkily. "Though how that rat-faced excrescence found it out I don't know."

"Let's take him to the luncheon tent, Jim," said Dick. "Perkins, go and ring up the police. Now, Tommy, get it off your chest. How did you spot this swab?"

"Mud," burbled Tommy. "Just mud. Mud on the ground; mud all over the place. And the jolly old law of gravity."

Carruthers, very tense and silent, was watching him intently.

"Where are they exactly, Carruthers?" he went on quietly.

"In the trees," said the other. "Chuck them over."

We watched him breathlessly as he took the trees out of his boots. In the hinge was a small plug, which he proceeded to unscrew with the point of a knife. And as soon as he'd got it out he held up the tree and out poured Lady Carrington's pearls. Then he did the same with the other, and out shot a variety of things, including a valuable tie-pin of Dick's.

"Of all the gall," spluttered Dick. "I'll have to have the spoons counted."

"Of that I assure you there is no need," said Carruthers affably. And to do the blighter justice, from then on he took things like a sportsman. For the time being he'd forgotten what was coming to him, and he was genuinely curious to find out where he'd made his mistake.

"Where all you blokes slipped up," began Tommy, "was over the jolly old ladder. You assumed that because it was lying on the ground outside Lady Carrington's window, the thief had got in that way. Not so, my hearties. The ladder was a blind."

"How did you spot that?" demanded Carruthers.

"Mud, laddie, mud. That's where you made your one and only bloomer. If you put a ladder into wet earth the mud will adhere to its legs up to the depth of the holes it makes. Possibly not as far. But by no conceivable hook or crook can it climb up some six inches above the depth of the hole. The holes you made were about three inches deep. There was mud on the legs for a good nine inches from the bottom."

A faint smile twitched round Carruthers' lips.

"Quick," he said quietly. "I congratulate you."

"So, you see, chaps," went on Tommy, "that altered the whole outfit. If the ladder was a blind, then the thief must be inside the house. There was another thing, too – that handkerchief with chloroform. Lady Carrington didn't feel sick: therefore the assumption was it hadn't been used. It was there in case of necessity, or possibly as a further blind. But if it hadn't been used, something else must have been employed to keep her quiet – a dope of sorts. You remember she said she fell asleep very quickly last night, which again pointed to someone inside the house. And my suspicions naturally fell on Carruthers, simply because he was the only bloke in the house who was a stranger.

"When I went and jollied you all up this morning I had a look at your basins. The one in Carruthers' room was full of brownish water where he'd washed the mud off his hands. So that was that as far as little Willie was concerned. I knew Carruthers had taken the pearls – but where were they? That was the point. And it struck me that the easiest way of finding out was to make him show us. If I was wrong, there was no damage done; if I was right, we nabbed the goods. So I invented the mythical valet, and installed our one and only Perkins in a cupboard where he could watch developments, trusting that the first thing Carruthers would do would be to see if the pearls were safe."

Jim Featherstone knocked out his pipe.

"Which I think proves my contention that Tommy is not such a fool as he looks."

We straightened out one or two points later; but he was absolutely right all through. Carruthers *had* doped Lady Carrington. He'd slipped it into a whisky and soda she had drunk before going to bed. He had specially wangled his introduction to Bob, knowing that Lady Carrington was always invited for the match. And he'd have got clean away with the pearls, and the other little trifles he'd lifted when he made a tour of the rooms, but for that little matter of mud. As it was, he got seven years, and I had to stump up a wedding present.

THAT BULLET HOLE
HAS A HISTORY

"A writing gentleman are you, sir? said the landlord, as he put a full tankard on the table in front of me. "Well, well – it takes all sorts to make a world."

I did not dispute such a profound truth, but concentrated on the contents of the tankard. A walking tour in the hilly part of Devonshire is thirsty work, and the beer tasted as good as it looked.

"Not that I hold much with it," he went on after a while. "I reckon that it's better to be up and doing than sitting down and spoiling good paper."

Against such an outrageous assault as that I felt I had to defend myself, and I pointed out to him that one had to put in a bit of up and doing oneself before beginning to spoil the paper.

"Not that I should think there's much doing beyond sleep in this village," I added sarcastically.

"That's just where you're wrong," he remarked triumphantly. "Why in that very chair you're sitting in a man was shot through the heart. Plugged as clean as a whistle, and rolled off the chair up against that table your beer is standing on, stone dead. And that" – he paused for a moment only to continue even more triumphantly – "is the man that did it."

He indicated a grey-haired man who was passing – a fine-looking old man who walked with a pronounced limp and leant heavily on a stick.

"Good evening, Mr Philimore," he called.

"Evening, Sam," answered the other, pausing and coming over towards the door of the inn outside which we were sitting.

He stopped for a few moments discussing local affairs, and I studied him covertly. A man of seventy-five I guessed, with the clear eye of one who has lived in the open. His great frame showed strength beyond the average, and even now it struck me that many a younger man would have found him more than a match physically.

He finished his discussion, and then, with a courteous bow that included me, continued his walk.

"Sleep, indeed!" snorted the worthy Sam. "Thirty years ago, sir, come next month, this village was more exciting than London."

"Look here, Sam," I said, "it strikes me that you'd better put your nose inside a pint of your excellent ale and tell me all about it."

He shouted an order through the door, and lit his pipe.

"You'll understand, sir," he began, when the potboy had brought the beer and he had sampled it, "that when the thing happened I was just flabbergasted. Couldn't make head nor tail of it, because I didn't know what it was all about. It was only afterwards when I began making inquiries and talking to this person and that, that the whole thing was clear from the beginning. And that's the way I'm going to tell you the story."

"And quite the right way, too," I assured him.

"It starts nigh on fifty-five years ago, when I was a nipper of ten, and John Philimore – him as you've just seen – a man of twenty-one. You can talk of good-looking men – and I've seen a tidy few in my life – but you can take it from me he came first. The girls were fair crazy about him, and well they might be. Tall, upstanding, strong as a giant – they don't breed 'em nowadays. There wasn't a man on the countryside could touch him at any sport, or at swimming. Why, I can remember seeing him swim out with a lifeline to a barque in distress in the October gales of 1868. Bit before your time, I reckon – but there's been no gales in these parts like 'em since.

"He lived up at Oastbury Farm, which had been his grandfather's and his great-grandfather's before him. Aye – and longer than that. Traced direct back from father to son for nigh on four hundred years was Oastbury with the Philimores. And John – he lived at home with his father, ready to take on when his time came.

"I've told you that all the girls were fair crazy about him, but John had eyes for only one – Mary Trevenna. And a proper match they were, too, in every way. Old Trevenna had Aldstock Farm – the place next to Oastbury – and though he wasn't as wealthy as the Philimores, he was quite comfortably off. And Mary was his only daughter, just as John was the only son, though he had a sister. Oh! it was a proper match! Just as John had eyes only for Mary, so she never looked at another man. I remember catching 'em one day when they thought no one was about, kissing and cuddling fine. And then John – he caught me, and I couldn't sit down for a week.

"Well – I must get on with it. When Mary was twenty, they were to get married. That was the arrangement, and that is what happened. John was twenty-two, and they were going to live in a small farm near Oastbury which his father had given them.

"It was a great wedding. The squire came – that's his present lordship's father – and everyone from the countryside. And after it was over they went off to Torquay for the honeymoon. Then they came back to the house where they were going to live, and things settled down normal again.

"Of course, you must remember, sir, that I was only a nipper at the time, helping my father in this very house. Them was the days before these new-fangled schemes of education, when folks held with a boy working and not filling his head with rubbish.

But little pitchers have long ears as they say, and I very soon finds out from what folks said that there was a baby on the way.

"John Philimore came in less and less – not that he was ever a heavy drinker, but after a while he hardly ever came in at all; and when he did it was only for a moment or two, and then he'd hurry off home. Not that things weren't going well, but a lad is apt to be a bit fazed over his first.

"A boy it would be – of course: for generations now the eldest child born to the Philimores had been a boy. And a rare fine specimen, too – with such parents. John's mother looked out the lace christening robe and all the old fal-lals the women like fiddling round with at such times. And at last Mary's time came, and it was a girl – as fine a child, so I heard tell, as anyone would have wished for. But it was a girl.

"Well, sir – I don't profess to account for it; Lord knows there was plenty more time for them to have half a dozen boys, but it seemed to prey on Mary's mind that she should be the first for so many generations to have a girl as her first-born.

"I remember old Doctor Taggart coming into the inn here one night, and leaning across the bar for his brandy and water. He and my father were alone, and they paid no attention to me.

" 'Sam,' he said – my father was Sam, too – 'Sam, that girl don't want to get well. There's nothing the matter with her; at least nothing serious. She just don't want to get well. I tell you I could shake her. Just mazed, she is, because it's a girl, and John near off his head.'

"And sure enough old Taggart was right. Ten days after the child was born, Mary Philimore died. She died in the afternoon at three o'clock, and with her death something must have snapped in John Philimore's brain.

"Never to my dying day shall I forget that evening. There was a bunch of people inside there, and naturally everyone was discussing it, when suddenly the door was flung open and John stood there swaying like a drunken man. He'd got no collar on;

his eyes were blazing – and his great fists were clenching and unclenching at his sides. He stood there staring round the room, which had fallen silent at his entrance, and then he let out a great bellow of laughter.

" 'A murderer!' he roared. 'That's what I am – a murderer. Confound you all! Give me some brandy.'

" 'Shame on you, John,' said one of the men. 'With Mary not yet cold.'

"And John hit him on the point of the jaw, and as near as makes no matter broke his neck.

" 'Brandy,' he shouted, 'or, by God! I'll take it!'

"And take it he did, for there was no stopping him. He tipped half the bottle down his throat, and once again he let out a roar of laughter, as he stood there with his back to the bar. He looked at the men bending over the chap he'd hit, and laughed and laughed and laughed.

" 'What's it matter if he's dead?' he cried. 'One or two – what's it matter? I've murdered Mary: what's Peter Widgeley to her? I tell you I've murdered her – my little Mary. What did it matter if it was a boy or girl? But she thought it did – and she's dead. And if they hadn't hidden the brat it would be dead too.'

"And then suddenly he grew strangely silent, and stared from one man to another. No one spoke: I guess they were all a bit scared. For maybe a minute you could have heard a pin drop in that room, and then John Philimore spoke again. He didn't shout this time: he spoke quite quiet. And in between his sentences he took great gulps of raw brandy.

"It's burnt on my brain, sir, what he said – and there it will remain. For on that night John Philimore cursed his Maker with blasphemy too hideous to think of. He cursed his Maker: he cursed his child: he cursed his father and, above all, he cursed himself. And when he'd finished he laid the empty bottle on a table, strode across the room looking neither to the right hand nor to the left, opened the door and went out into the night. And from that moment no man in this village saw him again for twenty years."

Mine host stared thoughtfully across the little harbour at two fishing boats beating in.

"A bad sailor, Bill Dennett. Always keeps too long on that tack. However, sir, as I was saying, John Philimore disappeared. From time to time there came news of him in different corners of the earth – and it wasn't good news. With a wild set he'd got in, and he was the wildest of the lot. From South Africa, from Australia, from over in America we heard of him at intervals – but only indirectly. He never wrote to his father, or to his sister – and it fair broke his mother's heart. For John was just the apple of her eye. She kept on hoping against hope that he'd walk in someday, and when the weeks passed, and the months and the years, she just faded out herself – though she was still a young woman.

"That was seven years after John went, and they buried her along with the rest of the Philimores. And then five years later the old man got thrown from his horse out hunting – and he died too – cursing his son on his deathbed for being the cause of his mother's death, even as John had cursed his father for being in part the cause of Mary's. A hard lot the Philimores – and always have been.

"And so for the first time Oastbury passed into the hands of a woman – John's sister, Ruth; though, of course, it was John's whenever he chose to return. If he'd been able to, the old man would have cut him out, and left it away from him – but he couldn't. But until John did return it was Ruth's, who went on living there with the innocent cause of all the trouble, who had been called Mary after her mother. She was twelve years old when her grandfather died, and even then gave promise of being as lovely as her mother. Of her father she knew nothing; she'd been told simply that he was abroad and no one could tell when he would return.

"On the death of the old man Ruth had written a letter to the last address at which her brother had been heard of, and she had caused advertisements to be put in the papers in Australia and South Africa. But after some months the letter came back to her, and there was no reply to the advertisements. In fact, there were a good many of us who began to think John Philimore was dead, and seeing how he had turned out, no bad riddance either.

"Well, the years went on, and Mary grew from a girl into a woman. And the promise as she'd given as a little 'un became a certainty. She was lovelier even than her mother had been, for there was a touch of the Philimore in her – in the way she stood, and in the way she looked at you. And in addition to her looks Mary stood to be a pretty considerable heiress. Old Trevenna – her grandfather – was ailing, and he had no kith nor kin but her. And if, as most of us thought, John Philimore was dead, then Oastbury became hers on her twenty-first birthday. For Ruth was only just in there as a guardian; Oastbury was John's till they proved him dead and then it passed to his child.

"So you'll see, sir, that Mary was due for Oastbury and Aldstock – and that in the days when farming was farming. It made her the biggest heiress round these parts, and the young fellows weren't exactly blind to the fact. Not that she weren't worth having without anything at all except her sweet self; but with them two farms chucked in like, the boys were fairly sitting up.

"But Mary wasn't going to be in any hurry. No one could say which way her fancy lay – not even her aunt; though it did seem sometimes as if it was towards young George Turnbury, whose father was a big miller in Barnstaple. Not that they were tokened, but when old Gurnet drew him in the sweepstake he stood drinks all round.

"A fine boy – young George – big and upstanding, who would come into a pretty penny of his own in time. And absolutely silly over Mary, as well he might be. And we was all beginning to think as things would be settled soon when the trouble began.

"I was standing at this very door – I'd been landlord then for nigh on two years – when I saw a stranger coming up the street. A great big fellow, he was, with a curious sort of roll in his walk, such as you often see in men who had been a lot at sea. As soon as he seed the sign over the door he made for it like a cat for a plate of fish. And I give you my word, sir, I got a shock when I saw his face. From his left temple, right down his cheek as far as his chin, ran a vivid red scar. It was an old one and quite healed, but it must have been the most fearful wound that caused it. For the rest, his skin was dark brown, his nose was hooked and his eyes a vivid blue.

" 'Hot work,' he said as he came up. 'I guess I'll have a gargle.'

" 'Very good, sir,' I said. 'And what shall it be?'

" 'Whisky,' he answered. 'And bring the bottle.'

"And I give you my word again, sir, I got another shock. He tipped out a tumbler and drank it neat, same as I'd take a glass of cider.

" 'Help yourself,' he said, and when he saw me take a little and fill up with water, he threw back his head and laughed.

" 'Why the devil don't you drink milk?' he cried.

" 'If I was to drink what you've just drunk with every customer,' I said short-like, 'I'd not be able to carry on my business.'

" 'Maybe you're right,' he answered, staring at me. 'No offence, anyway. But not having to carry on your business, I guess I'll have another.'

"He filled up his glass with neat whisky again, and then lay back in his chair, still staring at me with those blue eyes of his.

" 'Say, I guess you'll know,' he said after a moment. 'Is there a shack called Oastbury in this district?'

"Well, at that I pricked up my ears, for I'd placed him already as a man from foreign parts.

" 'There certainly is,' I said. 'If you go round the corner you can see Oastbury Farm upon the hill there.'

" 'I guess it will stop there,' says he, without moving. 'Good farm, is it?'

" 'It is accounted the best in these parts and one of the best in the whole West Country,' said I, and he nodded his head as if pleased with the news.

" 'May I ask, sir,' I went on, 'if you have by any chance news of John Philimore? I can see you come from foreign parts, and since you've asked about Oastbury, I thought you might know something of him.'

" 'Then your thoughts are correct,' he answered.

" 'For twenty years we've had no word of him direct,' I said, 'and there are those who say he's dead.'

" 'There are, are there?' he said, and finished his whisky. 'Well, they've backed a winner. John Philimore is dead right enough: he's been dead a year.'

" 'Good heavens!' I cried – for now that the news was confirmed it seemed a terrible thing. 'And what did he die of, sir?'

" 'An ounce of lead in a tender spot,' he answered shortly. 'Same as a good many other poor fools have died of. Say, now, there's a daughter of his alive, ain't there?'

" 'There is,' I said. 'Living at Oastbury Farm now. And if John Philimore is dead, the farm is hers. Leastways, it will be in a year, when she's twenty-one.'

" 'And what would happen, mister,' he said, 'if John had made a will leaving all he possessed to me?'

" 'It wouldn't be worth the paper it's written on,' I answered shortly. 'It's all tied up – see? John Philimore could no more leave Oastbury away from his daughter than he could give away Buckingham Palace.'

" 'Are you sure o' that?' he said with a sort of snarl.

" 'Of course I'm sure of it,' I answered. 'Didn't John's father go into the whole question after John ran off to Australia? That's what he wanted to do – leave Oastbury to his daughter – all tied up and secure. Went to Exeter, he did, to a big lawyer there, to see about it. But it couldn't be done. From eldest child to eldest child it's got to go – be it male or female. And so whatever wickedness John Philimore has done, he can't do his daughter out of Oastbury. It's hers – and remains hers.'

"I tell you, sir, I was beginning to dislike this man, and I spoke a bit short.

" 'And supposing,' said he, very quiet-like, 'this daughter of his should die before she's twenty-one?'

" 'Then,' I said, 'it would go to her aunt – John's sister. Will you be wanting any more whisky?'

" 'Yes – leave the bottle, and if I shout you'll know I want another.'

"With that I left him and went indoors. And half an hour later he was still sitting at the table staring across the harbour. Then he gives a shout, and out I goes.

" 'Can you give me a room here?' he says. 'I'll pay what you like, and give no trouble.'

"Well, business is business; and though I didn't fancy him as a guest, I said I'd fix him up.

" 'Good!' he cried. 'Then send out another bottle of whisky as a start. Oh! and by the way, is this wench married?'

" 'She is not,' I answered. 'But I expect she soon will be.'

" 'So do I,' he said, and laughed in a funny sort of way.

"She's all but tokened to young George Turnbury from Barnstaple,' I told him, but that only made him laugh the more.

"With that I went in and sent him out the second bottle of whisky. And then, what with one thing and another, and the chaps coming in for their evening drink, and telling them the news of John Philimore's death, I forgot all about him for a time.

"I reckons it must have been about nine o'clock when George Turnbury came in. He'd been up at Oastbury, I knew, because he had had his lunch in this house.

" 'Say, fellows,' he said, 'have any of you seen a queer-looking customer about the place? A great hook-nosed fellow with a huge red scar down his face?'

" 'It's the stranger,' I cried. 'The one who told me John Philimore was dead.'

" 'Dead?' cried George, staring at me. 'John Philimore dead?' For of course he hadn't heard the news.

" 'That's so,' I said. 'A year ago.'

" 'Good Lord!' he muttered, and I could see he was a bit moved. After all, though he'd never known John, he'd been up at his daughter's all the afternoon.

" 'Well, anyway,' he went on, 'I saw this man nosing round Oastbury, and I tell you I didn't like the look of him. So I passed the word to some of the hands, and Heaven help him if he tries any tricks!'

" 'In my life I've never relied overmuch on Heaven,' said a voice from the door, and there was the stranger, with his eyes fixed on George. As you can imagine, sir, it was a bit of an awkward moment, because we didn't know how much he'd heard.

" 'I've found that I'm quite capable of looking after myself, young man,' he continued, crossing the room and standing close to George. 'And now may I ask why you don't like the look of me?'

"George Turnbury got a bit red in the face.

" 'I'm sorry you should have heard that,' he said. 'I didn't know you were in the room.'

" 'I'm still waiting for an answer to my question, young man,' said the other quietly, though there was a nasty note in his voice.

"Young George, he drew himself up, for he had the devil of a temper of his own, and he didn't like the stranger's tone.

" 'You'll get the answer in a looking-glass,' he said, and turned his back on him. 'I guess it was a powerful cat you tried petting,' he flung over his shoulder.

"The stranger put out both his hands quite gently, and caught hold of George from behind just above each elbow. Now, George was a powerful lad, used to handling sacks of corn, and I shall never forget the look of blank amazement that spread over his face. It must have been a quarter of a minute they stood there without movement, and the reason was plain to us all. George couldn't move; he was as powerless as a child in that man's grasp. We could see him struggling so that the sweat broke out on his forehead, and there was hardly a tremor in that stranger's hands. And then the stranger laughed.

" 'It wasn't a cat, little boy,' he said. 'It was the slash of a cutlass. And the man who did it died as he did it. It was a much stronger man than you, little boy. But as far as you're concerned, don't be rude any more, or I might have to whip you.'

"And with that he let George go and swung round on me.

" 'Send me up a bottle of whisky,' he cried. 'I'm going to my room.'

"For a while after he left no one spoke. George – who had a proper pride in himself – was well-nigh crying with shame and mortification at having been made to look such a fool before us all. And, of course, a thing like that was bound to get around, if only as a measure indicating the stranger's strength. But as the days went on it was forgotten in the much more important affairs that were happening up at Oastbury. It had us all beat; we couldn't make head nor tail of 'em.

"For this stranger pretty well lived up there, and what Mary Philimore or her aunt could see in him was beyond us. He still kept on his room here; he still got through his two bottles of whisky a day, and sometimes three. But for the rest of the time he was at Oastbury.

"George was pretty near off his head about it all; seemed to think he'd got some hold over Mary – this man with the scar. And sure enough two or three times when I seed her, she seemed to have a terrible hunted look in her sweet eyes.

"Then a month after he'd arrived we heard the news. At first no one would believe it; but it was true right enough. Mary had tokened herself to this man with the scar, whose name we now knew was Henry Gaunt.

"I tell you, sir, it had us all knocked endwise. For Mary, that sweet girl, to marry this whisky-drinking bully, who was old enough to be her father, seemed a horrible sin. And once it was settled, what little mark of decency he had kept on to start with disappeared. He took a delight in picking quarrels and insulting people. He nearly killed poor old Dick, the policeman, one night – and only just escaped prison by the skin of his teeth.

"That sobered him up a bit, and he was more careful in future. But even then he was a devil. Chaps as had come to this house for years, and their fathers before them, stayed away, because they were afeared of Gaunt. And this was the man Mary was going to marry.

"Time went on and the wedding was due in a fortnight. And then one morning I was standing in the door there thinking things over, when again I seed a stranger coining up the street. The house was empty; Gaunt was up at Oastbury – but this stranger reminded me in a way of him. The same build – the same roll in his walk, and I thought to myself, I thought, 'Good Lord! This ain't another such as Gaunt.'

"And then as he got nearer I began to rub my eyes. I must be wrong, of course, but it surely was a staggering likeness to John Philimore.

" 'Hullo, Sam!' he sung out. 'Forgotten me, I suppose. I know it's you; you're so like your father.'

" 'Good God!' I said, all mazed-like; 'it's John Philimore!'

" 'The very same,' he answered. 'And why not?'

" 'But we was told you were dead, sir,' I cries.

" 'And who told you that?' he says, smiling.

" 'Why, Henry Gaunt,' I answers. 'Him as is staying here now.'

"The smile had left his face, and he stared at me speechless.

" 'Do you mean a man with a great red scar down his face?' he said in a terrible voice.

" 'That's the one,' I told him. 'And not only is he staying here, but he's tokened to your daughter.'

" 'What!' he roared, and I thought he was going to strike me. Then he pulled himself together. 'Come inside and tell me all about it. But – wait a moment. Where is he now?'

" 'Up at Oastbury,' I said, and I've never seen such a look of devilish rage on a man's face before or since.

"Well, I took him inside, and I told him all I knew. And when I'd finished he got up.

" 'Sam,' he said, 'I rely on you. Not a word to a soul that I'm back. Above all, not a word to that devil incarnate, Henry Gaunt.'

" 'You have my word, sir,' I said. 'And if you can get rid of him, I, for one, will be profoundly thankful.'

" 'I'll get rid of him all right,' he answered quietly. 'Usually back here at six, you say?'

" 'That's when he begins his second bottle,' I told him, and with that he left.

"Naturally, I was fair bursting with the news, but I kept my word and didn't breathe a hint to a soul. And as the afternoon wore on I got in such a condition of excitement at what was going to happen, that I gave old Downley, what always drank ginger ale, a double whisky by mistake. At a quarter to six Gaunt came in and, sitting down in the chair you're in, he ordered his usual bottle. In a foul temper he was over something or other and he sat there glowering across the harbour. There were two or three others drinking over at that table, and by this time my knees were shaking under me as six o'clock drew nearer.

"Five minutes to – and young George Turnbury passed down the road on the way to the station.

" 'Hi, you – you young swab,' sung out Gaunt. 'Come here!'

"George, he took no notice and just walked on, when, would you believe it, sir? that devil pulled out a revolver and fired. George told us afterwards that he felt the wind of the bullet past his ear – it was so close.

" 'Next time I'll hit you,' said Gaunt, 'unless you stop!'

"George stopped.

" 'Now, you young cockerel, is it you who has been closeted all the afternoon with the girl I'm going to marry?'

" 'It was not,' said a stern voice behind him. 'It was I.'

"And there was John Philimore standing just behind Gaunt with the muzzle of his revolver pressed into the devil's neck.

" 'And if you move, Gaunt; if you try any of your foul tricks, I'll blow the top of your head off, as sure as there's a God above.'

"Gaunt's face was a study. He'd gone quite white, and the scar looked like a streak of bright red paint, while in his eyes there was the look of an animal at bay, a sort of snarling fear.

" 'Is it you, John Philimore?' he said, moistening his lips, for with that gun in his neck he dursn't look round to see.

" 'Who else would it be, Gaunt?' said John. 'You see, you didn't kill me after all, though it was touch and go, Gaunt – touch and go. If two prospectors hadn't come along soon after you cleared out with what was left of the water, having shot me from behind, you would have killed me, Gaunt.'

"Young George, he started forward in a rage.

" 'You foul swine!' he shouted, but Gaunt heeded him not. There was only one thing he could think of at the moment, and that was that his sin had found him out. And ceaselessly he moistened his lips with his tongue.

" 'And then, Gaunt,' went on John Philimore in a terrible voice, 'having killed me as you thought, you came to my home. You knew all about it, for I'd told you – and you thought it would be a fine way of spending the rest of your foul life. And when you found it was entailed, and you couldn't get it by forgery – then, Gaunt, your infamous brain conceived a plan which would have done the devil himself credit. You went to my daughter, and told her that I wasn't really dead; that you'd lied when you said so – lied on purpose. You said that I was in prison for life for murder and bush-ranging: that I'd been guilty of unnameable crimes; that you had proof of it. And then, Gaunt, you told her the price of your silence. You knew our pride: you knew she'd do anything rather than that our name should be disgraced. And so you blackmailed her into the unthinkable sacrifice of marrying you. Can you tell me, Gaunt, of any single reason why I shouldn't kill you where you sit?'

"Gaunt laughed harshly, though his eyes roved wildly from side to side as if seeking some way of escape.

" 'One very good one,' he snarled. 'They'll hang you if you do.'

" 'True,' answered John Philimore. 'Then I'll flog you, Gaunt – flog you here and now till the blood drips off you. And to save bother I shall lash you up. Sam,' he called out to me, 'you'll find a rhinoceros whip in my grip. Get it.'

"And then, sir, it happened – so quickly that one could scarce see. Of a sudden two shots rang out, and we saw John Philimore sink to the ground. And even as he fell on one side of the chair, Gaunt rolled off and fell on the other.

"We rushed up to them, young George Turnbury first of us all. And John, he looked up at him with a smile.

"Go up, young George,' he said, 'and tell Mary that the wedding can take place, but the bridegroom will be different.'

" 'Are you hurt, sir?' cried George.

" 'Not so badly as Henry Gaunt,' he answered. "We looked at the man with the scar on his face, and he was dead. Shot through the heart – plugged clean as a whistle.

"Well, sir, that's the story. John Philimore was shot through the groin: maybe you noticed he still limps. And young George, he married Mary. But that shows you we don't always sleep in this village."

THE IDOL'S EYE

1

"Personally, I don't consider there's a word of truth in the whole thing," said Fenton, dogmatically. "All this mystery and spook stunt was started by hysterical old women, and has been kept alive by professional knaves, who fill their pockets at the expense of fools."

He drained his port, and glared round the table as if challenging anyone to dispute his assertion.

"There was a silly old aunt of mine," he continued, thrusting his heavy-featured face forward, "who bought a house down Camberley way two or three years ago. Admirable house: just suited the old lady. Special room facing south for the canaries and parrots, and all that sort of thing." He helped himself to another glass of port. "She hadn't been in the house a fortnight before the servants gave notice. They weren't going to stop on, they said, in a house where noises were heard at strange hours of the night, and where the clothes were snatched off the cook's bed. So the old thing wrote to me – I was managing her affairs for her – and asked what she should do. I told her that I'd come down and deal with the noises, and that if anyone started pulling my bedclothes off he'd get a thick ear for his trouble."

Fenton laughed, and, leaning back in his chair, thrust his hands into his trousers pockets. "Of course there were noises," he continued. "Show me any house – especially an old one –

where there ain't noises at night. The stairs creaked – stairs always do: boards in the passages contracted a bit and made a noise – boards always do. And as for the cook's bedclothes, having once seen the cook I didn't wonder they came off in the night. She must have weighed twenty stone, and nothing less than full-size double sheets could have been expected to remain tucked in. But do you suppose it was any good pointing these things out to the old dear? Not on your life! All she said to me was: 'Harry, my boy: there are agencies at work in this world of which we have no knowledge. You may not be able to feel with them; some of us can. And it is written in the Book that they are evil.' "

Again Fenton laughed coarsely. "Twaddle! Bunkum. The only agent that she felt was the house agent, who was charmed at the prospect of a second commission so soon."

"She moved, did she?" said Lethbridge, our host.

"Of course she did," jeered Fenton. "And the last I heard of the house was that it had been taken by a retired grocer with a large family who were perfectly happy there." He thumped his fist on the table. "The whole thing is entirely imagination. If you sit at the end of a dark passage, when the moon is throwing fantastic shadows, and imagine hard enough that you're going to see a ghost, you probably will. At least you'll fancy you see something. But that's not a ghost. There's nothing really there. You might as well say that the figures you see in a dream are real."

"Which raises a very big question, doesn't it?" said Mansfrey, thoughtfully. He was a quiet man with spectacles, who had so far taken little part in the conversation. "Even granted that what you say is correct, and I do not dispute it, you cannot dismiss imagination in quite the same manner as you do a dream. It may well be that half the so-called ghosts which people see or hear are merely imagination: but the result on the people is the same as if they were there in reality." His blue eyes were fixed on Fenton mildly, and he blinked once or twice. "It takes all sorts to make a world, and everyone is not so completely devoid of imagination as you are, Fenton."

"I don't know that I am completely devoid of imagination," said Fenton. "I can see as far into a brick wall as most men, where a business proposition is concerned. But if you mean that I'm never likely to see a ghost, you're quite right." He was staring at Mansfrey, and his face was a little flushed. It struck me as he sat there half-sprawling over the table, what a coarse animal he was. And yet rumour had it that he was very popular with a certain type of woman.

Mansfrey sipped his port, and a slight smile played round his lips. Lethbridge noticed it and made a movement as if to join the ladies. For Mansfrey's smile was deliberately provocative, and Fenton was not a congenial companion if provoked – especially after three glasses of port. His voice, loud enough at ordinary times, became louder: the bully in him, which was never far from the surface, flared out.

"Ghosts," said Mansfrey, gently, "are the least of the results of imagination. Even if you did see one, Fenton, I don't expect it would worry you much."

His mild blue eyes were again fixed on the other man. "It is not that manifestation of the power of mind that I was particularly thinking of."

Fenton gave a sneering laugh. "Then what was it?" he asked. "Trying to walk between two lampposts and finding there was only one?"

"Personally," answered Mansfrey, "I have never suffered that way." Lethbridge looked at me uncomfortably, but Mansfrey was speaking again. "It was the power of mind over matter with regard to bodily ailments that I was thinking of."

"Good heavens!" jeered Fenton, "you don't mean to say that you're a Christian Scientist?"

"Up to a point, certainly," answered the other. "If it is possible, and we know on indisputable proof that it is, for a man to deliberately decide to die when there is nothing the matter with him, and having come to that decision to sit down on the ground and put it into effect – surely the contrary must be still more feasible. For in the case of the native who dies, his mind is acting against nature: in the case of the man who tries to cure himself his mind is acting with nature."

"Those natives who die in that manner have always been seen by somebody else's brother-in-law," answered Fenton. "I'll believe it, Mansfrey, when I see it for myself."

"I doubt if you would," said Mansfrey. "You'd say the man was malingering even when he was in his coffin."

Once again I glanced at Lethbridge. It almost seemed as if Mansfrey, usually the mildest of men, was deliberately going out of his way to annoy Fenton.

"And I suppose," he continued, after a pause, "that you absolutely disbelieve in the ill luck that goes with certain houses and other inanimate objects – such as the Maga diamond, for instance?"

"Absolutely," answered Fenton. "And if I had the money I would pay a thousand pounds to anyone who would prove me wrong – " Then he laughed. "I thought you were reputed to be a scientist, Mansfrey! Funny sort of science, isn't it? Do you honestly mean to tell me that you believe a bit of carbon like the Maga diamond has the power to bring bad luck to its owner?"

"The last four owners have died violent deaths," remarked Mansfrey, quietly.

Fenton snorted. "Coincidence," he cried. "Good heavens! man, you're talking like an hysterical nursemaid."

"When up against the standard of pure knowledge," returned Mansfrey, mildly, "quite a number of people talk like hysterical nursemaids. When one reflects how little one knows, I sometimes wonder why even the cleverest man ever speaks at all." He started fumbling in his waistcoat pocket. "But talking of the Maga diamond, I've got something here that might interest you."

He produced a little chamois-leather bag, and untied the string that kept it closed. Then before our astonished gaze he tipped out on to the tablecloth what appeared to be a large ruby. It was a cut stone, and in the light it glowed and scintillated with a thousand red flames.

"Pretty thing, isn't it?" said Mansfrey.

"My dear fellow," cried Lethbridge, leaning forward, "is it real? If so, it must be worth a fortune. I'm some judge of precious stones, but I've never dreamed of anything to approach that."

"Glass," laughed its owner. "A particularly beautiful tint of red glass. No – it's not a historic jewel that I've got here, Lethbridge, but something which bears on what we have been discussing." His mild eyes once more sought Fenton's face. "This piece of glass, so the story runs, was originally the eye of an idol in one of the most sacred shrines in Lhasa. The Tibetans, as you know, are a very religious race – and this particular idol was apparently the 'big noise' amongst all their gods. Some young fools, on a shooting trip, managed to get to Lhasa – no mean feat, incidentally, in itself – and not content with that they violated this most sacred temple, and stole the eye of the god."

Fenton gave a shout of laughter. "Good lads," he cried. "That's the stuff to give the troops."

Mansfrey looked at him gravely. "They were discovered by the priests," he continued, "and had to run for their lives. All quite usual, you see: the good old historic story of fiction. Even the curse comes in, so as not to spoil the sequence. I, of course, have only heard it fifteenth hand, but I give it to you as I got it. The thing is harmless, unless allowed to remain in the hand, or up against a man's bare flesh for a certain length of time. How long I don't know. The sailor I got it from was a bit vague himself – all he wanted to do was to get rid of it as quickly as he could. But if, so the yarn goes, it remains for this necessary period of time in a man's hand or up against him somewhere – the man dies."

Fenton shook with amusement. "And do you believe that twaddle?" he demanded.

"I don't know," said Mansfrey, slowly. "There are one or two very strange stories about it." He prodded the glass gently with his finger, and the ruby lights shivered and danced till it seemed as if it was on fire. "A Danish sailor stole it from the man who sold it to me, on the voyage home. He was an enormously powerful, healthy fellow, but he was found dead the next morning with the thing inside his shirt. My sailor friend got it from a Chinaman in Chefoo. The Chink's assistant had recently stolen it out of his master's shop. He had been found dead with it in his hand, and the Chink was frightened." Mansfrey smiled, and put the bit of glass back in its bag. "Just two yarns of many, and they're all the same. Anybody who holds it, or lets it touch him for too long, dies. And dies to all appearances a natural death."

"And you really believe that twaddle?" said Fenton, again, even more offensively than before.

Mansfrey shrugged his shoulders. "I don't know whether I do or don't," he answered. "I myself have tested the thing; and as far as I can see, it is just a piece of ordinary red glass, but – " Again he shrugged his shoulders, and then replaced the leather bag in his pocket.

"Do you mean to say that you've been too frightened to hold the thing in your hand and prove that it's rot?" cried Fenton. He turned to Lethbridge. "Well, I'm hanged! And in the twentieth century. Chuck the bauble over here, Mansfrey. I'll sleep with it in my hand tonight, and give it back to you tomorrow morning at breakfast."

But Mansfrey shook his head. "Oh, no, Fenton," he said, "most certainly not. If anything *did* happen, I should never forgive myself."

The opposition only served to make Fenton more determined than ever, and more objectionably rude into the bargain. Personally, I had been surprised at Mansfrey carrying such a thing about with him – it did not fit in with what I knew of the man at all; but I was even more surprised at his reluctance to allow Fenton to have it. It was preposterous that he could really believe there was any danger to be feared from holding a piece of coloured glass in one's hand, and yet for five or ten minutes he remained obdurate.

Then, suddenly, he gave in. "Very well, Fenton," he remarked, "you shall have it. But don't say I didn't warn you."

Fenton laughed. "If your preposterous stories were to be believed, and came true in my case, I gather I shouldn't be in a condition to say much. But my ghost shall come and haunt you, Mansfrey. I'll pull off your bedclothes, and rattle chains in the passages."

We all laughed, and shortly after Lethbridge rose. As he got to the door he paused and looked at us doubtfully. "Of course it's all rot, and only a joke – but I think we might as well postpone telling the ladies until Fenton gives it back tomorrow at breakfast. My wife is such a nervous woman, don't you know. Probably come running along to your room, Fenton, every half hour to see that you're still snoring."

Fenton gave one of his usual bellows, and in a few minutes we had all settled down to bridge.

2

It was Fenton himself who insisted on his hand being tied up with a pocket handkerchief. The four of us were standing talking in his room before turning in: in fact, Mansfrey had already completed the first part of his toilet by donning a smoking jacket of striking design.

"Bring out your bally bit of glass, my boy," boomed Fenton, jovially, "and put it right there." He held out a hand like a leg of mutton. "Then I'll close my fist, and afterwards you tie my hand with a handkerchief, so that I can't open it in the night."

But the idol's eye was not immediately forthcoming. "I tell you candidly, Fenton," said Mansfrey, "I wish you'd give it up. I don't believe myself that there *is* anything in it, but somehow – " His eyes were blinking very fast behind his spectacles; he seemed the picture of frightened indecision.

Fenton laughed and clapped him on the back; and to be clapped on the back by Fenton is rather like being kicked by a mule. I have had experience of both, and I know.

"You funny little man," he cried, and prepared to do it again, until Mansfrey discreetly withdrew out of range. "You funny little man – blinking away there like a startled owl. You know, Lethbridge, I do really believe that he fancies there's something in his blessed old glass eye from Lhasa. Give it to me, you silly ass," he said to Mansfrey. "I'll show you." To say that Fenton's speech was thick would be to exaggerate, but as I sat on the edge of his dressing-table, smoking a cigarette, I could not help recalling that, though Lethbridge and I had each had one whisky and soda during the evening, while Mansfrey had drunk only plain Vichy, the tantalus was nearly empty when we came to bed. Fenton was, in fact, in a condition when, for peace all round, it was better not to annoy him.

Apparently the same idea had struck Lethbridge, for he turned to Mansfrey and nodded his head. "Give it to him, old boy, and let's get to bed. I'm dog tired."

"Very well," answered Mansfrey. "I'll get it. It is in my waistcoat pocket."

Slowly, almost reluctantly, he left the room, and went along the passage to his own. While we waited, Fenton got into his pyjamas, and by the time Mansfrey returned he was already in bed.

"Here it is," said Mansfrey, holding out the little bag. "But I wish you wouldn't, Fenton."

"Oh! confound you and your wishes," said Fenton, irritably, stretching out his hand. "Put it there, little man, put it there."

The piece of glass rolled out of the bag, and lay for a moment glittering scarlet in Fenton's huge palm. Then his fingers closed over it, and Lethbridge tied a handkerchief round his fist.

"I'll give it back to you at breakfast, Mansfrey," he said, turning over on his side. "And you can prepare to be roasted, my lad, properly roasted. Good night, you fellows: turn out the light, one of you, as you go."

I closed the door behind me, and strolled towards my own room. It was next to Mansfrey's, and I stopped for a moment talking to him.

"What a great animal that fellow is," I remarked.

He did not reply at once, and I glanced at him. He was standing quite still, with his pale blue eyes fixed on Fenton's room, from which already I fancied I heard the snores of the heavy sleeper.

"Animal is not a bad description of him," he answered, thoughtfully. "Not at all bad. Good night."

He stepped inside his door and closed it, and it was only as I switched off my own light that it struck me that Mansfrey's eyes had never blinked as he stood looking at Fenton's door. And blinking was a chronic affliction of his.

I seemed only to have been asleep a few minutes when I was awakened by the light being switched on. Lethbridge was standing by my bed, looking white and shaken.

"My God! man," he said, as I blinked up at him. "He's dead!"

"Who is?" I cried foolishly, sitting up in bed.

"Why, Fenton," he answered, and the whole thing came back to my mind.

"Fenton dead!" I looked at him horror-struck. "He can't be, man: there must be some mistake."

"I wish to God there was," he answered hoarsely. "Mansfrey's with him now – almost off his head."

I reached for my dressing-gown, and glanced at the time. It was just half-past four.

"I'll never forgive myself," he went on, as I searched for my slippers. "That fool story of Mansfrey's made a sort of impression on me, and I couldn't sleep. After a while I got out of bed and went to Fenton's room. I listened outside, and you know how he used to snore. There wasn't a sound: absolute silence." He wiped his forehead with a shaking hand. "I don't know – but I got uneasy. I opened the door and went in. Still not a sound. Then I switched on the light." Lethbridge shuddered. "There he was, lying in bed, absolutely motionless. I went over to him, and put my hand on his heart. Not a movement: he was dead."

I stared at him speechlessly, and then together we went towards Fenton's room. The door was ajar, and as we pushed it open Mansfrey, who was standing by the dead man, turned his white, stricken face towards us.

"Not a trace of life," he whispered. "Not a trace." He ran his hands through his hair, blinking at us despairingly. "What a fool I was, what an utter fool, to show him that thing."

"Oh! rot, man," said Lethbridge, roughly. "It can't have been that paltry bit of red glass. He's dead now, poor fellow, but he was a gross liver, and there's no getting away from the fact that he drank too much last night. Probably heart failure."

But Mansfrey only shook his head, and stared miserably out of the window to where the first faint streaks of dawn were showing in the sky.

"The point is, what we're going to do now," went on Lethbridge. He held up the hand holding the idol's eye, and then let it fall again with a shudder.

"Ring up a doctor at once," said Mansfrey. "He's dead, but you must send for one."

"Yes," said Lethbridge, slowly, "I suppose we must. Er – the only thing is – er – " he looked awkwardly from Mansfrey to me, "this – er – bit of glass. You know what local people are, and the sort of things that – er – may be said. I mean, it will be a little hard to account for the poor fellow being found dead with this bauble in his hand, all tied up like this. The papers will get hold of it, and we shall have a crowd of confounded reporters buzzing round, trying to nose out a story."

Mansfrey blinked at him in silence. "You suggest," he said at length, "that we should take it out of his hand?"

"I do," said Lethbridge, eagerly. "After all, the poor chap's dead, and we've got the living to consider. It's bad enough having a death in the house at all: it'll be perfectly awful if it's turned into a nine days' newspaper wonder. I mean, it isn't as if there was any question of foul play," he glanced apologetically at Mansfrey, "we all of us are equally concerned, and it *can* only be a very strange and gruesome coincidence. What do you say, Mayhew?"

"I quite agree," I answered. At the time I was engaged in a big deal, and I was certainly not anxious for notoriety – even of a reflected nature – in the papers. "I suggest that we remove the stone, and that we destroy it forthwith by smashing it to pieces and throwing the bits into the pond."

Lethbridge gave a sigh of relief, and started to unfasten the handkerchief. "One moment," interrupted Mansfrey, "with all due regard for both your interests, my case is not quite the same as yours. We are not all equally concerned. The thing is mine: I gave it to him." He blinked at us apologetically. "I've got to think of the years to come, when the momentary unpleasantness will be forgotten, and you two – almost unconsciously – may begin to wonder whether it *was* a coincidence." He silenced our quick expressions of denial with a smile. "You may," he said, "and I prefer not to risk it. And so I will only agree to your proposal on one condition, and that is that one or other of you send the thing to some good analytical chemist and have it tested. I *know* that it is glass; I want you to *know* it too."

"Right," said Lethbridge, who would willingly have promised anything, so long as he was allowed to remove the glass eye. "I quite see your point of view, Mansfrey." He was busy untying the knot in the handkerchief. "Perhaps Mayhew will take it up tomorrow to town with him, when he goes."

At length the handkerchief was removed, and with obvious distaste Lethbridge forced back the fingers. There lay the glass, clouded a little by the moisture of the dead man's hand – but still glittering with its devilish red light. Then suddenly the arm relaxed and the idol's eye rolled on to the carpet.

"My God!" said Lethbridge, hoarsely, "put the vile thing away, Mansfrey, and let's send for a doctor."

"The bag is on my table," he answered. "I'll put it in." With his handkerchief he picked the thing up, and carried it away.

Lethbridge turned to me. "I don't often drink at this hour of the night," he said, "but when I've rung up the doctor, I'm going to open a bottle of brandy. I want it."

We tidied up the clothes, and with a last look at the great body lying motionless on the bed, we went out softly, locking the door behind us.

An hour later the doctor came and made his examination. By this time, of course, the whole house knew, and there was no question of any more sleep. The women had foregathered in Mrs Lethbridge's room, and we three men waited for the doctor downstairs. He came, after only a short time in the dead man's room, and helped himself to a cup of tea.

"It may be necessary," he said, "to hold a post-mortem. You say that he was perfectly fit last night?"

"Perfectly," said Lethbridge.

"Forgive my putting the question," continued the doctor, "but did he have much to drink?"

"He was always a very heavy drinker and eater," answered Lethbridge, and both Mansfrey and I nodded in agreement.

"So I should have imagined," commented the doctor. "I have no doubt in my mind that, though he looked a strong, healthy man, we shall find he was pretty rotten inside. Brought on by over-indulgence, you know. He was essentially the type that becomes liable to fits later in life. Most unpleasant for you, Mr Lethbridge. I'll do everything I can to spare you unnecessary inconvenience. But I'm afraid we shall have to have a post-mortem. You see, there's no obvious cause of death."

Lethbridge saw him to the door, and shortly after we heard his car drive off.

"May Heaven be praised," said Lethbridge, coming back into the room, "that we took that glass thing out of his hand, and that we didn't mention it to the women last night." He sat down and wiped his forehead. "Chuck that brandy over, Mansfrey; I want another."

Thus ended the tragic house-party. At nine o'clock I left for town, with the idol's eye in my pocket. I took it to a chemist and asked him to submit it to any tests he liked, and tell me what it was. Later in the evening I called for it, and he handed it back across the counter.

"As far as I can see, sir," he remarked, "it is simply a piece of ordinary red glass, of not the slightest value save for its rather peculiar shape."

I thanked him and took it home with me. The next day I returned it to Mansfrey with a brief note containing the chemist's report, and a suggestion that he should drop it into the Thames.

Lethbridge sent me a cutting from the local paper giving an account of the inquest and the result of the post-mortem.

"Death from natural causes," was the verdict; and gradually, in the stress of reconstructing a business which had suffered badly during the war, the matter passed from my head. Occasionally the strange coincidence came back to my mind and worried me: occasionally I even wondered whether, indeed, there was some deadly power in that piece of red glass: whether in a far-off Tibetan temple strange priests, performing their sinister rites round a sightless idol, kept count in some mysterious way of their god's revenge. Then I would laugh to myself and recall the doctor's words when he had made his brief examination of Fenton – "We shall find he was pretty rotten inside."

And so, but for a strange freak of fate, the matter would have ended and passed into the limbo of forgotten things. Instead of which – but the devil of it all is, I don't know what to do.

Two days ago I wandered casually into Jones' curio shop just off the Strand. At times I have picked up quite good bits of stuff there, and I frequently drop in on the chance of a bargain.

"I've got the very thing for you, Mr Mayhew," he said as soon as he saw me. "A couple of bits of old Sheffield. Just wait while I get them."

He disappeared into the back of the shop and left me alone. I strolled round, looking at his stuff, and in one corner I found a peculiarly ugly carved table, standing on three gim-crack legs. Ordinarily, I should merely have shuddered and passed on: but something made me stop and look at it a little more closely. Its proud designer, presumably in order to finish it off tastefully, had cut four holes in the top, and into these four holes he had placed four pieces of coloured glass – yellow, blue, green, and red. Mechanically I touched them, and to my surprise I found the red one was loose. Still quite mechanically I worked it about, and finally took it out.

A minute later Jones found me staring dazedly at something in my hand, which, even in the dim light of the shop, glowed and scintillated like a giant ruby.

"Here are those two bits of plate, Mr Mayhew," he remarked. Then he saw what I had in my hand, and glanced at the table. "Don't worry about that. It's been loose ever since I got it. I must seccotine it in some day."

"Tell me, Mr Jones," I endeavoured to speak quite calmly, "where did you get this from?"

"What – that table? A Mr Mansfrey asked me to try and sell it for him months ago: you know, the gentleman who's just written that book on poisons. Not that I've got any hope of obliging him, for it's a horrible-looking thing, I think."

A thousand wild thoughts were rushing through my brain as I stood there, with the dealer watching me curiously. If that bit of red glass came out of a table, it had never adorned an idol's face in Tibet. And as it *had* come out of a table, it proved that Mansfrey had lied. Why?

"I will take that table," I said to the astounded dealer. "I'll give you five pounds for it. Send it round at once."

"Shall I put that red thing in, sir?" he asked.

"No," I answered, "I'll keep this."

I strode out of the shop and into the Strand. Why had Mansfrey gone to the trouble of inventing that long tissue of falsehood? Why? The question rang ceaselessly through my brain. Why should a writer on poisons and an able, clever man – I had heard of Mansfrey's new book – take the trouble to lie steadily throughout an evening, unless he had some object in view?

I turned into my club, and sat down to try and puzzle things out. And the more I thought of it the less I liked it.

At length I rose and, going to a table, wrote a note to Mansfrey asking him to come round and see me at my flat. He came last night – and as I said before, I don't know what to do.

Straight in front of him as he came into the room I had placed the table. The hole for the red glass was empty, the piece itself was in the centre of the mantelpiece. He stopped abruptly and stared at the little table: then he turned and the gleaming red thing in front of the clock caught his eyes. Then he looked at me, blinking placidly with a faint smile on his face.

"I didn't know you knew Jones," he said, sinking into an easy chair, and lighting a cigarette.

"I should like an explanation, Mansfrey," I remarked, sternly.

"What of? Fenton's death? My dear fellow – surely it was quite obvious from the first. I killed him." He still blinked at me with his mild blue eyes.

"You killed him!" I almost shouted.

"Hush, hush!" He held up a deprecating hand. "Not so loud, please. Of course I killed him, as I had always intended to do. He was one of the type of carrion who was not fit to live. He ruined my sister!" For a moment he had ceased blinking: then he went on again quite calmly: "But why should I weary you with personal history? Is there anything else you'd like to know?"

"A lot," I said. "Of course, your reason is a big extenuating circumstance, and undoubtedly Fenton was a blackguardly cad – but that does not excuse you, Mansfrey, for murdering him."

"I absolutely disagree," he returned, gently. "The law would have given me no redress, so I had to make my own."

"Of course," I said, after a pause, "I shall have to tell Scotland Yard. I mean, I can't possibly condone such a thing."

He smiled peacefully and shook his head. "I don't think I would if I were you," he murmured. "Who was it who begged Fenton not to take the idol's eye in his hand – ?" He glanced at the glass on the mantelpiece. "It bore a striking resemblance to that thing you've got there, now I come to look at it. But, who was it? Why, me. Who overruled me? Well – neither you nor Lethbridge backed me up, anyway. Who was it suggested removing it before the doctor came? I think I am right in saying it was Lethbridge. Who insisted on a chemical analysis? I did. Who had it carried out? You, and I have the chemist's report in my desk. What was the result of the post-mortem and the coroner's inquest? Death from natural causes: no trace of poison." He blinked on placidly. "Oh! no, my friend, I don't quite see you going to Scotland Yard. In the extremely improbable event of that august body not regarding you as a lunatic, you would inevitably, and Lethbridge also, be regarded as my accomplices in the matter. You see, between you, in all innocence, you compromised yourselves very awkwardly – very awkwardly indeed." He rose to go.

"How did you kill him?" I demanded.

"A rare and little-known poison," he answered. "You'll find something about it in my new book. Probably the most deadly in the world, for it leaves no trace. It kills by shock, which induces heart failure. I dipped that glass – er – I mean the idol's eye, which is so like that bit of glass – into a solution of the poison before putting it in his hand. Then the next morning I dipped it in another solution. You considerately left it with me for some hours – a minute was all I required. From experiments I have carried out on animals, I should think he died in about half an hour. Er – good night."

The door closed behind him, and I sat staring at the red bauble glittering in the light. Then in a fit of rage I took it to the window and hurled it into the street below. It broke into a thousand fragments and Mansfrey – who had just left the front door – looked up and smiled.

"Er – good night," he called, and I could imagine those blue eyes blinking mildly.

And the devil of it all is, as I mentioned previously – I don't know what to do.

A QUESTION OF IDENTITY

The reputation of Mason, Cartwright and Mason is too well known to need emphasizing. To do so would be rather like alluding to the solvency of the Bank of England. Mention them as your solicitors, and no further reference for a business deal is necessary. And yet it is nevertheless a fact that John Mason, senior member of the firm, did, on one occasion, wittingly and with full knowledge thereof, compound a felony. And it is a further fact that his doing so has never caused him one sleepless night, nor is it ever likely to. Neither Peter Mason, his son, nor Edward Cartwright, his partner for thirty years, knows anything about it: it is his own private secret and it will go with him to the grave. And this was the way of it...

It was in the year 1835 that William, tenth Earl of Olford, being dissatisfied with his lawyer, transferred his affairs to John Mason's father. It was doubtless an honour and a compliment, but it was not altogether an unmixed blessing. Like all the Olfords the tenth Earl had the devil of a temper, and since – again like all the Olfords – his ideas on expenditure with regard to income were a little optimistic, John Mason's father had sometimes been heard to express a profound wish that the honour had been bestowed elsewhere.

He died in 1850, did the tenth Earl, twelve years before John Mason was born, so that his first acquaintance with the family was Richard, the eleventh holder of the title. And he was twenty-five when his father, who was getting on in years, took him down to Olford Towers to introduce him to the Earl.

"My young hopeful, Lord Olford," said the old lawyer. "We've got to have a Mason in the firm, and another few years will see me through."

The Earl shook hands with a grip that made John Mason wince, though he was a rowing man of no mean repute.

"Glad to meet you, my boy. And I hope you'll look after our affairs as well as your father has done. But you'll find it difficult."

"I'll do my best, my lord," John answered, and then the other two plunged into business.

It was always the same, as he found out afterwards – the place. With Richard, Olford Towers was an obsession. It was his religion, almost his very soul. And for an hour that morning John Mason sat and listened while the other two went into facts and figures. Once or twice the imperious will of the Earl flashed out when his father raised objections, only to be succeeded immediately by a charming smile and, "You're right, old friend, as usual."

And then, just as they had finished, the door opened and a boy of ten came into the room. No need to ask who he was: the likeness, even at that age, to his father was amazing. The same keen eyes and firm chin, the same look of inflexible pride. It was the little Viscount Carslake, the future twelfth Earl and his father's only child.

At the moment, however, any thought of the future was relegated to the background by the very obvious present. A cut under one eye, some bleeding knuckles, and a large tear in his shirt proclaimed the fact that there had been trouble.

"What have you been up to, young fellow?" said his father quietly.

"I found Joe Mercer hitting his puppy," answered the boy, "and I told him to stop. And he wouldn't."

"So, you fought him, did you?"

"Well, of course I did, father," said the boy simply.

"Did you beat him?"

The boy nodded.

"He said he'd had enough, and promised he wouldn't hit the puppy again."

"Good boy," said the Earl, "now go and tidy yourself up before your mother sees you."

The door closed behind the child, and the Earl turned with twinkling eyes to the other two.

"Young Mercer is twelve and big for his age. 'Nil timent' – eh, what! 'Nil timent!' "

"They fear nothing": the motto of the Olfords. And that was the other half of their religion. Never mentioned, naturally, merely accepted as a matter of course. "Nil timent." Once in years to come, when John Mason had relieved his father, he happened to go one day to the portrait gallery. They were all there – all the men of the line of Olford – staring down from the walls; all, that is, save one. And where his portrait should have been there was a gap. Without thinking he asked the obvious question.

"It is put away somewhere," said the Earl. "A pity, because it is the most valuable of all as a painting. But we have indisputable proof that he was guilty of cowardice at the time of the Civil War."

And that was enough: the blank space marked the unforgivable sin. Libertines, gamblers, drunkards – all were represented; but for a coward there could only be the oblivion of an attic.

It was during the Boer War that Richard died, and Viscount Carslake became the twelfth Earl. He was in South Africa at the time – a subaltern in the early twenties. And as John Mason wired him the news he breathed a silent prayer that he would pull through all right. For five hundred years the title had descended from father to son, and now there was a chance of the line being broken. Broken badly, too, for the new Earl's nearest male relatives were second cousins.

There were two brothers – Spencer by name – and John Mason had hardly been aware of their existence till they turned up at the funeral. The elder, Harold, was a very decent fellow: to the younger, Stephen, he took an instant dislike. He was a shifty-eyed, ferret-nosed young man, with an unhealthy looking skin, and he habitually spoke with a slight snuffle. However, even if the worst happened in Africa, Stephen would come into the picture, and Harold, though not a true Olford, would make a very fair substitute. And John Mason was a very exacting judge. More and more as the years passed had he become wrapped up in the family. In fact, he was more like an elder brother to the youngster at the front than a legal adviser. And he wanted an elder brother pretty badly at times. He was a wild boy, bubbling over with life and spirits – a true Olford, and there had been one or two awkward scrapes. One at Eton touching a little matter of gambling; and another at Sandhurst concerning breaking bounds and an unlawful supper party at one of the local hotels.

It was touch and go in the latter case as to whether he wasn't expelled, and his father was furious.

"An Olford," he roared, "sneaking out like a damned footman to drink bad port with fifth-rate chorus girls. By Gad! sir, I never thought I'd say it, but I'm glad your mother is dead."

It blew over and they patched it up, but things were never quite the same again. Their wills were both too imperious, and the atmosphere at Olford Towers stifled the boy. Not that he didn't love the place, but it was only natural that he couldn't feel for it at his age in the way his father did. He wanted freedom and big spaces. Olford Towers could come later. He wanted life with a capital L, not the comparative stagnation of a great country seat.

And so when he returned to England, the war over, John Mason was not altogether surprised at his decision. He heard it while they were sitting over the port at the end of dinner. A day of business lay behind them, and once or twice from little remarks he had guessed that something of the sort was coming.

"You know I've sent in my papers, John: no peace soldiering for me."

John Mason sipped his wine.

"What do you propose to do?"

"Get out of England," cried the other. "Man! there are a million places in this world that I want to see, a million things to do. Life's all too short as it is, so why waste another moment. But I'm not going as the Earl of Olford in a de luxe suite on a P & O. I don't mind sticking to Hector, since it's my name, but from tomorrow onwards yours truly becomes Hector Latham."

"And all this?" asked John Mason, with a little wave of his hand round the room.

"Can wait. I'll come back to it in time, John; never fear about that. But first I've got to live. Lord! old man, yarning with some of those irregulars out there, I've just marvelled at the life most of us live."

"And supposing you don't come back?" said John Mason quietly, "then what about all this?"

"It will go presumably to that fellow you told me about – Harold Spencer," answered the other. "I've never seen him, but you say he's a decent fellow. I know what you're driving at, John. You want me to marry, and have an heir. But if I do that how the devil can I go off and do what I want to do? I'll marry when I come back, old man; there will be plenty of time then. And you can look after the place for me. I won't have it let, I love the old pile too much for that. And if I want any money I'll cable you from time to time. But I'll not want much."

And so a few days later, Hector, twelfth Earl of Olford, disappeared, and in the log of a wind-jammer bound from South

Shields to Sydney, the fact that one Hector Latham had booked a passage by nominally signing on as second steward, was duly entered.

From then on for ten years John Mason heard from him periodically. From South America, China, New Zealand, there came short messages. Sometimes, not often, there was a request for money to be cabled; generally it was just a notification that he was still alive. And it was in June, 1912, that he received a cable which brought a smile of satisfaction to his face.

"Wire hundred pounds. Leaving for home, *Bellonia*."

And it had been handed in at Auckland.

The hundred pounds were duly dispatched; preparations were at once started at Olford Towers to welcome the returning owner. The end of July, reflected John Mason, should see him in England again; and on the second of that month the *Bellonia* was reported lost with all hands on board.

At first he could hardly grasp it; he just sat in his chair staring dazedly at the paper in his hands. Then feverishly he rang up Lloyd's. Yes, he was told, as far as they could make out it was only too true. The whole thing at the moment was wrapped in mystery, and they really knew no more than he did. She had apparently encountered the most fearful weather, and had got into difficulties. Her SOS had been picked up by three other boats, but when they reached the place indicated there was no sign of her. Moreover the last SOS had broken off abruptly in the middle of the message.

He got hold of a passenger list, hoping against hope that Hector might have changed his mind at the last moment and not travelled in the *Bellonia*. But a glance at the names confirmed his worst fears. Evidently, since he was coming home, he had decided to travel under his real name, for the Earl of Olford was at the top of the column.

So he hadn't come back as he said he would. Fate had decided otherwise. The unbroken line had got to be severed. Of course there were legal formalities as to presumption of death; months dragged by before they were concluded. But in no one's mind was there the slightest doubt as to what had happened. Not a word came to break the silence; it was just one of those mysteries of the sea, which, in this world, will never be explained.

And so in due course, Harold Spencer became the thirteenth Earl, with a singularly charming young wife as his Countess. They had been married about a year, and a son had just appeared on the scene, when the war in France broke out. And the first batch of Kitchener's Army included Harold; it did not include his brother Stephen. That ferret-faced gentleman preferred to fight from an office stool, and succeeded in wangling it successfully. He even gave a watery snuffle when Harold was ripped to pieces by a machine gun at Loos; and felt aggrieved when a dry-eyed woman holding a baby boy of a year in her arms called him a coward to his face.

The fourteenth Earl of Olford – that baby boy; and Stephen, the shifty-eyed, found strange thoughts coming into his tortuous mind. Just supposing the child died, and children do die, he would be the Earl. Measles or something like that.

It would be very nice to be the Earl of Olford – very nice indeed. Sometimes, as he polished his chair, he almost forgot the dangers he incurred from Zeppelin raids, in the wonderful train of thought that the idea conjured up. Stephen, Earl of Olford –

But the baby didn't die; it grew into a sturdy, straight-backed little boy. And John Mason, rising sixty himself now, watched the child with discerning eyes, even as in days gone by he had watched Hector. He felt if anything a keener sense of responsibility towards the house of Olford than ever before; it was his job to see that the spirit of those keen-faced men was carried on, just as if the line had not been broken.

And the mother helped him wonderfully. She too, seemed to realise the bigness of the issue, and the place her sonnie had to fill in the world.

He was eight years old when she took him to see the gap on the wall in the picture gallery. And he listened to her with wide-open eyes as she told him why there was no picture.

"But what did he do, mummie?" asked the boy eagerly.

"I don't know quite what he did, darling," she answered. "Perhaps Uncle John can tell you next time he comes down. Anyway, he was a coward, and that's a terrible thing."

"Daddy wasn't a coward," said the child proudly.

And with a little cry she caught him up and kissed him.

"Of course he wasn't, my pet," she whispered, "and you've got to be like daddy – never afraid of anything."

"Uncle Stephen is afraid," announced the boy gravely. "He was afraid of Rollo when he barked at him the other day. I don't like Uncle Stephen, mummie, he looks at me so funnily sometimes."

"Don't think about him, darling," said his mother.

"Do you like Uncle Stephen, mummie?" he pursued.

"Not very much, old man, but we won't talk about him."

"He didn't fight, did he, mummie, in daddy's war?"

"No, darling, he didn't fight in daddy's war. He was afraid."

"So he was a coward like that gentleman whose picture is hidden?"

Involuntarily she smiled; but much as she disliked Stephen, the conversation was becoming dangerous with an outspoken young man of eight. So she frowned reprovingly.

"Yes, but you must never tell him so, old chap, because that's rude. And you mustn't be rude to people older than yourself."

They went off to play a game, but those few words lingered in her mind – "He looks at me so funnily sometimes."

It was true; she had noticed it herself. It was very rarely that he came near them; even Stephen's rhinoceros-like hide was not

205

impervious to the icy contempt she felt for him. But on the last occasion it had seemed to her that his face had worn a peculiar gloating look: as if he was in possession of some secret which boded ill for her – and her Robin.

She realised, of course, as well as he did, that he would become Earl if anything happened to Robin; but, unpleasant specimen though he was, she did him sufficient credit to believe that he would never attempt to harm the boy. In the first place, he was far too much afraid for his own skin. Still, she felt vaguely worried, and one day she went so far as to mention the matter to John Mason.

"Perhaps it's foolish of me, Uncle John, and yet there are times when I can't help being uneasy. All his life Stephen has been a wrong 'un; Harold always used to admit it openly, and wonder where the kink in him came from. And when I realise that it's only Robin's life that stands between him and all this – "

"But, Marcia, my dear, what could he do?" said John Mason reassuringly. "This is a civilised country, and nothing short of killing the child would be of any use to him."

"Oh! I know! I know! Put it down to the illogical woman's brain if you like. But what I feel is that the wish is there, and if the opportunity came who knows what would happen? I don't say that it's likely to, but it might. After all, children have been kidnapped before now."

She paused and stared over the great park, and John Mason saw a strange look come into her eyes – the look which, in days gone by, he had seen so often in the faces of men and women who had lost their all in France – the look of a great pride.

"I've got proud of this place," she went on slowly. "Heaven knows how proud. It's not for myself; it's for Robin. I know we're not the direct line, but that can't be helped. And I've tried to make him worthy of the name; I've put my whole soul, my whole life into it. Harold was worthy; those fierce men upstairs would all say that. And Robin's going to be; he is now. But Stephen! Why, the hidden picture in the attic would cry aloud if he came here. It's all that, as well as the fact that he's my baby."

They were strolling through the Copthorne Spinney, their feet making no sound on the soft turf, when suddenly John Mason clutched her arm and dragged her behind a clump of undergrowth.

"Look!" he muttered. "Don't move; don't let them see you."

And had the woman not been engrossed in the scene in front of her, she would have noticed that every vestige of colour had left his face.

In a little clearing in front of them stood a tall, sunburnt, black-bearded man, holding a struggling small boy in each hand, whilst facing him was Robin.

"Not two to one," he said in a deep, pleasant voice. "That's not fair. Now, who are you, young fellow?" he asked Robin.

"I'm Lord Olford," said Robin, "and I'll thrash them both if you'll let them go."

The big man stared at the child curiously; then he laughed.

"Of course, you'll thrash them both," he agreed. "But one at a time. Take this one first."

He propelled a wriggling victim forward, and Robin set on him furiously.

"Well done," said the man gravely, as after about a minute the boy turned and ran away. "Now the other."

Once again Robin fought like a young tiger cat, but this time it was a longer affair. Robin was getting tired, and the other boy was bigger. And it was only John Mason's restraining hand that prevented the devoted mother from hurling herself into the fray.

"Now then – stop it, both of you," remarked the big man at length. "Shake hands; that's quite enough."

The two children shook hands sheepishly, and the man solemnly helped Robin on with his coat.

"You cut off out of it," he said to the other boy, who did so with alacrity. "Well, young fellow; so you're Lord Olford, are you? What's your other name?"

"Robin. They were teasing me about it; calling me a bird," he announced. "That's why I fought."

"Quite right," agreed the man. "Nil timent; has anyone ever told you what that means?"

"Of course," answered the boy proudly. " 'They fear nothing.' That's our motto. And my mummie always says I must never be afraid. None of the Olfords ever are. My daddy wasn't afraid, and he was Lord Olford before me. He was killed in the war."

"Was he?" said the man quietly.

"But my Uncle Stephen was a coward. He didn't go to daddy's war. He was like the man in the picture at home who isn't allowed to be there because he was a coward, too. I asked Mummie what he did, but she didn't know."

"I'll tell you what he did, young fellow," said the man. "There was a king in England called Charles the First. And the king was hidden from a man called Cromwell. And the man in the picture knew where the king was because the king trusted him. And then, to save his own life, he went and told Cromwell, so that the king was very nearly caught. So that's why we put his picture in the attic, Robin."

He broke off as a tall and graceful woman came out into the clearing. Robin, with a cry of "Mummie", had run to her, and over the child's head their eyes met.

"Who are you?" said the woman slowly. "You seem to know a lot of the Olford history."

"It is a fairly well-known one, madam," he returned gravely. "May I congratulate you on the present holder of the title?"

She frowned a little; the appearance of this stranger was not altogether prepossessing.

"Uncle John," she said, turning round – but John Mason seemed to have disappeared.

"I suppose you know you're trespassing?" she went on abruptly.

The black-bearded man smiled.

"Please forgive me," he said. "At any rate I got Robin a fair fight."

"The road is through there," she remarked, haughtily, and still with the same faint smile the stranger turned and left her. Again she looked round for John Mason, but there was no sign of him, and at length she led Robin back to the house.

"He suddenly came, Mummie; off the road – just as we were fighting. Wasn't he a nice man?"

"I don't want you to go so far away, darling, when you're by yourself. There are all sorts of tramps and nasty people about."

She hardly heard his indignant defence of his new friend: all sorts of vague fears were darting through her mind. Ingratiating strangers who enticed children away; gipsies. Coming to think of it, he had looked like a gipsy. And was it mere coincidence that Stephen was now paying one of his rare visits to Olford Towers? A tutor: she'd have to get a tutor. Robin was getting too old to be left any longer to his own devices.

And even as she hurried Robin back to have arnica applied to his bruises, John Mason and Hector, Earl of Olford, met face to face.

"It can't be, but it is," said John Mason, and his voice was shaking.

"Aye! old John, it is – right enough," answered the other, quietly. "I told you I'd come back, didn't I? I wonder you recognised me, for I'm altered more than you."

"I think it was seeing you with Robin, Hector. The first time I saw you, you'd just licked Joe Mercer. D'you remember?"

"I remember," said the other. "The beginning of one's life – and now the end."

"What do you mean, Hector – the end? You're only forty-eight."

"Is that all? I suppose it is. For all that, John – it's the end. I've got about six months at the most to go."

John Mason laughed incredulously, and then grew silent. For there was that in the eyes of the man to whom he spoke which forbade disbelief.

"Tell me," he said at length. "I know nothing."

"There's not much to tell, John," said the other. "You thought, of course, that I went down when the *Bellonia* sank. Well, as you can see for yourself, I didn't. She struck something during that appalling storm – possibly a derelict – and sank in two minutes. And I found myself with three of the deck hands clinging to some superstructure that had been carried away. Mercifully the water was warm, because we were adrift for three days. Gradually the sea went down; the pitiless sun came out, and we began to wish that we'd died quickly like the others. And then, one of the other three went mad, and dived overboard. It lightened the load a bit, but beyond that it didn't help, because anyway, we had no water. I think we were all just about following his example, when we sighted land. It was an island, John, with a few peaceful natives on it. I think they'd only seen a white man once before; later on we managed to talk to them a bit. And the island was miles out of the beaten track."

He leaned back suddenly against the tree and seemed to fall asleep, and John Mason stared at him in amazement.

"What's the matter, Hector?" he cried.

With an effort the other opened his eyes.

"That's what the others died of," he said heavily. "It's a sort of sleeping sickness, I suppose. The natives die of it too, but they're more or less immune. Water or something on the island. John, I must sleep."

He sat down on the ground and rolled on his side. And for over an hour did John Mason sit beside him waiting. It needed no expert now to see that he spoke the truth; the grey tinge of his face told its own tale. He woke as suddenly as he had fallen asleep.

"How long was I asleep, John?" he demanded.

"Over an hour," said John Mason. "You'll come straight up with me to a specialist, of course."

The Earl of Olford smiled faintly.

"I don't think so, old man," he answered. "I'll die in peace, thanks. It saps one's vitality; one doesn't want to do anything – except sleep. It'll be two hours soon, John, and a shorter time between the bouts. And at last one will never wake up. I've watched the others. And when the first boat in ten years did come, I almost decided to let her go without me. But there was one thing stronger than this cursed germ: my will to see the place again. To die here, John; and to see my successor. For I can't do the other thing I told you I would – marry. It's too late for that. But I wouldn't want a better kid anyway than Robin – so what does it matter? It's not for long, and they needn't turn out. I'll leave you to explain it to Robin's mother."

His eyes closed again, but he pulled himself together with an effort.

"An element of humour in being ordered off my own ground, John," he laughed. "But a fine woman. Let's go to the house. I want to see it, John; I want to see it. It bored me in the old days, but now it's my life, or what's left of it. And we'll get someone down to put my face on canvas. Shave off this beard, buy some decent clothes, and die like an Olford. Come on, old friend, I want to set foot in my home again. Great Scott! Who's this?"

For the shifty-eyed, ferret-nosed youngster with the unhealthy skin had developed true to type, and the Earl of Olford watched Stephen Spencer taking his morning walk much as a man watches a noisome insect. Stephen Spencer glanced curiously at the big black-bearded man in such deep conversation with John Mason, and for a moment paused as if to speak. Then he seemed to think better of it, and with a little nod to the lawyer he shuffled on and disappeared.

"Who the devil is that?" repeated Hector.

"He's Robin's uncle, and your heir should anything happen to Robin," said John Mason. "What's the matter, Hector? What are you looking like that for?"

"You say that he would be the heir if anything happened to Robin," said the other slowly.

"Certainly," answered John Mason. "He's Robin's next of kin in the male line."

"Then what was he doing talking to the most villainous-looking ruffian a mile or so down the road there? I passed him this morning – though he didn't see me. He was so engrossed in his conversation."

"Are you sure, Hector?" cried the other.

"Of course, I'm sure," snapped Lord Olford. "You can't mistake a man with a face like that. John, little sportsmen who climb trees and run wild – can easily break their necks. In a big place like this who is to tell? A broken neck can always be made to look accidental."

"My God!" muttered John Mason, and his face was white. "But we've got no proof, Hector."

"And a damned lot of good proof would be – once it's happened. Don't be a fool, John; don't be a fool."

For a while they fell silent, pacing up and down over the soft turf.

"Granted you're right, Hector," said the lawyer at last, "or even supposing you're wrong, it doesn't alter things. In fact – now that you've come back it makes them easier. Any designs that Stephen may have on Robin are useless now. He gains nothing from the death of the boy. You've got to do it; you've got to see a specialist. Don't you see that you must marry. Marry and have a son. When Marcia knows you're back – that it's you

– she won't mind. She feels in a sense just a steward for the Olfords."

Lord Olford nodded gravely.

"We could not ask for a better. She must continue."

"But how can she, Hector?" cried John Mason irritably. "Don't you see – "

"I see nothing, John, except one thing. And that is that for me to have a child would be a crime, suffering as I am from this disease. And in any event I might not succeed before I died – or it might be a girl. And what then? We have only postponed things. Robin would still be threatened by the same danger."

"You mustn't assume on that," said the lawyer. "Just because you saw him talking to a tramp – "

"I'm not risking it," remarked the Earl calmly.

"You'll have to," answered John Mason. "You can't shut the boy up."

And the other's deep-set eyes gleamed strangely.

"True, John; you can't shut the boy up. But there are other ways of killing a cat than drowning it."

He smiled grimly, as if amused by some sudden thought, and John Mason stared at him gravely. Only too well did he know the futility of argument once the other had made up his mind, but he made one final attempt.

"What is the use of all this discussion?" he cried. "Come back to the house now with me, and make yourself known. And if you want to, you can put the fear of God into Master Stephen."

And then he shrugged his shoulders despairingly; the other wasn't even listening.

"It's a difficult proposition, John; very difficult," he remarked slowly. "Even with a reptile of that type one would like to have some proof. And I, as you say, have none."

"And what if you could get proof, Hector? What would you do then?"

"The removal of Stephen would assist matters," answered the Earl calmly. "I feel certain no one would miss him."

"But good heavens, man," spluttered John Mason, "you're in England. And I'm not anxious to see the Earl of Olford ending his days on the gallows."

"You won't, John; I can promise you that. We've died most ways, but never by hanging, so far. And I don't propose to start. No, John, there shall be no disgrace – if by any chance I find that what I suspect is the truth. Only I mustn't be recognised; that's vital. I'm a wanderer, John; a tramp – and tramps may do what the Earls of Olford may not."

"But, Hector," protested the other feebly, only to be silenced with an impervious wave of the hand.

"Your word, John – your word of honour – that you will not divulge to a living soul that you have met me this morning, until you hear further from me."

And John Mason gave his word.

"Good. Come back here at three, and wait for me. I'm going to find that man. So long, old friend."

And at three o'clock the lawyer returned, his mind made up. All through lunch his determination had strengthened to insist upon being released from his promise. If Hector was dying, then it was his right to die at Olford Towers.

"Now it's my life, or what's left of it."

He had heard the note of yearning in the wanderer's voice as he spoke. Besides, it was absurd; it was illegal; it was out of the question. John Mason slashed viciously at a nettle with his stick. Fanciful, too; just because Stephen had spoken to some tramps. He'd watched him snuffling over his food at lunch; there was no nerve in that quarter for conspiracy. The thing was ridiculous…

And yet – was it? What had Marcia said to him only that morning? Was it so ridiculous after all?

"All his life Stephen has been a wrong 'un."

Her words came back to him as he sat with his back up against a tree waiting for Hector. Supposing – just supposing – And at that moment he heard the sound of two shots fired not far away.

At first he took no notice – a keeper after rabbits or something. And then a hoarse shout brought him scrambling to his feet.

"Help! Murder!"

With pounding heart he ran in the direction of the cry, forcing his way through the undergrowth. And it was Jenkins, the keeper – white in the face and shaking – who saw him and shouted again.

"Mr Mason, sir; come here, for goodness sake!"

"What is it?" gasped the lawyer. "What's happened?"

"It's up there, sir – behind them bushes," stammered the keeper. "And I seed the whole thing as clear as I sees you now. Mr Spencer was a-standing there talking to a man – talking very earnest like. And I wondered to myself what he could be saying to a dirty-looking tramp like that, when suddenly the bushes parted behind them, and a great, big, black-bearded man stepped out. And then I give you my word, sir, it all 'appened so quick that I'm all mazed still. This black-bearded man, he 'it the tramp on the point of the jaw, and the tramp 'e fell like a log. Then he drew a pistol and shot Mr Spencer through the 'eart."

"I heard two shots, Jenkins," said John Mason quietly.

"I'm coming to that, sir," cried the man. " 'E shot Mr Spencer through the 'eart and then 'e walked back a few paces and stared for a moment or two at the house, over yonder. And then he blew his brains out."

There was only one possible verdict, of course. It was true that the tramp's evidence was unsatisfactory, but he was a man of low brain, and the exact topic of the conversation he had been having with Mr Stephen Spencer was really immaterial. In fact, what little interest there was in the case centred round one point. And it was to John Mason that the coroner addressed himself in his endeavour to elucidate it.

"Owing to the manner in which this man killed himself he is, as you know, Mr Mason, unrecognizable. Now, from what Lady Olford has told me you saw him on the very morning of the tragedy."

"That is so," assented John Mason.

"Then can you throw any light on to the question of his identity?"

And John Mason's reply came without hesitation:

"I never saw the man before in my life."

FER DE LANCE

Ceaselessly the machine went on. It worked somewhat on the principle of a moving staircase. An endless canvas band, lying loosely over cross-pieces placed at intervals, formed a series of ever-advancing cradles, which vanished, each with its load, into the hold. Then the band, flattening out underneath for its return journey, came back for more.

Everything worked with the smoothness born of long practice. Overhead the garish spluttering arc lights hissed, throwing crude shadows on train and boat alike. Occasionally with the harsh clanging of a bell the engine would move forward a few yards, in order to bring the opening of another truck opposite the loading machine. A moment's respite while the train moved, and then down to it again. No pause, no respite: the SS *Barare* was loading bananas, and it was an all-night job. Stem after stem of the fruit – still green – was carried out of the truck by natives and placed each in its separate moving cradle, only to be seized by other natives inside the ship and stowed away in the hold.

Seated on a raised stand was an unshaven, bleary-eyed man. In front of him was a pad on which he checked the number of stems loaded; just as he had checked them for years – or was it centuries? Bananas: millions of stems of bananas had he recorded on paper – until the word banana drove him frantic. He loathed bananas with a loathing that passed description. On the occasions when he had *delirium tremens* – and they were not

217

infrequent – no imaginary animals haunted him. He was denied a rat of any hue. Only bananas: bananas of all shapes and sizes and colours thronged in on his bemused brain, till the whole world seemed full of them.

He was a strange personality – this unkempt checker, and how he had held his job for nearly three years was stranger still. Perhaps the answer could only have been given by the quiet, clean-cut man who was his boss – a strange personality himself. For rumour had it that on one occasion, when a ship was loading, the boss had gone on board as usual. And as he reached the top of the companion he ran straight into a certain Austrian nobleman, who gave a startled gasp of amazement before drawing himself up and bowing punctiliously. Rumour had it also that that same nobleman, having paced the deck with him for a while, was heard to call him "Sir."

An ill-assorted pair, one would have thought – a drunken, down-and-out Englishman and a man whom an Austrian of ancient family called "Sir." And perhaps the reason lay in the fact that the epithet "down-and-out" is only relative. Once the crash has come, a bond of sympathy exists between those who crash, even though their falls are of different height.

The Englishman called himself Robinson when he was sober enough to remember. At other times he was apt to give a different name. The boss called himself Barlock, which, as a name, had certain advantages. It left one in doubt as to the nationality of its owner. And the two men had arrived at Port Limon about the same time in very different capacities. Barlock was taking over a responsible post in the Union Fruit Company, that vast American concern whose tentacles stretch into every corner of the West Indies and Central America. Robinson was merely drunk. He arrived as a deckhand in an old tramp, and, being temporarily mislaid when she sailed again, was left behind without lamentation or regret. And acquaintance between the two men started almost at once in a somewhat peculiar way.

Barlock was wandering round the big railway shed, which was to be the scene of his labours for the next few years, and as he stepped behind some barrels he walked on the other man.

"Don't apologise," remarked Robinson, getting unsteadily to his feet. "I'm used to it. Would you tell me if a bilge-laden old tub, whose name escapes me for the moment, has sailed?"

"If you mean the *Corsica*," said the other, "she sailed about six hours ago."

"It would appear, then, that I have been left behind. Not that it matters in the slightest degree. I have long given up any attempt at regularity in my habits. One small point, however, might be of interest. Where am I?"

Barlock smiled faintly: there was a certain whimsical note in the other's voice that amused him.

"This is Port Limon," he answered. "And in the event of your geography having been as much neglected as mine was, Port Limon is in Costa Rica."

"Costa Rica," said the other, thoughtfully. "Its exact position on the globe is a little beyond me at the moment, but, provided it possesses a bar, it fulfils all my requirements."

He shambled off, leaving the other staring after him. A gentleman obviously: equally obviously a drunkard. And for a moment or two Barlock wondered how the mixture would be digested by the narrow strip of civilisation that lies at the bottom of the densely wooded hills which make up the greater part of the republic. Then with a shrug of his shoulders he went about his lawful occasions.

For a week he saw Robinson no more. Then one night he found him standing at his elbow. A banana train had just creaked into the station, its bell clanging furiously. Natives were lethargically replacing greasy packs of cards in their pockets; Port Limon's justification for existence came to a groaning standstill. No bananas: no Port Limon.

"It is incredible," remarked Robinson, "that human stomachs can consume such inordinate quantities of vegetable matter. I am not a banana maniac myself, unless they are soaked in rum. And even then – why spoil the rum? But when one sees that train, and realises that there are other trains in other places all carrying bananas, one takes off one's hat in silent homage to the world's eaters. By the way, I suppose you haven't the price of a drink on you?"

A sudden idea struck Barlock.

"I have not," he said, shortly. "But I'll give you a job of work. Go and help load them. You'll get the same rate of pay as the natives."

For a moment the other hesitated: it was black man's work. Then finding Barlock's steady eye fixed on him, he gave a short laugh and peeled off his coat. And thus began his personal acquaintance with bananas. Began also a strange relationship between the two men.

Friendship it could hardly be called. Their positions were too widely separated. Barlock was the boss; Robinson a paid hand doing coolie work. But through the long nights, whilst the loading went monotonously on, sometimes the difference between them disappeared. They became just two white men amongst a crowd of blacks. Moreover, they became two white men of the same interests and station. Away from the railway shed it was different. Barlock, by reason of his job, belonged to the club, and could enjoy what social life the place afforded; Robinson was down and out, living native fashion. But under the hissing arc lights the two men met on a common ground – bananas.

And then there occurred an incident which insensibly brought them nearer to one another. If a competition open to the world for the number of snakes to the square yard was instituted, Costa Rica would be very near the top of the list. Moreover, her representatives would not be of the harmless variety. And it so happens that on occasions members of the fraternity go to ground in the bunches of fruit as they lie stacked beside the railway line, waiting to be picked up by the train. The snake hides itself along the stem, and may or may not be discovered at the up-country siding. If it is, it is promptly dispatched; if it is not, it makes the journey to Port Limon. And so at that terminus the danger is an ever-present one, especially as the snake, after having jolted down the line in a stuffy truck, is not in the best of tempers on its arrival.

It all happened very, quickly – some six months after Robinson's introduction to his new trade. He had just taken a big stem of fruit from the man standing in the opening of the truck, when a native beside him gave a shout. He had a momentary glimpse of a wicked yellow head curving out of the fruit in his arms: then there came the thud of a stick, and he dropped the bunch.

He looked up a little stupidly to find Barlock standing beside him, the stick still grasped in his hand. And for a few moments the two men stared at one another in silence, whilst a native completed the good work on the platform.

"*Fer de Lance*," said Barlock, curtly. "Lucky I had a stick."

"Thanks," muttered Robinson, staring at the dead body of perhaps the most deadly brute in existence. "Thanks. Though I wonder if it was worthwhile."

"Don't talk rot," said Barlock, even more curtly, and moved away.

The incident was over; a *Fer de Lance* was dead. Robinson was alive. And there were still bananas to load. But when one man has saved another man's life, it is bound to make some difference in their relationship. And though nothing changed outwardly, though they still remained boss and paid hand, under the surface there was an alteration.

"Thanks once more," said Robinson, as the empty train pulled out the next morning. He had followed Barlock to his room in the station, and was standing in the open door. "You were deuced quick with that stick."

"Not much good moving by numbers when there is a bone-tail about," said Barlock with a laugh.

"So you're of the breed, are you?" Robinson stared at the other man. "I always thought you were by the set of your shoulders. By numbers. God! how it brings things back. Do you know our immortal songster? I've got a new last line to one of his things: –

> 'Gentlemen rankers out on the spree,
> Damned from here to eternity.
> God have mercy on such as we,
> Ba – na – na.'

I load the damned things to the rhythm."

Barlock looked at him thoughtfully.

"What regiment?" he asked after a moment.

"Thirteenth Lancers," said the other. "And you?"

"Austrian Cavalry of the Guard," answered Barlock.

"Of course, I knew you weren't English," said Robinson, "though you speak it perfectly. So we went through that performance on different sides. Funny life, isn't it? Look here, I don't want to be impertinent or unduly curious. The reason for me is obvious: I can't keep away from the blasted stuff. But you – you don't drink."

Barlock smiled grimly.

"Have you ever thought, my friend, of the difference it makes when the last two o's are lopped off a man's income? The gap between fifty thousand and five hundred is considerable."

"So that's it, is it?" said Robinson, and began to laugh weakly. "And our mutual life-belt is that rare and refreshing fruit the banana."

Suddenly he pulled himself together.

"By the way, there's just one thing I'd like to say. I don't suppose the situation is ever likely to arise, but it may do. There's a lot of tourist traffic passes through – and one never knows. I'm dead."

"I don't quite follow," said Barlock, quietly.

"I should have thought it was easy," remarked the other. "But I'll be more explicit. Six or seven years ago a regrettable accident took place. An extremely drunken man fell over Waterloo Bridge into the River Thames, and the only thing that was ever recovered was his hat. Wherefore after prolonged search the powers decided that the owner of the hat had been drowned. The powers that be were wrong, but it would be a pity if they found out. There would be complications."

Barlock turned away abruptly; there are moments when a man may not look on another man's face.

"I see," he said, after a pause. "Your secret is safe with me."

"Complications," repeated Robinson, dully. "Damnable complications. Well – I'll be pushing on. Thanks again for that snake business."

He slouched off down the platform, and for a time the Austrian stood staring at his retreating back. Damnable complications: the words rang in his brain. Then, with a little shrug of his shoulders, he closed his door. For when one's job is to unload bananas by night, it is necessary to sleep by day.

It was a year afterwards that the official belief concerning Robinson was very nearly justified. Two trains came in, were unloaded and departed again, but of Robinson there was no sign. And after the second, Barlock made inquiries. It was not the first time that Robinson had missed a train, but never before had it been more than that. And the result of Barlock's inquiries was short and to the point. A more than usually fierce drinking bout, coupled with the intense heat – it was the end of July – had just about finished him off. In fact, Barlock's native informant stated that he was, in all probability, already dead. However, if the boss wished he would lead him to the house where the sick man was.

The boss did wish, though once or twice on the way he almost repented and turned back. There are degrees of filth and stench even in the native quarters of Port Limon, and it seemed to Barlock that his destination reached the lowest abyss in the scale. Verminous dogs slunk garbaging along the refuse-strewn gutter; naked children, the flies swarming round them, stared at him with wide-open eyes as he picked his way along the road. And over everything, like a hot wet blanket, pressed the tropical heat.

He thought with longing of the club at the other end of the town, where what breeze there was came fresh from the sea, and where a man could wallow in the water through the stifling afternoon. After all, this man meant nothing to him. What was he save a broken-down waster belonging to a nation largely responsible for his own present condition? And then he laughed a little cynically. Whatever Robinson was he knew that he was going through with it. White is white, however far down it has sunk.

At last his guide turned through a ramshackle gate from which a short path, which was evidently the household dustbin, led to a dilapidated shanty. Seated outside the front door was a vast negress, who grinned expansively on seeing the white man. Her lodger was about the same, she told him, and would his honour walk in if he wished to see him. Barlock did so, dodging some hens that walked out simultaneously. And once again he almost chucked it. If the smell outside was bad, there at any rate it was not confined. But in the hovel he had just entered it was concentrated to such an extent that it produced a feeling of physical nausea. And then, as he stood there for a moment or two undecided, there came a hoarse voice from a room beyond.

"Steady, lads – steady! They're coming on again."

One of the breed, and they had gone through that performance on different sides. Yes – it had its humorous side, without doubt. Barlock crossed the room, and pulled aside a dirty hanging. Different sides, perhaps – but both were the same colour.

More hens scuttled out as he stood in the opening. The sick man was lying on some reeds in the corner, and as Barlock crossed to him he glanced up. His eyes showed no trace of recognition, and his visitor saw at once that matters were serious. It was a question of a doctor, and a doctor quickly.

Then his eyes caught sight of something that lay beside the sick man; he bent over him and removed it. And Robinson, delirious as he was, was not so far gone that that escaped him. He cursed foully, and tried to snatch it out of Barlock's hand, only to fall back weakly on the rushes.

"Listen, Robinson," said Barlock, speaking slowly and distinctly. "I'm going to get a doctor."

But the sick man only muttered and mouthed, and glared at his visitor with a look of venomous hatred.

"Now, you old devil," continued Barlock to the negress who had come shambling in, "if I find he has any more of this, you'll be sorry. Police after you, unless you're careful. I go get doctor."

He strode out, leaving the old woman shaking like a mountain of jelly. Then, having smashed to bits a bottle of illicit native spirit, he went in search of the one tolerable doctor the place boasted of. By luck he found him taking his siesta, and dragged him out despite his protests. And between them they saved what was left of Robinson.

Barlock did most of it. For hours on end when he was free did he sit beside the sick man, listening to his ravings – and in the course of those ravings learning the truth. And after a while a great pity for the wretched derelict took hold of him. For the first time he found out Robinson's real name, and truly the crash was greater than he had guessed. And for the first time he found out that there was a woman involved.

At last came the day when the fever died out, and the sick man opened sane eyes to the world.

"Hullo!" he said, staring at Barlock, "have I been talking out of my turn?"

"Don't worry about that," answered the other quietly. "I'm the only person who has heard. And it's safe with me."

"You know who I am?" persisted Robinson, and Barlock nodded.

"Yes – I know who you are," he answered.

"You know I'm married. Or rather" – the smile was a little pitiful – "was married."

"I gathered so," said Barlock. "Look here – we'll talk it all over when you're a bit stronger. You go to sleep now."

Robinson shut his eyes wearily.

"Damnable complications," he muttered. "That's why I'm dead. Because Ulrica has married again."

And at that it was left. A fortnight later Robinson reported for duty again, but now there was a difference. The fever had left its indelible mark: the physical labour required for that continuous carrying of heavy bunches of fruit was beyond his powers. And so Barlock promoted him; he became assistant checker. Seated on his raised stand, he checked on the pad in front of him the number of stems loaded, and he went on checking them as each ship came in. Until in the fullness of time the SS *Barare* arrived, and, as usual, it was an all-night job.

Leaning over the ship's rail, watching the scene, was a tall, fair-haired man. He was smoking, and every line of his figure breathed that lazy contentment which only a good cigar can give. Occasionally a faint smile flickered round his lips, at some monkey-like contortion of one of the niggers, but for the most part his face was that expressionless mask which is the hallmark of a certain type of Englishman.

Suddenly his eyes narrowed: he leaned forward, staring into the crowd below.

"Good God!" he muttered, "it can't be. But it is, by Jove!"

Barlock was coming up the gangway, and the tall, fair-haired man moved along the deck so that the two met at the top.

"But what astounding luck!" he cried. "My dear Baron – how are you? And what are you doing here?"

The faintest perceptible frown showed for a moment on Barlock's forehead.

"How are you, Lord Rankin?" he said. "But if you don't mind – not Baron. My name here is just Barlock."

The other stared at him in puzzled amazement.

"My dear fellow," he stammered, "I don't quite follow."

"And yet it's fairly easy," answered Barlock. "Financial considerations made it necessary for me to work. So I now superintend the loading of bananas for the Union Fruit Company. And since the job, though honest and homely, is hardly one that I ever saw myself doing in the past, I decided, temporarily at any rate, to drop my title."

"Well, I'm damned!" said the other, a little awkwardly. "You stagger me, my dear chap. One thing, however, is perfectly clear. Whatever your name is here, to me you are Baron von Studeman, who was amazingly good to a young military attaché in Vienna. And I insist – first on your having a drink, and second on your meeting Ulrica."

"Ulrica!" said Barlock, standing of a sudden very still.

"My wife," explained the other. "I've been married seven years, old boy. Her young hopeful is below now, safely tucked up in the sheets."

But Barlock's eyes were fixed on the back of an unshaven, bleary-eyed man who was checking stems of bananas on a pad.

Seven years: an uncommon name like Ulrica. Had the unexpected happened?

And then a peculiarity in the other's phrasing struck him.

"*Her* young hopeful!" he said with a slight smile.

"Yes," answered Lord Rankin. "My wife had been married before. He was drowned, leaving her with a boy two years old."

Once again Barlock stared at the man with the pencil below.

"I see," he heard himself saying. "By the way, did you ever meet your wife's first husband?"

Lord Rankin raised his eyebrows. Loading bananas did not seem to have increased the Baron's tact.

"I did not," he said curtly, and changed the conversation.

But Barlock hardly heard what he was saying. The unexpected *had* happened. Back to his mind came the remembrance of that day when Robinson had stood in the doorway of his office. He saw once more the look on his face, heard once more those low-breathed words, "Damnable complications." And unless he did something the complications had arrived.

He tried to force himself to think clearly – to get the salient facts in his brain. There, on the dock, within fifteen yards of where he stood, was a man whose wife and child were on board the boat. At any moment Lady Rankin might appear, and what was going to happen then? For even if she did not recognise him, he would be bound to recognise her.

"Excuse me for a few minutes," he said. "There are one or two things I must see to on the quay."

"You'll come back?" cried the other, and Barlock nodded. At all costs he must speak to Robinson.

He went swiftly down the gangway, and crossed to the stand where he sat.

"Hullo, my noble boss!" said Robinson. "You seem a little agitated."

"Look here, Robinson," he said, quietly, "you've got to pull yourself together. Something that you have long feared has happened."

For a moment the other stared at him uncomprehendingly; then he sat up with a jerk.

"You mean that – "

"I mean that Lord Rankin is on board."

"And Ulrica?"

"Yes, she is on board, and your son."

"My God!" Mechanically he was ticking off the bunches as they passed. "My God!"

"Don't look round," went on Barlock. "Rankin is leaning over the rail now, and Lady Rankin has just joined him."

He watched the other stiffen, till the sweat dripped off his forehead on to the paper in front of him.

"If I could only see her once again," he muttered. "And the boy."

"But you mustn't," said Barlock, quietly. "Of course – you mustn't."

"Of course I mustn't," repeated Robinson, dully. "Why – no; you are right."

"So keep your back turned, Robinson," continued Barlock.

"Yes, I'll keep my back turned, Barlock. But tell me how she is looking, Barlock, and whether she still has that quaint little trick of hers of throwing her head sideways when she laughs. Go and talk to her, Barlock – while I go on counting bananas. And if maybe she did drop her handkerchief, why, I don't think she'd miss it much, would she, Barlock?"

"Hell!" grunted the other as he turned away. "You poor devil."

"Come along," came Lord Rankin's cheery hail. "We'll go and split a bottle."

"One thousand three hundred and twenty-one bunches up to date," said Robinson, with a twisted grin. "Yes – go and split a bottle, Barlock."

And with the feeling that the whole night was a dream from which he would wake soon, the Baron von Studeman went to split a bottle. It increased, that sense of unreality, as the three of them sat in the smoking-room, till he became conscious that his host was looking at him curiously. And he realised he was speaking at random and must pull himself together.

"All natives, I suppose?" said Rankin. "Don't you find it damned boring? Except that fellow you were talking to, who looked white."

"I rather think he is white," he answered, slowly. "As white as you or I."

It came unexpectedly, the sudden commotion on the platform outside. There was a hoarse shouting from the natives, and then some excited babbling.

"Probably only a snake," said Barlock, reassuringly. "They always lose their heads when one arrives in the bananas. Hullo! who is this young man?"

Standing in the open doorway was a small figure arrayed in a large dressing-gown.

"I say, mummie," remarked an enthusiastic treble voice, "I've had a priceless time. They've just walloped a snake."

"Tommy!" cried his mother. "You naughty boy! Why aren't you in bed?"

"That funny machine woke me up," answered the child. "So I put my head out to look. And then I saw all the bananas. So I thought I'd go and see what was happening. There was such a nice gentleman sitting on a stool who wanted to know if I'd shake hands with him."

Barlock rose a little abruptly and stared out into the darkness.

"What's this about a snake, young fellah?" said Lord Rankin.

"Well, daddie, just as I was talking to this gentleman, somebody suddenly gave a shout. And I looked round, and there was a yellowy-green snake on the platform close to me. And the gentleman sort of fell out of his chair, and the snake bit him in the hand."

"What's that you say, laddie?" Barlock's voice seemed to come from a distance. "The snake bit him in the hand?"

"Why, yes," said the child. "And then he was so funny. He said, 'I used to field in the slips, old man,' and then he went away ever so quickly, while the natives killed the snake."

"Well, come to bed at once now," cried his mother. "It's nearly midnight."

She bustled him out, leaving the two men alone.

"Young devil," chuckled Lord Rankin. "Not going yet, von Studeman, are you?"

"For a little," returned the other evenly. "I will come back later."

But he searched for twenty minutes before he found Robinson. A glance told him it was too late. The end was very near. He had been bitten in the wrist, and nothing could be done.

"A bonnie kid, Barlock," he said, feebly. "I'm glad I saw him. Just got my hand there in time. It was one thousand seven hundred and thirty – "

The voice died away, and the man called Robinson lay still.

"A very narrow escape for the boy." It was an hour later, and the Baron von Studeman was standing with Lord Rankin on deck. "The snake was a *Fer de Lance*, one of the most deadly in the world. They generally remain in the bananas until the stem is lifted out. But this one apparently escaped in the truck; anyway, it was loose on the platform. And but for – Robinson's quickness, the kid would now be dead."

"Good God! It would have broken his mother's heart," said the other. "Where is this man, Robinson? Because I must thank him."

"I don't think you quite realise what happened, Rankin," said the Baron, quietly. "Robinson received the bite intended for the boy in his own wrist."

The other stared at him speechlessly.

"You don't mean – " he stammered, and the Baron nodded gravely.

"My God!" repeated the other. "This is too awful. Poor devil! Dead!"

He paced up and down in his agitation.

"Anything I could have done for him I would. You see, von Studeman, I didn't tell you before. But my wife's first husband was the most frightful waster. And it broke her up badly before he was drowned. Made her put everything into the kid. If anything had happened to him, I don't know what she'd have done. And this poor chap – dead. I can't get it somehow. Look here, I must do something. He was probably not too well off, and you could help me here. What about giving a present to his wife? He was married, I suppose?"

A queer smile flickered round the lips of the Baron von Studeman.

Below him the machine went on ceaselessly, for the SS *Barare* was loading bananas and it was an all-night job.

"Married?" he said. "Not that I'm aware of."

THE GREEN DEATH
Part 1

1

"And why Major Seymour, do they call you 'Old Point of Detail'?"

The tall, spare man, with a face tanned by years in the tropics, turned at the question, and glanced at the girl beside him. At the time when most boys are still at school, force of circumstances had sent him far afield into strange corners of the earth – a wanderer, and picker-up of odd jobs. He had done police work in India – he had been on a rubber plantation in Sumatra. The Amazon knew him and so did the Yukon, while his knowledge of the customs of tribes in Darkest Africa – the very names of which were unknown to most people – was greater than the average Londoner has of his native city. In fact, before the war it would have been difficult to sit for an evening in one of those clubs which spring into being in all corners where Englishmen guard their far-flung inheritance without Bob Seymour's name cropping up.

Then had come the war, and in the van of the great army from the mountains and the swamps which trekked home as the first shot rang out, he came. As his reward he got a DSO and one leg permanently shortened by two inches. He also met a girl – the girl who had just asked him the question.

He'd met her just a year after the Armistice, when he was wondering whether there was any place for a cripple in the lands that he knew. And from that day everything had changed. Even to himself he wouldn't admit it; the thought of asking such a glorious bit of loveliness to tie herself to a useless has-been like himself was out of the question. But he let the days slip by, content to meet her occasionally at dinner – to see her, in the distance, at a theatre. And now, for the first time, he found himself staying under the same roof. When he'd arrived the preceding day and had seen her in the hall, just for a moment his heart had stopped beating, and then had given a great bound forward. She, of course, knew nothing of his feelings; of that he felt sure. And she must never know; of that he was determined. The whole thing was out of the question.

Of course – naturally. And the only comment which a mere narrator of facts can offer on the state of affairs is to record the remark made by Ruth Brabazon to a very dear friend of hers after Bob Seymour had limped upstairs to his room.

"That's the man, Delia," she said, with a little smile. "And if he doesn't say something soon, I shall have to."

"He looks a perfect darling," remarked the other.

"He is," sighed Ruth. "But he *won't* give me the chance of telling him so. He thinks he's a cripple."

With which brief insight into things as they really were, we can now return to things as Bob Seymour thought they were. Beside him, on a sofa in the hall, sat the girl who had kept him in England through long months, and she had just asked him a question.

"The Old, I trust, is a term of endearment," he answered, with a smile, "and not a brutal reflection on my tale of years. The Point of Detail refers to a favourite saying of mine with which my reprobate subalterns – of whom your brother was quite the worst – used to mock me."

"Bill is the limit," murmured the girl. "What was the saying?"

"I used to preach the importance of Points of Detail to 'em," he grinned. "One is nothing; two are a coincidence; three are a moral certainty. And they're very easy to see if you have eyes to see them with."

"I suppose they are, Old Point of Detail," she replied, softly.

Was it his imagination or did she lay a faint stress on the Old?

"It was certainly a term of endearment," she continued deliberately; "if what Bill says is to be believed."

"Oh! Bill's an ass," said Seymour, sheepishly.

"Thank you," she remarked, and he noticed her eyes were twinkling. "I've always been told I'm exactly like Bill. I know we always used to like the same things when we were children." She rose and crossed the hall. "Time to dress for dinner, I think."

In the dim light he could not see her face clearly; he only knew his heart was thumping wildly. Did she mean – ? And then from halfway up the stairs she spoke again.

"Two are certainly a coincidence," she agreed, thoughtfully. "But the third would have to be pretty conclusive before you could take it as a certainty."

2

"Well, Major Seymour, hitting 'em in the beak?" The Celebrated Actor mixed himself a cocktail with that delicate grace for which he was famed on both sides of the Atlantic.

"So–so, Mr Trayne," returned the other. "All the easy ones came my way."

The house-party were in the hall waiting for dinner to be announced, but the one member of it who mattered to Bob had not yet appeared.

"Rot, my dear fellow," said his host, who had come up in time to hear his last remark. "Your shooting was magnificent –

absolutely magnificent. You had four birds in the air once from your guns."

"Personally," murmured the Celebrated Actor, "it fails to appeal to me. Apart from my intense fright at letting off lethal weapons, I have never yet succeeded in hitting anything except a keeper or – more frequently – a guest. I abhor violence – except at rehearsals." He broke off as a heavy, bull-necked man came slowly down the stairs. "And who is the latest addition to our number, Sir Robert?"

"A man who did me a good turn a few weeks ago," said the owner of the house, shortly. "Name of Denton. Arrived only half an hour ago."

He moved away to introduce the newcomer, and the Actor turned to Bob Seymour.

"One wonders," he remarked, "whether it would be indiscreet to offer Mr Denton a part in my new play. Nothing much to say. He merely drinks and eats. In effect, a publican of unprepossessing aspect. One wonders – so suitable."

He placed his empty glass on the table and drifted charmingly away towards his hostess; leaving Bob Seymour smiling gently. Undoubtedly a most suitable part for Mr Denton.

And then, quite suddenly, the smile died away. Bill Brabazon, who was standing near the fireplace, had turned round and come face to face with the newcomer. For a moment or two they stared at one another – a deadly loathing on their faces; then with ostentatious rudeness Denton turned his back and walked away.

"My God! Bob," muttered Bill, coming up to Seymour. "How on earth did that swine-emperor get here?"

His jaw was grim and set, his eyes gleaming with rage; and the hand that poured out the cocktail shook a little.

"What's the matter, Bill?" said Seymour, quietly. "For Heaven's sake, don't make a scene, old man!"

"Matter!" choked Bill Brabazon. "Matter! Why – "

But any further revelations were checked by the announcement of dinner, and the party went in informally. To his delight, Bob Seymour found himself next to Ruth, and the little scene he had just witnessed passed from his mind. It was not until they were half-way through the meal that it was recalled to him by Ruth herself.

"Who is that dreadful-looking man talking to Delia Morrison?" she whispered.

"Denton is his name," replied Seymour, and every vestige of colour left her face.

"Denton," she muttered. "Good Heavens! it can't be the same." She glanced round the table till she found her brother, who was answering the animated remarks of his partner with morose monosyllables. "Has Bill – "

"Bill has," returned Seymour, grimly. "And he's whispered to me on the subject. What's the trouble?"

"They had the most fearful row – over a girl," she explained, a little breathlessly. "Two or three months ago. I know they had a fight, and Bill got a black eye. But he broke that other brute's jaw."

"Holy smoke!" muttered Seymour. "The meeting strikes the casual observer as being, to put it mildly, embarrassing. Do you know how the row started?"

"Only vaguely," she answered. "That man Denton got some girl into trouble, and then left her in the lurch – refused to help her at all. A poor girl – daughter of someone who had been in Bill's platoon. And he came to Bill."

"I see," said Seymour, grimly. "I see. Bill would."

"Of course he would!" she cried. "Why, of course. Just the same as you would."

"I suppose that isn't pretty conclusive?" he said, with a grin. "As a third point, I mean."

But Ruth Brabazon had turned to the Celebrated Actor on her other side. He had already said, "My dear young lady," five times without avail, and he was Very Celebrated.

Neglected for the moment by both his neighbours, Bob proceeded to study the gentleman whose sudden arrival seemed so inopportune. He was a coarse-looking specimen, and already his face was flushed with the amount of wine he had drunk. Every now and then his eyes sought Bill Brabazon vindictively, and Seymour frowned as he saw it. Denton belonged to a type he had met before, and it struck him there was every promise of trouble before the evening was out. When men of Denton's calibre get into the condition of "drink-taken", such trifles as the presence of other guests in the house do not deter them from being offensive. And Bill Brabazon, though far too well-bred to seek a quarrel in such surroundings, was also far too hot-tempered to take any deliberate insult lying down.

Suddenly a coarse, overloud laugh from Denton sounded above the general conversation, and Ruth Brabazon looked round quickly.

"Ugh! what a horrible man!" she whispered to Bob. "How I hate him!"

"I don't believe a word of it," he was saying, harshly. "Fraud by knaves for fools. For those manifestations that have been seen there is some material cause. Generally transparent trickery." He laughed – again, sneeringly.

For a second or two there was an uncomfortable silence. It was not so much what the man had said, as the vulgar, ill-bred manner in which he had said it, and Sir Robert hastily intervened to relieve the tension.

"Ghosts?" he remarked. "As impossible a subject to argue about as religion or politics. Incidentally, you know." he continued, addressing the table at large, "there's a room in this house round which a novelist might weave quite a good ghost story."

"Tell us, Sir Robert." A general chorus assailed him, and he smiled.

"I'm not a novelist," he said, "though for what it's worth I'll tell you about it. The room is one in the new wing which I used to use as a smoking-room. It was the part built on to the house by my predecessor – a gentleman, from all accounts, of peculiar temperament. He had spent all his life travelling to obscure places of the world; and I don't know if it was liver or what, but his chief claim to notoriety when he did finally settle down appears to have been an intense hatred of his fellow-men. There are some very strange stories of the things which used to go on in this house, where he lived the life of an absolute recluse, with one old man to look after him. He died about forty years ago."

Sir Robert paused and sipped his champagne.

"However, to continue. In this smoking-room in the new wing, there is an inscription written in the most amazing jumble of letters by the window. It is written on the wall, and every form of hieroglyphic is used. You get a letter in Arabic, then one of Chinese, then an ordinary English one, and perhaps a German. Well, to cut a long story short, I took the trouble one day to copy it out, and replaced the foreign letters – there are one or two Greek letters as well – by their corresponding English ones. I had to get somebody else to help me over the Chinese and Arabic, but the result was, at any rate, sense. It proved to be a little jingling rhyme, and it ran as follows: –

' When 'tis hot, shun this spot.
When 'tis rain, come again.
When 'tis day, all serene.
When 'tis night, death is green.' "

Sir Robert glanced round the table with a smile.

"There was no doubt who had written this bit of doggerel, as the wing was actually built by my predecessor – and I certainly didn't. That's a pretty good foundation to build a ghost story on, isn't it?"

"But have you ever seen anything?" inquired one of the guests.

"Not a thing," laughed his host. "But" – he paused mysteriously – "I've smelt something. And that's the reason why I don't use the room any more.

"It was a very hot night – hotter even than this evening. There was thunder about – incidentally, I shouldn't be surprised if we had a storm before tomorrow – and I was sitting in the room after dinner reading the paper. All of a sudden I became aware of a strange and most unpleasant smell: a sort of fetid, musty, rank smell, like you get sometimes when you open up an old vault. And at the same moment I noticed that the paper I held in my hand had gone a most peculiar green colour and I could no longer see the print clearly. It seemed to have got darker suddenly, and the smell became so bad that it made me feel quite faint.

"I walked over to the door and left the room meaning to get a lamp. Then something detained me, and I didn't go back for an hour or so. When I did the smell was still there, though so faint that one could hardly notice it. Also the paper was quite white again." He laughed genially. "And that's the family ghost; a poor thing, but our own. I'll have to get someone to take it in hand and bring it up-to-date."

"But surely you don't think there is any connection between this smell and the inscription?" cried Denton.

"I advance no theory at all." Sir Robert smiled genially. "All I can tell you is that there is an inscription, and that the colour green is mentioned in it. It seemed to me most certainly that my paper went green, though it is even more certain that I did not die. Also there is at times in this room this rather unpleasant smell. I told you it was a poor thing in the ghost line."

The conversation became general, and Ruth Brabazon turned to Bob, who was thoughtfully staring at his plate.

"Why so preoccupied, Major Seymour?"

"A most interesting yarn," he remarked, coming out of his reverie. "Have a salted almond, before I finish the lot."

3

To have two hot-tempered men who loathe one another with a bitter loathing in a house-party is not conducive to its happiness. And when one of them is an outsider of the first water, slightly under the influence of alcohol, the situation becomes even more precarious. For some time after dinner was over Bill Brabazon avoided Denton as unostentatiously as he could, though it was plain to Bob Seymour and Ruth that he was finding it increasingly difficult to control his temper. By ten o'clock it was obvious, even to those guests who knew nothing about the men's previous relations, that there was trouble brewing; and Sir Robert, who had been told the facts of the case by Bob, was at his wits' end.

"If only I'd known," he said, irritably. "If only someone had told me. I know Denton is a sweep, but he did me a very good turn in the City the other day, and, without thinking, I asked him to come and shoot some time. And when he suggested coming now, I couldn't in all decency get out of it. I hope to Heaven there won't be a row."

"If there's going to be, Sir Robert, you can't prevent it," said Seymour. "I'm sure Bill will do all he can to avoid one."

"I know he will," answered his host. "But there are limits, and that man Denton is one of 'em. I wish I'd never met the blighter."

"Come and have a game of billiards, anyway," said the other. "It's no use worrying about it. If it comes, it comes."

When they had been playing about twenty minutes, Ruth Brabazon and Delia Morrison joined them, the billiard-room being, as they affirmed, the coolest room in the house.

"We'll have rain soon," said Sir Robert, bringing off a fine losing hazard off the red. "That'll clear the air."

And shortly afterwards his prophecy proved true. Heavy drops began to patter down on the glass skylight, and the girls heaved a sigh of relief.

"Thank goodness," gasped Ruth. "I couldn't have stood – " She broke off abruptly and stared at the door, which had just opened to admit her brother. "Bill," she cried, "what's the matter?"

Bob Seymour looked up quickly at her words; then he rested his cue against the table. Something very obviously was the matter. Bill Brabazon, his tie undone, with a crumpled shirt, and a cut under his eye on the cheek-bone, came into the room and closed the door.

"I must apologise, Sir Robert," he said, quietly, "for what has happened. It's a rotten thing to have to admit in another man's house, but the fault was not entirely mine. I've had the most damnable row with that fellow Denton – incidentally he was half-drunk – and I've laid him out. An unpardonable thing to do to one of your guests, but – well – I'm not particularly slow-tempered, and I couldn't help it. He went on and on and on – asking for trouble: and finally he got it."

"Damnation!" Sir Robert replaced his cue in the rack. "When did it happen, Bill?"

"About half an hour ago. I've been outside since. Meaning to avoid him I went to the smoking-room in the new wing, and I found him there examining that inscription by the window. I couldn't get away – without running away. I suppose I ought to have."

An uncomfortable silence settled on the room, which was broken at length by Sir Robert.

"Where is the fellow now, Bill?"

"I haven't seen him – not since I socked him one on the jaw. I'm deucedly sorry about it," he continued, miserably, "and I feel the most awful sweep, but – "

He stopped suddenly as the door was flung open and the Celebrated Actor rushed in. The magnificent repose which usually stamped his features was gone: it was an agitated and frightened man who stood by the billiard table, pouring out his somewhat incoherent story. And as his meaning became clear Bill Brabazon grew white and leaned against the mantelpiece for support.

Dead – Denton dead! That was the salient fact that stood out from the Actor's disjointed sentences.

"To examine the inscription," he was saying. "I went in to examine it – and there – by the window…"

"He can't be dead," said Bill, harshly. "He's laid out, that's all."

"Quick! Which is the room?" Bob Seymour's steady voice served to pull everyone together. "There's no good standing here talking – "

In silence they crossed the hall, and went along the passage to the new wing.

"Here we are," said Sir Robert, nervously. "This is the door."

The room was in darkness and in the air there hung a rank, fetid smell. The window was open, and outside the rain was lashing down with tropical violence. Bob Seymour fumbled in his pocket for a match; then he turned up the lamp and lit it. Just for a moment he stared at it in surprise, then Ruth, from the doorway, gave a little stifled scream.

"Look," she whispered. "By the window – "

A man was lying across the window-sill, with his legs inside the room and his head and shoulders outside.

"Good Heavens," muttered Sir Robert, touching the body with a shaking hand, "I suppose – I suppose – he *is* dead?"

But Seymour apparently failed to hear the remark.

"Do you notice this extraordinary smell?" he said at length.

"Damn the smell," said his host, irritably. "Give me a hand with this poor fellow."

Seymour pulled himself together and stepped forward as the other bent down to take hold of the sagging legs.

"Leave him alone, Sir Robert," he said, quickly. "You must leave the body till the police come. We'll just see that he's dead, and then – "

He picked up an electric torch from the table and leant out of the window. And after a while he straightened up again with a little shudder.

It was not a pretty sight. In the light of the torch the face seemed almost black, and the two arms, limp and twisted, sprawled in the sodden earth of the flower-bed. The man was quite dead, and they both stepped back into the middle of the smoking-room with obvious relief.

"Well," said Brabazon, "is he – ?"

"Yes – he's dead," said Seymour, gravely.

"But it's impossible," cried the boy, wildly. "Why, that blow I gave him couldn't have – have killed the man."

"Nevertheless he's dead," said Seymour, staring at the motionless body, thoughtfully. Then his eyes narrowed, and he bent once more over the dead man. Ruth, sobbing hysterically, was trying to comfort her brother, while the rest of the house-party had collected near the door, talking in low, agitated whispers.

"Bob – Bob," cried Bill Brabazon, suddenly, "I've just remembered. I couldn't have done it when I laid him out. I told you I was walking up and down the lawn. Well, the light from this room was streaming out, and I remember seeing his shadow in the middle of the window. He must have been standing up. The mark of the window-sash was clear on the lawn."

Seymour glanced at him thoughtfully. "But the light was out, Bill. How do you account for that?"

"It wasn't," said the other, positively. "Not then. It must have gone out later."

"We'll have to send for the police, Sir Robert," said Seymour, laying a reassuring hand on the boy's arm. "Tell them everything when they come."

"I've got nothing to hide," said the youngster, hoarsely. "I swear to Heaven I didn't do that."

"We'd better go," cried Sir Robert. "Leave everything as it is. I'll ring the police up."

With quick, nervous steps he left the room, followed by his guests, until only Seymour was left standing by the window with its dreadful occupant. For a full minute he stood there, while the rain still lashed down outside, sniffing as he had done when he first entered. And, at length, with a slight frown on his face, as if some elusive memory escaped him, he followed the others from the room, first turning out the light and then locking the door.

4

It was half an hour before the police came, in the shape of Inspector Grayson and a constable. During that time the rain had stopped for a period of about twenty minutes; only to come on again just before a ring announced their arrival.

The house-party were moving aimlessly about in little scattered groups, obsessed with the dreadful tragedy. In the billiard-room Ruth sat with her brother in a sort of stunned silence; only Bob Seymour seemed unaffected by the general strain. Perhaps it was because, in a life such as his, death by violence was no new spectacle; perhaps it was that there was something he could not understand.

Who had blown the light out? That was the crux. Blown – not turned. The Celebrated Actor was very positive that the light had not been on when he first entered the room. It might have been the wind, but there was no wind. A point of detail – one. And then the smell – that strange, fetid smell. It touched a chord of memory, but try as he would he could not place it.

His mind started on another line. If the boy, in his rage, had struck the dead man a fatal blow, how had the body got into such a position? It would have been lying on the floor.

"Weak heart," he argued. "Hot night – gasping for breath – rushed to window – collapsed. That's what they'd say."

He frowned thoughtfully; on the face of it quite plausible. Not only plausible – quite possible.

"Major Seymour!" Ruth's voice beside him made him look up. "What can we do? Poor old Bill's nearly off his head."

"There's nothing to do, Miss Brabazon – but tell the truth," said Seymour, gravely. "What I mean is," he explained, hurriedly, "you've got to impress on Bill the vital necessity of being absolutely frank with the police."

"I know he didn't do it, Bob," she cried, desperately. "I know it."

Bob! She'd called him Bob. And such is human nature that for a moment the dead man was forgotten.

"So do I, Ruth," he whispered, impulsively. "So do I."

"And you'll prove it?" she cried.

"I'll prove it," he promised her. Which was no rasher than many promises made under similar conditions.

"Thank goodness you've come, Inspector." Sir Robert had met the police at the door. "A dreadful tragedy."

"So I gather, Sir Robert," answered the other. "One of your guests been murdered?"

"I didn't say so on the 'phone," said Sir Robert. "I said – killed."

The inspector grunted, "Where's the body?"

"In the smoking-room." He led the way towards the door.

"I've got the key in my pocket," said Seymour; and the inspector looked at him quickly.

"May I ask your name, sir?" he remarked.

"Seymour – Major Seymour," returned the other. "I turned out the light and locked the door while Sir Robert was telephoning for you, to ensure that nothing would be moved.

The inspector grunted again, as Seymour opened the door and struck a light.

"Over in that window, Inspector – " began Sir Robert, only to stop and gape foolishly across the room.

"I don't quite understand, gentlemen," said Inspector Grayson, testily.

"No more do I," muttered Bob Seymour, with a puzzled frown.

"I left him lying, as we found him, half in and half out of the window," said Seymour. "His legs were inside, his head and shoulders from the waist upwards were outside."

It was the constable who interrupted him. While the others were standing by the door he had crossed to the window and leaned out.

"Here's the body, sir," he cried. "Outside in the flower-bed."

PART 2

1

The inspector went quickly to the window and peered out; then he turned and confronted Sir Robert and Seymour.

"He's dead right enough *now*," he said, gravely. "It seems a pity that you gentlemen didn't take a little more trouble to find out if he was in the first place. You might have saved his life."

"Hang it, man!" exploded Seymour, angrily, "do you suppose I don't know a dead man when I see one?"

"I don't know whether you do or don't," answered the other, shortly. "But I've never yet heard of a dead man getting up and moving to an adjacent flower-bed. And you say yourself that you left him lying over the window-sill."

For a moment an angry flush mounted on the soldier's face, then with an effort, he controlled himself. On the face of it, the inspector was perfectly justified in his remark: dead men do not move. The trouble was that Bob Seymour had felt the dead man's heart and his pulse; had turned the light of his torch from close range into his eyes. And he *knew* that he had made no mistake; he *knew* that the man was dead when he turned out the light and left the room. He *knew* it; but – dead men do not move. What had happened in the room during the time they were waiting for the police? The key had been in his pocket: who had moved the body? And why? Not Bill Brabazon: that he knew.

With a puzzled frown he crossed slowly towards the two policemen, who were hauling the limp form through the open window. And once again he paused and sniffed.

"That smell again, Sir Robert," he remarked.

"What smell?" demanded the inspector, as they laid the dead man on the floor.

"Don't you notice it? A strange, fetid, rank smell."

The inspector sniffed perfunctorily. "I smell the ordinary smell of rain on dead leaves," he remarked. "What about it?"

"Nothing, except that there are no dead leaves in June," returned Seymour, shortly.

"Well, sir," snorted the inspector, "whether there are dead leaves or not, we've got a dead man on the floor. And I take it he wasn't killed by a smell, anyway."

In the full light of the room Denton was an even more unpleasant sight than when he had lain sprawling over the window-sill. The water dripped from his sodden clothing and ran in little pools on the floor; the dark, puffy face was smeared with a layer of wet earth. But it was not at these details that Bob Seymour was staring: it was an angry-looking red weal round the neck just above the collar that riveted his attention. The inspector, taking no further notice of the two spectators, was proceeding methodically with his examination. First he turned out all the pockets, laying the contents neatly on the table; then, with the help of the constable, he turned the body over on its face. A little fainter, but still perfectly discernible, the red weal could be traced continuously round the neck; and after a while the inspector straightened up and turned to Sir Robert.

"It looks as if he had been strangled, sir," he remarked, professionally. "I should imagine from the size of the mark that a fairly thin rope was used. Have you any idea whether anyone had a grudge against him? The motive was obviously not robbery."

"Strangled!" cried Sir Robert, joining the other three. "But I don't understand." He turned perplexedly to Bob Seymour, who was standing near the window absorbed in thought. Then, a little haltingly, he continued: "Unfortunately there was a very severe row between him and another of my guests earlier in the evening."

"Where did the row take place?"

"Er – in this room."

"Was anyone else present?"

"No. No one heard them quarrelling. But Mr Brabazon, the guest in question, made no secret about it – afterwards. He told us in the billiard-room that – that they had come to blows in here."

"I would like to see Mr Brabazon, Sir Robert," said the inspector. "Perhaps you would be good enough to send for him."

"I will go and get him myself," returned the other, leaving the room.

"A very remarkable affair," murmured Seymour, as the door closed behind his host. "Don't you agree with me, inspector?"

"In what way?" asked the officer, guardedly.

But the soldier was lighting a cigarette, and made no immediate answer. "May I ask," he remarked at length, "if you've ever tried to strangle a man with a rope? Because," he continued, when the other merely snorted indignantly, "I have. During the war – in German East Africa. And it took me a long while. You see, if you put a slip-knot round a man's neck and pull, he comes towards you. You've got to get very close to him and kneel on him, or wedge him in some way so that he can't move, before you can do much good in the strangling line."

"Quite an amateur detective, Major Seymour," said the inspector condescendingly. "If you will forgive my saying so, however, it might have been better had you concentrated on seeing whether the poor fellow was dead."

He turned as the door opened, and Bill Brabazon came in, followed by Sir Robert.

"This is Mr Brabazon, Inspector," said the latter.

The officer eyed the youngster keenly for a moment before he spoke. Then he pointed to a chair, so placed that the light of the lamp would fall on the face of anyone sitting in it.

"Will you tell me everything you know, Mr Brabazon? And I should advise you not to attempt to conceal anything."

"I've got nothing to conceal," answered the boy, doggedly. "I found Denton in here about half-past ten, and we started quarrelling. I'd been trying to avoid him the whole evening, but there was no getting away from him this time. After a while we began to fight, and he hit me in the face. Then I saw red, and really went for him. And I laid him out. That's all I know about it."

"And what did you do after you laid him out?"

"I went out into the garden to cool down. Then when the rain came on, I went to the billiard-room and told Sir Robert. And the first thing I knew about this," with a shudder he looked at the dead body, "was when Mr Trayne came into the billiard-room and told us."

"Mr Trayne? Who is he, Sir Robert?"

"Another guest stopping in the house. Do you wish to see him?"

"Please." The inspector paced thoughtfully up and down the room.

"The light was on, wasn't it, Bill, when you left the room?" said Seymour.

"It was. Why, I saw his shadow on the lawn, as I told you."

"Did you?" said the inspector, watching him narrowly. "Would you be surprised to hear, Mr Brabazon, that this unfortunate man was strangled?"

"Strangled!" Bill Brabazon started up from his chair. "Strangled! Good God! Who by?"

"That is precisely what we want to find out," said the inspector.

"But, good heavens! man," cried the boy, excitedly, "don't you see that that exonerates me. I didn't strangle him: I only hit him on the jaw. And that shadow I saw," he swung round on Seymour, "must have been the murderer."

"You wish to see me, Inspector?" Trayne's voice from the doorway interrupted him, and he sat back in his chair again. And Seymour, watching the joyful look on Bill's face, knew that he spoke the truth. His amazement at hearing the cause of death had been too spontaneous not to be genuine. In his own mind Bill Brabazon regarded himself as cleared: the trouble was that other people might not. The majority of murderers have died, still protesting their innocence.

"I understand that it was you, Mr Trayne, who first discovered the body," said the inspector.

"It was. I came in and found the room in darkness. I wished to study an inscription by the window to which Sir Robert had alluded at dinner. I struck a match, and then – I saw the body lying half in half out over the sill. It gave me a dreadful shock – quite dreadful. And I at once went to the billiard-room for assistance."

"So whoever did it turned out the light," said the inspector, musingly. "What time was it, Mr Trayne, when you made the discovery?"

"About half-past eleven, I should think."

"An hour after the quarrel. And in that hour someone entered this room either by the window or the door, and committed the deed. He, further, left either by the window or the door. How did you leave, Mr Brabazon?"

"By the door," said the youngster. "The flower-bed outside the window is too wide to jump."

"Then if the murderer entered by the window, he will have left footmarks. If he entered by the door and left by it the presumption is that he is a member of the house. No one who was not would risk leaving by the door after committing such an act."

"Most ably reasoned," murmured Seymour, mildly.

But the inspector was far too engrossed with his theory to notice the slight sarcasm in the other's tone. With a powerful electric torch he was searching the ground outside the window for any trace of footprints. The mark in the ground where the body had lain was clearly defined; save for that, however, the flower-bed revealed nothing. It was at least fifteen feet wide; to cross it, leaving no trace, appeared a physical impossibility. And after a while the inspector turned back into the room and looked gravely at Sir Robert Deering.

"I should like to have every member of the house-party and all your servants in here, Sir Robert, one by one," he remarked.

"Then you think it was done by someone in the house, Inspector?" Sir Robert was looking worried.

"I prefer not to say anything definite at present," answered the official, guardedly. "Perhaps we can start with the house-party."

With a shrug of his shoulder, Sir Robert left the room, and the inspector turned to the constable.

"Lend a hand here, Murphy; we'll put the body behind the screen before any of the ladies come in."

"Great Scott! man," cried Seymour. "What do you want the ladies for? You don't suggest that a woman could have strangled him?"

"You will please allow me to know my own business best," said the other, coldly. "Shut and bolt the windows, Murphy."

The rain had stopped as the policeman crossed the room to carry out his orders. And it was as he stood by the open window, with his hands upraised to the sash, that he suddenly stepped back with a startled exclamation.

"Something 'it me in the face, sir," he muttered. Then he spat disgustedly. "Gaw! What a filthy taste!"

But the inspector was not interested – he was covering the dead man's face with a pocket handkerchief, and after a moment's hesitation, the constable again reached up for the sash, and pulled it down. Only the soldier had noticed the little incident, and he was staring like a man bereft of his senses at a point just above the policeman's head.

"Don't move," he ordered, harshly. "Stand still, constable."

With a startled look the policeman obeyed, and Seymour stepped over to him. And then he did a peculiar thing. He lit a match and turned to the inspector.

"Just look at this match, Inspector," he murmured. "Burning brightly, isn't it?" He moved it a little, and suddenly the flame turned to a smoky orange colour. For a moment or two it spluttered; then it went out altogether.

"You can move now, constable," he said. "I didn't want any draught for a moment." He looked at Inspector Grayson with a smile. "Interesting little experiment that – wasn't it?"

Grayson snorted. "If you've quite finished your conjuring tricks, I'll get on with the business," he remarked. "Come along over here, Murphy."

"What is it, Bob?" Bill Brabazon cried, excitedly.

"The third point, Bill," answered the other. "Great Scott! what a fool I've been. Though it's the most extraordinary case I've ever come across."

"Think you can reconstruct the crime?" sneered the inspector.

"I don't think – I know," returned the other quietly. "But not tonight. There's the rain again."

"And might I ask what clues you possess?"

"Only one more than you, and that you can get from Sir Robert. I blush to admit it, but until a moment ago I attached no importance to it. It struck me as being merely the foolish jest of a stupid man. Now it does strike me quite in that light. Ask him," he continued, and his voice was grim, "for the translation of that inscription under the window. And when you've got that, concentrate for a moment on the other end of the dead man – his trousers just above the ankles."

"They're covered with dirt," said the inspector, impressed, in spite of himself, by the other's tones.

"Yes – but what sort of dirt? Dry, dusty, cobwebbed dirt – not caked mud on his knees. Immense amount of importance in dirt, Inspector."

But Mr Grayson was recovering his dignity. "Any other advice?" he sneered.

"Yes. Hire a man and practise strangling him. Then buy a really good encyclopædia and study it. You'll find a wealth of interesting information in it." He strolled towards the door. "If you want me I shall be in the billiard-room. And, by the way, with regard to what I say about strangling, don't forget that the victim cannot come towards you if his feet are off the ground."

"Perhaps you'll have the murderer for me in the billiard-room," remarked the inspector, sarcastically.

"I'm afraid not," answered the other. "The real murderer, unfortunately, is already dead. I'll look for his accomplice in the morning."

With a slight smile he closed the door and strolled into the hall. The house-party were being marshalled by Sir Robert preparatory to their inquisition; the servants stood huddled together in sheepish groups under the stern eye of the butler.

"Have you found out anything, Major Seymour?" With entreaty in her eyes, Ruth Brabazon came up to him.

"Yes, Miss Brabazon, I have," answered the man, reassuringly. "You can set your mind absolutely at rest."

"You know who did it?" she cried, breathlessly.

"I do," he answered. "But unfortunately I can't prove it tonight. And you mustn't be alarmed at the attitude taken up by the inspector. He's not in a very good temper, and I'm afraid I'm the cause."

"But does he think – ?"

"I should hesitate to say what great thoughts were passing through his brain," said Seymour. "But I have a shrewd suspicion that he has already made up his mind that Bill did it."

"And who did do it, Bob?" She laid her hand beseechingly on his arm as she spoke.

"I think it's better to say nothing at the moment," he answered, gently. "There are one or two points I've got to make absolutely certain of first. Until then – won't you trust me, Ruth?"

"Trust you! Why, my dear – " She turned away as she spoke, and Bob Seymour barely heard the last two words. But he did *just* hear them. And once again the dead man was forgotten.

2

"May I borrow your car, Sir Robert? I want to go to London and bring back a friend of mine – Sir Gilbert Strangways." Bob Seymour approached his host after breakfast the following morning. "I'll have to be back by three, in time for the inquest, and it's very important."

"Strangways – the explorer! Certainly, Seymour; though I'm not keen on adding to the house-party at present."

"It's essential, I'm afraid. They can only bring in one verdict this afternoon – Murder. That ass Grayson was nosing round this morning, and he, at any rate, is convinced of it."

"What – that Bill did it?" muttered the other.

"He's outside there now, making notes."

"You don't think the boy did it, do you, Seymour?"

"I *know* he didn't, Sir Robert. But to prove it is a different matter. May I order the car?"

"Yes, yes of course. Anything you like. Why on earth did I ever ask the poor fellow down here?" Sir Robert walked agitatedly up and down the hall. "And anyway, who did do it?" He threw out his hands in despair. "He can't have done it himself."

"All in good time, Sir Robert," said the other gravely. "The lucky thing for you is that you have practically never used that room."

"What do you mean?" muttered his host, going a little white.

"If you had, the chances are that this house-party would never have taken place," answered Seymour. "At least, not with you as the host."

"My God!" cried the other. "You don't mean to say that there's anything in that inscription!"

"It's the key to everything," returned the other, shortly. "To put it mildly, your predecessor had a peculiar sense of humour."

Ten minutes later he was getting into the car, when Inspector Grayson appeared round the corner.

"You won't forget the inquest is at three, Major Seymour?" he said, a trifle sharply.

"I shan't miss it," answered the soldier.

"Found the murderer yet?" asked the detective.

"Yes – this morning," returned the other. "Haven't you?"

And the officer was still staring thoughtfully down the drive long after the car had disappeared round a bend. This confounded soldier seemed so very positive, and Grayson, who was no fool, had been compelled to admit to himself that there were several strange features about the case. The inscription on the wall he had dismissed as childish; from inquiries made in the neighbourhood, Sir Robert Deering's predecessor had obviously been a most peculiar specimen. Not quite all there, if reports were to be believed. To return to the case, however, a complete *alibi* had been proved by every single member of the household, save one kitchen maid, Mr Trayne, and – Bill Brabazon. The kitchen maid and Mr Trayne could be dismissed – the former for obvious reasons, the latter owing to the impossibility of having done the deed in the time between leaving the drawing-room and arriving in the billiard-room with the news. And that left – Bill Brabazon. Every single line of thought led ultimately, to – Bill Brabazon. Motive, opportunity, capability from a physical point of view – all pointed to him. A further exhaustive search that morning of the flower-bed outside the window had revealed no trace of any footprint; it was impossible that the murderer should have entered by the window. Therefore – he shrugged his shoulders. The house-party again – and Bill Brabazon. Blind with fury, as he admitted himself, he had first knocked the dead man down and then strangled him, turning out the light lest anyone should see. Then, taking off the rope, he had left him, almost, but not quite, dead on the floor. In a last despairing gasp for air, Denton had staggered to the window and collapsed – still not quite dead. Finally, he had made one more convulsive effort, floundered on the flower-bed, and had there died.

Such was the scene as Inspector Grayson reconstructed it, and yet he was far from satisfied. Why strangle? An un-English method of killing a man. Still – facts were facts – the man *had* been strangled. Un-English or not, that was the manner in which he had met his death; and since suicide could be ruled out, only murder remained. If the soldier could prove it was not young Brabazon – well and good. Until he did, Mr Grayson preferred to bank on facts which were capable of proof.

The result of the coroner's inquest was a foregone conclusion. Death after strangulation, with a rider to the effect that, had prompt assistance been given on the first discovery of the body, life might have been saved.

Bob Seymour, seated beside another lean, suntanned man, heard the verdict with an impassive face. He had given his evidence, confining it to the barest statement of fact; he had advanced no theory; he had not attempted to dispute Inspector Grayson's deductions. Once he had caught Ruth's eyes fixed on him beseechingly, and he had given her a reassuring smile. And she – because she trusted him – knew that all was well; knew that the net which seemed to be closing so grimly round her brother would not be fastened. But why – why didn't he tell them now how it was done? That's what she couldn't understand.

And then, when it was all over, Bob and his friend disappeared in the car again.

"There's no doubt about it, Bob," said Strangways. "What a diabolical old blackguard the man must have been."

"I agree," answered Seymour, grimly. "One wishes one could get at him now. As it is, the most we can do is to convince our mutton-headed friend Grayson. I owe the gentleman one for that rider to the verdict."

The car stopped first at a chemist's, and the two men entered the shop. It was an unusual request they made – cylinders of oxygen are generally required only for sick rooms. But after a certain amount of argument, the chemist produced one, and they placed it in the back of the car. Their next errand was even stranger, and consisted of the purchase of a rabbit. Finally, a visit to an ironmonger produced a rose such as is used on the end of a hosepipe for watering.

Then, their purchases complete, they returned to the house, stopping at the police-station on the way. Grayson came out to see them, a tolerant smile on his face. Yes, he would be pleased to come up that evening after dinner.

"Do you want to introduce me to the murderer, Major?" he asked, maliciously.

"Something of the sort, Inspector," said Seymour. "Studied that encyclopædia yet?"

"I've been too busy on other matters – a little more important," answered the other, shortly.

"Good," cried Seymour, genially. "By the way, when you want to blow out a lamp what is the first thing you do?"

"Turn down the wick," said Grayson.

"Wise man. I wonder why the murderer didn't."

And for the second time that day, Inspector Grayson was left staring thoughtfully at a retreating motor-car.

It was not till after dinner that Bob Seymour reverted to the matter which was obsessing everyone's mind. Most of the house-party had left; only Mr Trayne and Ruth and her brother remained. And even the Celebrated Actor had been comparatively silent throughout the meal, while Bill had remained sunk in profound gloom. Everything at the inquest had pointed to him as the culprit; every ring at the bell and he had imagined someone arriving with a warrant for his arrest. And Bob had said nothing to clear him – not a word, in spite of his apparent confidence last night. Only Ruth still seemed certain that he would do something; but what could he do, exploded the boy miserably, when she tried to cheer him up. The evidence on the face of it was damning.

"About time our friend arrived, Gilbert." Bob Seymour glanced at his watch, and at that moment there came a ring at the bell.

"Who's that?" said Bill, nervously.

"The egregious Grayson, old boy," said Bob "The experiment is about to begin."

"You mean – " cried Ruth, breathlessly.

"I mean that Sir Gilbert has kindly consented to take the place of Denton last night," said Bob, cheerfully. "He'll have one or two little props to help him, and I shall be stage-manager."

"But why have you put it off so long?" cried Bill, as the inspector came into the room.

" 'When 'tis day. All serene,' "quoted Bob. "Good evening, Mr Grayson. Now that we are all here, we might as well begin."

"Just as well," agreed the inspector, shortly. "What do we begin with?"

"First of all a visit to the smoking-room," answered Seymour. "Then, except for Sir Gilbert Strangways, we shall all go outside into the garden."

In silence they followed him to the scene of the tragedy.

"I trust you will exonerate me from any charge of being theatrical," he began, closing the door. "But in this particular case the cause of Mr Denton's death is so extraordinary that only an actual reconstruction of what happened would convince such a pronounced sceptic as the inspector. Facts are facts, aren't they, Mr Grayson?"

The inspector grunted non-committally. "What's that on the floor?" he demanded.

"A cylinder of oxygen, and a rabbit in a cage," explained Seymour, pleasantly. "Now first to rearrange the room. The lamp was on this table – very possibly placed there by the dead man to get a better view of the inscription under the window; so that we may proceed to what happened.

"First, Inspector, Mr Brabazon entered the room and, as he has already described, he and Mr Denton came to blows, with the result that he laid Denton out. Then Mr Brabazon left the room, as I propose we shall do shortly. And, after a while, Mr Denton came to his senses again, and went to the window for air, just as Sir Gilbert has done at the present moment."

"You can't prove it," snapped Grayson.

"True," murmured Seymour. "Just logical surmise – so far; from now onwards – irrefutable proof. The murderer is admirably trained, I assure you. Are you ready, Gilbert?"

"Quite," said Strangways, bending down and picking up the rabbit-cage, which he placed on the table by the lamp.

"Perhaps, Inspector, you would like to examine the rabbit?" remarked Seymour. "No! Well, if not, I would just ask you to notice Sir Gilbert's other preparations. A clip on his nose; the tube from the oxygen cylinder in his mouth."

"I don't understand all this, Major Seymour," cried Grayson, testily. "What's the rabbit for, and all this other tommy-rot?"

"I thought I'd explained to you that Sir Gilbert is taking the place of the murdered man last night. The tommy-rot is to prevent him sharing the same fate."

"Good God!" The inspector turned a little pale.

"Shall we adjourn to the garden?" continued Seymour, imperturbably. He led the way from the room. "I think we'll stand facing the window, so that we can see everything. Of course, I can't guarantee that the performance will be *exactly* the same; but it will be near enough, I think. Nor can I guarantee *exactly* when it will start." As he spoke they reached a point facing the window. The lamp was burning brightly in the room, outlining Sir Gilbert's figure as he stood facing them, and with a little shudder Ruth clutched her brother's arm.

"Even so did Denton stand last night." Seymour's even voice came out of the darkness. "You see his shadow on the grass, and the shadow of the sash; just as Mr Brabazon saw the shadow last night, Inspector."

Silence settled on the group; even the phlegmatic inspector seemed impressed. And then suddenly, when the tension was becoming almost unbearable, Sir Gilbert's voice came from the window.

"It's coming, Bob."

They saw him adjust his nose-clip and turn on the oxygen; then he stood up as before, motionless, in the window.

"Watch carefully, Inspector," said Seymour. "Do you see those dark, thin, sinuous feelers coming down outside the window? Like strands of rope. They're curling underneath the sash towards Sir Gilbert's head. The lamp – look at the lamp – watch the colour of the flame. Orange – where before it was yellow. Look – it's smoking; thick black smoke; and the room is turning green. Do you see? Now the lamp again. It's going out – even as it went out last night. And, by this time last night, Inspector, Denton, I think, was dead; even as the rabbit on the table is dead now. Now watch Sir Gilbert's shirt front."

"Great Heavens!" shouted Sir Robert. "It's going up."

"Precisely," said Bob. "At the present moment he is being lifted off his legs – as Denton was last night; and if at this period Denton was not already dead, he could not have lasted long. He would have been hanged."

"Oh Bill, it's awful!" cried Ruth, hysterically.

"Then came the rain," continued Seymour "I have here the hosepipe fitted with a rose." He dragged it nearer the window, and let it play on the side of the house as far up as the water would reach. Almost at once the body of Sir Gilbert ceased rising; it paused as if hesitating; then with a little thud, fell downwards half in half out of the window, head and arms sprawling in the flower-bed.

"And thus we found Mr Denton last night, when it was still raining," said Seymour. "All right, Gilbert?"

"All right, old boy!" came from the other.

"But if he's all right," said the inspector, wonderingly, "why wasn't the other?"

"Because Sir Gilbert, being in full possession of his senses when the hanging process stared, used his hands to prevent strangulation. To continue – the rain ceased. We were out of the room waiting for your arrival, Mr Grayson, and while we were out – Look! Look!"

Before their eyes the top part of Sir Gilbert's body was being raised till once again he stood straight up. Then steadily he was drawn upwards till his knees came about the level of the sill, when, with a sudden lurch, the whole body swung out and then back again, while the calves of his legs drummed against the outside of the house. "Do you remember the marks on the trousers, Inspector? And then the rain came again." Seymour turned on the hose. Once more the body paused, hesitated, and then crashed downwards into the flower-bed.

"All right, Gilbert?"

"All right," answered the other. "Merely uncomfortably wet." He rose and came towards them.

"And now, Inspector," murmured Seymour mildly, "you know exactly how Mr Denton was killed."

"But good Lord! gentlemen," said Grayson, feebly, "what was it that killed him?"

"A species of liana," said Sir Gilbert. "In my experience absolutely unique in strength and size – though I have heard stories from the Upper Amazon of similar cases. It's known amongst the natives as the Green Death."

"But is it an animal?"

"You've asked me a question, Inspector," said Sir Gilbert, "that I find it very difficult to answer. To look at – it's a plant – a climbing plant, with long, powerful tendrils. But in habits – it's carnivorous, like the insect-eating variety in England. It's found in the tropical undergrowth, and is incidentally worshipped by some of the tribes. They give it human sacrifices, so the story goes. And now I can quite believe it."

"But, hang it, sir," exploded the inspector, "we aren't on the Upper Amazon. Do you mean to say that one of these things is here?"

"Of course. Didn't you see it? It's spread from the wall to the branches of that old oak."

"If you remember, Inspector, I pointed it out to you this morning," murmured Seymour, mildly. "But you were so engrossed with the flower-bed."

"But why did the lamp go out?" asked Ruth breathlessly.

"For the same reason that the rabbit died," said Bob. "For the same reason that the match went out last night, and gave me the third clue. From each of the tendrils a green cloud is ejected, the principal ingredient of which is carbon dioxide – which is the gas that suffocates. The plant holds the victim, and they suffocate him. Hence the oxygen and the nose-clip; otherwise Sir Gilbert would have been killed tonight. By the way, would you like to see the rabbit, Inspector?"

"I'll take your word for it, sir," he grunted, shortly. "Only, why the devil you didn't tell me this last night I can't understand."

"I'd have shown you – only the rain had come on again. And you must admit I advised you to get an encyclopædia."

3

"Bob, I don't understand how you did it," cried Ruth.

It was after breakfast the following morning, and the sound of axes came through the open window from the men who were already at work cutting down the old oak tree.

The other laughed. "Points of detail'," he said, quietly. "At first, before the police arrived, I thought it possible that Bill had been responsible for his death. I thought he'd hit him so hard that the man's heart had given out, and that in a final spasm he'd staggered to the window and died. It struck me as just conceivable that Denton had himself blown out the lamp, thinking it made it hotter. But why not turn it out? And would he have had time if he was at his last gasp? Then the police came, and the body had moved. I *knew* the man was dead when he was lying over the sill, though I hadn't seen the mark round his neck. I therefore knew that some agency had moved the body. That agency must have been the murderer – anyone else would have mentioned the fact. Therefore it couldn't have been Bill, because he was in the billiard-room the whole time, and I'd locked the door of the smoking-room. Then I saw the mark round his neck – strangled. But you can't strangle a powerful man without a desperate struggle. And why should the strangler return after the deed was committed? Also there were no footmarks on the flower-bed. Then I noticed the grey dust on his trousers just below the knee, and underneath the window outside, kept dry by the sill, which stuck out, was ivy – dusty and cobwebby as ivy always is. How had his legs touched it? If they had – and there was nowhere else the dirt could have come from – he must have been lifted off the ground. Strangulation, certainly, of a type – hung. The dirt had not been there when we first found the body lying over the sill. And if he'd been hung – who did it? And why hang a dead man? What had happened between the time Bill left the room and the police found the body? A heavy shower of rain, during which we found the body; then clear again, while we were out of the room; then another shower, when the police found the body. And then I thought of the rhyme: –

> 'When 'tis hot, shun this spot;
> When 'tis rain, come again.'

"Could it be possible that there was some diabolical agent at work, who stopped, or was frustrated, by rain? It was then I saw the green cloud itself over the constable's head – the cloud which extinguished my match.

"Incredible as it seemed, I saw at once that it was the only solution which fitted everything – the marks on the back of his trousers below the knee – everything. He'd been hung, and the thing that had hanged him had blown out the lamp – or extinguished it is a more accurate way of expressing it – even as it extinguished my match. The smell – I'd been searching my memory for that smell the whole evening, and it came to me when I saw that green gas – it's some rank discharge from the plant, mixed with the carbon dioxide. And I last saw it, and smelt it, on the Upper Amazon ten years ago. My native bearers dragged me away in their terror. There was a small animal, I remember, hanging from a red tendril, quite dead. The tendril was round its neck, exuding little puffs of green vapour. So I got Gilbert to make sure. That's all."

"But what a wicked old man he must have been who planted it!" cried the girl, indignantly.

"A distorted sense of humour, as I told our host," said Bob, briefly, starting to fill his pipe.

"Bill and I can never thank you enough, Major Seymour," said the girl, slowly, after a long silence. "If it hadn't been for you – " She gave a little shudder, and stared out of the window.

"Some advantages in wandering," he answered lightly. "One does pick up odd facts. Suppose I'll have to push off again soon."

"Why?" she demanded.

"Oh, I dunno. Can't sit in England doing nothing."

"Going alone?" she asked, softly.

"Do you think anybody would be mug enough to accompany me?" he inquired, with an attempt at a grin. Dear Heavens! If only he wasn't a cripple –

"I don't know, I'm sure," she murmured.

"You'd want your three points of detail to make it a certainty, wouldn't you? We only reached the coincidence stage two nights ago."

"What do you mean, Ruth?" he whispered, staring at her.

"That for a clever man – you're an utter fool. With a woman one is a certainty. However, if you'll close your eyes, I'll pander to your feeble intellect. Tight, please."

And it was as the tree fell with a rending crash outside that Ruth Brabazon found that, at any rate as far as his arms were concerned, Bob Seymour was no cripple. And Bob – well, a kiss is pretty conclusive. At least, some kisses are.

SAPPER

THE BLACK GANG

Although the First World War is over, it seems that the hostilities are not, and when Captain Hugh 'Bulldog' Drummond discovers that a stint of bribery and blackmail is undermining England's democratic tradition, he forms the Black Gang, bent on tracking down the perpetrators of such plots. They set a trap to lure the criminal mastermind behind these subversive attacks to England, and all is going to plan until Bulldog Drummond accepts an invitation to tea at the Ritz with a charming American clergyman and his dowdy daughter.

BULLDOG DRUMMOND

'Demobilised officer, finding peace incredibly tedious, would welcome diversion. Legitimate, if possible; but crime, if of a comparatively humorous description, no objection. Excitement essential… Reply at once Box X10.'

Hungry for adventure following the First World War, Captain Hugh 'Bulldog' Drummond begins a career as the invincible protectorate of his country. His first reply comes from a beautiful young woman, who sends him racing off to investigate what at first looks like blackmail but turns out to be far more complicated and dangerous. The rescue of a kidnapped millionaire, found with his thumbs horribly mangled, leads Drummond to the discovery of a political conspiracy of awesome scope and villainy, masterminded by the ruthless Carl Peterson.

SAPPER

BULLDOG DRUMMOND AT BAY

While Hugh 'Bulldog' Drummond is staying in an old cottage for a peaceful few days duck-shooting, he is disturbed one night by the sound of men shouting, followed by a large stone that comes crashing through the window. When he goes outside to investigate, he finds a patch of blood in the road, and is questioned by two men who tell him that they are chasing a lunatic who has escaped from the nearby asylum. Drummond plays dumb, but is determined to investigate in his inimitable style when he discovers a cryptic message.

THE FEMALE OF THE SPECIES

Bulldog Drummond has slain his arch-enemy, Carl Peterson, but Peterson's mistress lives on and is intent on revenge. Drummond's wife vanishes, followed by a series of vicious traps set by a malicious adversary, which lead to a hair-raising chase across England, to a sinister house and a fantastic torture chamber modelled on Stonehenge, with its legend of human sacrifice.

SAPPER

THE FINAL COUNT

When Robin Gaunt, inventor of a terrifyingly powerful weapon of chemical warfare, goes missing, the police suspect that he has 'sold out' to the other side. But Bulldog Drummond is convinced of his innocence, and can think of only one man brutal enough to use the weapon to hold the world to ransom. Drummond receives an invitation to a sumptuous dinner dance aboard an airship that is to mark the beginning of his final battle for triumph.

THE RETURN OF BULLDOG DRUMMOND

While staying as a guest at Merridale Hall, Captain Hugh 'Bulldog' Drummond's peaceful repose is disturbed by a frantic young man who comes dashing into the house, trembling and begging for help. When two warders arrive, asking for a man named Morris – a notorious murderer who has escaped from Dartmoor – Drummond assures them that they are chasing the wrong man. In which case, who on earth is this terrified youngster?

OTHER TITLES BY SAPPER AVAILABLE DIRECT
FROM HOUSE OF STRATUS

Quantity		£	$(US)	$(CAN)	€
☐	ASK FOR RONALD STANDISH	6.99	11.50	15.99	11.50
☐	THE BLACK GANG	6.99	11.50	15.99	11.50
☐	BULLDOG DRUMMOND	6.99	11.50	15.99	11.50
☐	BULLDOG DRUMMOND AT BAY	6.99	11.50	15.99	11.50
☐	CHALLENGE	6.99	11.50	15.99	11.50
☐	THE DINNER CLUB	6.99	11.50	15.99	11.50
☐	THE FEMALE OF THE SPECIES	6.99	11.50	15.99	11.50
☐	THE FINAL COUNT	6.99	11.50	15.99	11.50
☐	THE ISLAND OF TERROR	6.99	11.50	15.99	11.50
☐	JIM BRENT	6.99	11.50	15.99	11.50
☐	JIM MAITLAND	6.99	11.50	15.99	11.50
☐	JOHN WALTERS	6.99	11.50	15.99	11.50
☐	KNOCK-OUT	6.99	11.50	15.99	11.50
☐	MUFTI	6.99	11.50	15.99	11.50
☐	THE RETURN OF BULLDOG DRUMMOND	6.99	11.50	15.99	11.50
☐	SERGEANT MICHAEL CASSIDY R E	6.99	11.50	15.99	11.50
☐	TEMPLE TOWER	6.99	11.50	15.99	11.50
☐	THE THIRD ROUND	6.99	11.50	15.99	11.50

ALL HOUSE OF STRATUS BOOKS ARE AVAILABLE FROM GOOD BOOKSHOPS
OR DIRECT FROM THE PUBLISHER:

Internet: www.houseofstratus.com including author interviews, reviews, features.

Email: sales@houseofstratus.com please quote author, title and credit card details.

Hotline: UK ONLY: 0800 169 1780, please quote author, title and credit card details.
INTERNATIONAL: +44 (0) 20 7494 6400, please quote author, title and credit card details.

Send to: House of Stratus Sales Department
24c Old Burlington Street
London
W1X 1RL
UK

Please allow for postage costs charged per order plus an amount per book as set out in the tables below:

	£(Sterling)	$(US)	$(CAN)	€(Euros)
Cost per order				
UK	2.00	3.00	4.50	3.30
Europe	3.00	4.50	6.75	5.00
North America	3.00	4.50	6.75	5.00
Rest of World	3.00	4.50	6.75	5.00
Additional cost per book				
UK	0.50	0.75	1.15	0.85
Europe	1.00	1.50	2.30	1.70
North America	2.00	3.00	4.60	3.40
Rest of World	2.50	3.75	5.75	4.25

PLEASE SEND CHEQUE, POSTAL ORDER (STERLING ONLY), EUROCHEQUE, OR INTERNATIONAL MONEY
ORDER (PLEASE CIRCLE METHOD OF PAYMENT YOU WISH TO USE)
MAKE PAYABLE TO: STRATUS HOLDINGS plc

Cost of book(s): ———————— Example: 3 x books at £6.99 each: £20.97

Cost of order: ———————— Example: £2.00 (Delivery to UK address)

Additional cost per book: ———— Example: 3 x £0.50: £1.50

Order total including postage: ———— Example: £24.47

Please tick currency you wish to use and add total amount of order:

☐ £ (Sterling)   ☐ $ (US)   ☐ $ (CAN)   ☐ € (EUROS)

VISA, MASTERCARD, SWITCH, AMEX, SOLO, JCB:

☐ ☐ ☐ ☐ ☐ ☐ ☐ ☐ ☐ ☐ ☐ ☐ ☐ ☐ ☐ ☐ ☐ ☐

Issue number (Switch only):

☐ ☐ ☐

Start Date: **Expiry Date:**

☐ ☐ / ☐ ☐   ☐ ☐ / ☐ ☐

Signature: _____

NAME: _____

ADDRESS: _____

_____

POSTCODE: _____

Please allow 28 days for delivery.

Prices subject to change without notice.
Please tick box if you do not wish to receive any additional information. ☐

House of Stratus publishes many other titles in this genre; please check our website (**www.houseofstratus.com**) for more details.